34320000095936

LP FIC GALL, M
7/10/14
(Western)

UPPER SAN JUAN LIBRARY DISTRICT
SISSON LIBRARY
BOX 849   (970) 264-2209
PAGOSA SPRINGS, CO 81147-0849

THE MAN FROM BOOT HILL: BURYING THE PAST

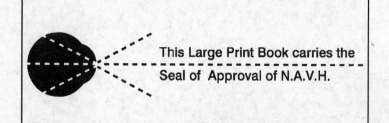

This Large Print Book carries the
Seal of Approval of N.A.V.H.

THE MAN FROM BOOT HILL: BURYING THE PAST

MARCUS GALLOWAY

THORNDIKE PRESS

A part of Gale, Cengage Learning

GALE
CENGAGE Learning·

Farmington Hills, Mich • San Francisco • New York • Waterville, Maine
Meriden, Conn • Mason, Ohio • Chicago

GALE
CENGAGE Learning®

Copyright © 2005 by Marcus Pelegrimas.
Thorndike Press, a part of Gale, Cengage Learning.

ALL RIGHTS RESERVED
This is a work of fiction. Names, characters, places, and incidents are products of the author's imagination or are used fictitiously and are not to be construed as real. Any resemblance to actual events, locales, organizations, or persons, living or dead, is entirely coincidental.
Thorndike Press® Large Print Western.
The text of this Large Print edition is unabridged.
Other aspects of the book may vary from the original edition.
Set in 16 pt. Plantin.

LIBRARY OF CONGRESS CATALOGING-IN-PUBLICATION DATA

Galloway, Marcus.
  The man from boot hill : burying the past / by Marcus Galloway. — Large print edition.
    pages ; cm. — (Thorndike Press large print western)
    ISBN 978-1-4104-6976-2 (hardcover) — ISBN 1-4104-6976-X (hardcover)
    1. Large type books. I. Title.
PS3607.A4196M363 2014
813'.6— dc23   2014007252

Published in 2014 by arrangement with Harper, an imprint of HarperCollins Publishers

Printed in the United States of America
1 2 3 4 5 6 7 18 17 16 15 14

To Mike and Marc.
With friends like these,
who needs a gang?

ONE

The Dakota Territories
1882

It had been a beautiful service.

Certain things could have gone better depending on who was asked, but all in all it was a fine ending to a fine life.

Raymond Hunt was a miner and retired lawman. A fever caught hold of him toward the end of the previous autumn and never let him go. His skin had gotten warmer to the touch and his dreams had gotten more frantic until the only way for him to get any rest was to drown his addled brain in liquor. His wife and both his children had done their best to comfort him. When it was the doctor's turn to step in, he did so admirably but none of it was good enough.

Death was like that. Once it set its sights upon a soul, there wasn't a whole lot to be done about it.

Raymond Hunt's death hadn't been a

cruelty. It had been a kindness. It brought an end to the nights of fitful sleep and the times he would wake up having to be reminded of the names he'd known his entire life. It marked the end of his family's heartache as Raymond eventually became a fond memory instead of a stranger wasting away in front of them.

It was a cool day in the spring of 1882 when Raymond's family gathered to see his body committed to the earth. Nestled in the hills of the southern Dakota Territories, the cemetery was a peaceful spot, no more than a half mile from a town named Switchback. There were stones carved into different shapes and sizes bearing names carved expertly into their faces. There were also simple wooden markers with names painted in a hasty scrawl. All of them were labors of love arranged in simple jagged rows.

Raymond's marker was one of the nicer stone ones planted in that hallowed ground thanks to the efforts of a stranger who'd ridden in to seek employment with the town's undertaker. He was a tall, slender man with dark hair shot through with the occasional strand of gray. He wasn't old, but he seemed to have done more than his share of living in the time he'd been around. As cold and off-putting as his eyes may have been, folks were eventually drawn to him by the soothing tone of his voice, which sounded like a rumble of thunder in the distance.

This man proved to be more than a simple gravedigger. In fact, he took part in nearly every duty performed by the regular undertaker as well as a few others. One of his talents was masonry and was taught to him by a father who'd been carving headstones his entire life.

This man's talent was able to shine thanks to the simple fact that Raymond's illness had taken so long to tear him apart that the doctor took to calling it a "condition." Folks in town, Raymond's family, even Raymond himself, knew he was going to get better. There was hope in people's eyes when they talked about him and his strength of will.

But the man in charge of carving the headstones didn't feel so hopeful.

He wasn't a cruel man and didn't share his doubts with anyone else. He'd just seen enough death in his life to recognize the sound of its steps when it approached. He'd seen Raymond once during the winter and after that, the stranger with the cold eyes had gone back to his workshop and started chipping at a fresh stone.

A week after that stone was finished, so

was Raymond Hunt.

When it had been revealed the day before the burial, the stone had gotten plenty of compliments. Tears of joy flowed from the widow's eyes and grateful, if somewhat weary, smiles came onto the faces of Raymond's children as they shook the ravaged hand that had carved Raymond's marker.

Time and talent.

That was all it had taken for a simple miner to receive the finest headstone in any cemetery a hundred miles in any direction. After the preacher was finished with his sermon and the simple wooden box had been lowered into its hole, folks stood in silence to study that marker as if they were taking in a work of art.

The seconds ticked by and folks drifted away to move on with their lives, but a few remained to pay their last respects. Among them were Raymond's oldest son and the wife he'd left behind.

"I don't know how to thank you, Nicolai," the widow said. She was a woman in her early fifties who seemed at least five years younger since her husband had passed on. The love she had for her husband saw to it that she deteriorated right along with him when he'd been ill. Now, after death's most recent visit to Switchback, a weight had been lifted from her shoulders. Her eyes were always kind, yet they became even kinder as she gazed upon the downcast face of the gravedigger.

The gravedigger smiled. The compliment was nice, but something else was even nicer. It had been a while since he'd heard his name spoken out loud properly without being shortened to Nick. "No need to thank me, ma'am," he said. "I'm just doing my job."

Raymond's son stepped forward and extended his hand. "You've done so much for us, Nick. We really appreciate it. I know my father's smiling down on this beautiful marker you made for him. If there's anything we can do, just name it."

Nick shook the younger man's hand and gave him a polite, yet subtle smile.

The wind blew around them, tugging at the edges of jackets and the hems of skirts as it passed. The family wore their finest dark clothes. Nick wore more practical garb consisting of plain denim work pants, a rumpled white shirt, and a midlength jacket made from thick cotton that was about the same color as the dirt now surrounding Raymond Hunt. He would have dressed more formally, but there was still some work to be done and Nick was the man to do it.

Besides, he'd worn his finest the day before at Raymond's showing.

Thinking of the previous day, Nick's head snapped up slightly and he reached into his jacket's inner pocket. "That reminds me, I forgot to give you something yesterday at the wake."

The widow was already shaking her head. "Oh, I couldn't accept anything from you, Nicolai. You've done so much already."

"It's just a simple token," Nick said, removing a small, square object from his pocket. "Just something to help you through the difficult times you may experience after your loss."

The object Nick took from his pocket was a book small enough to fit in his palm. Bound in black leather, its pages were trimmed in gold. Although the front of the book was stamped with the words HOLY BIBLE, it didn't seem nearly thick enough to be the entire volume.

"It's a Mourner's Bible," Nick explained. "There's passages in there to help ease your mind. You can keep it with you for the difficult days."

After flipping through the small book and reading one of the passages, the widow clutched it to her heart and fought to hold back a fresh batch of tears. "Thank you," she said. "I already miss him so much."

Nick reached out to pat her on the shoulder, but stopped himself before allowing himself to make contact with her. The twitch was a reflex and seemed to affect him more than anyone else. No matter how much time had passed, it was doubtful that the reflex would ever fade.

Nick's right hand looked more like gnarled wood than flesh and bone. The ring finger was nothing more than a nub and the tip of the middle finger was missing from the top knuckle up. Nick also hid away his left hand which was missing half of its little finger.

"Would you like to stay a bit longer with him?" Nick asked, shifting as though the wind had taken on a sudden chill.

"No. I don't think so. He needs to be . . ." She trailed off when she looked over to her husband's grave. Although some dirt had been thrown on top of the coffin as part of the ceremony, there was still plenty of shoveling to be done. Pulling in a breath, she steeled herself and tightened her grip around her new bible. "I'll let you finish. Thanks again."

Raymond's son watched as his mother turned and walked away. After that, he lifted his nose to the wind and filled his lungs slowly. The air smelled like freshly turned earth and wildflowers. Although he smiled at the soothing scent, he quickly pushed the faint trace of joy from his face.

"How long have you been in town, Nick?" he asked without looking at the other man.

Nick shrugged. "A couple months."

"Where did you live before?"

"A lot of places. Came up through Nebraska after heading through Kansas and Missouri."

Truth be told, there was a bit more to it than that. Nick's stay in Nebraska had been a lot more than just a pause to water the horses and throw back a few drinks. There had been some trouble in a town named Jessup. That trouble had come from a man named Skinner.

Actually, Skinner was more animal than man and had bared his teeth while Nick had been in town. Nick and Skinner had had some history of their own, but in the end none of those details mattered. All that did matter was that things had gotten bloody.

Real bloody.

Nick was forced to fight back or be killed in a way that only an animal could kill. A wild man like Skinner tended to be known in the shadier circles and when Nick was able to put Skinner into the ground, that set off plenty of repercussions of its own.

14

Nick thought he could ride far enough away to escape those repercussions.

At least, he'd thought that until now.

"You sound like you came from farther than that," Raymond's son said, cutting in on Nick's thoughts.

Nick didn't have to ask what the younger man was talking about. Having arrived in America as a small child and raised by a man who only spoke English when absolutely necessary, he'd never been able to fully shed the accent of his homeland. As a kid, he'd all but mastered his new language but every so often the past crept into his voice to add a subtle curl to his words.

Whatever inflection the younger man had heard, Nick knew it wasn't much. Years of practice had seen to that. Shrugging he said, "We're all mutts in this country."

"Yeah," the younger man said with a bit of a chuckle. "I guess you're right about that. The reason I asked was because you never did strike me as the sort of man who made his living as a gravedigger." Wincing as though he'd dodged a backhand, he shook his head and quickly added, "Not that I don't appreciate all you can do, it's just that —"

"I know," Nick cut in. "Maybe you should make sure your mother gets home all right."

"I'll do that. Maybe someday I'll learn what brought you all the way to Switch-back."

Nick shrugged and picked up the shovel which had been lying nearby. It was a subtle way to end the conversation and it almost seemed to work. Almost, but not quite.

Although the younger man turned and started to leave, he stopped next to Raymond's headstone and looked back at Nick. "Sometimes it just seems like there's a shadow over you. I know I only met with you a few times lately to arrange everything here, but I noticed it. Actually," he said, stepping a little closer to Nick while leaning in, "I noticed him."

With that last word, the younger man nodded toward the edge of the cemetery that faced away from town. The horizon was a rolling landscape of hills and ridges, some of which were smooth and graceful while others looked more like a giant's backbone jutting from the ground. Against that backdrop, the shape of a single figure stood out dramatically even though that figure was as still as the rocks behind him.

"Yeah," Nick said after a quick glance in that direction. "I noticed him too."

The younger man's eyes darted back and forth between Nick and that other figure. It seemed as though he was searching for some kind of connection between the two. Very quickly, however, he decided not to think about it too hard. "He's not from around here, Nick. I asked around after I saw him lurking across the street from the parlor where you work and nobody knew who he was."

"Could be anyone," Nick said as he hefted the shovel in both hands, scooped up some dirt and tossed it into the grave. "Maybe he's just passing through."

"He . . ." Cutting himself short, the younger man dropped his voice to a whisper. "He's wearing a gun."

"It's nothing. Your family's left, so why don't you tend to them? I'll finish up here."

"But he's been watching you. Switchback's a small town. Others have noticed. The way he stares at you, he looks —"

Nick fixed his eyes upon the younger man in a way that added a layer of cold to the swirling breeze. "It's nothing. Go tend to your family and I'll finish up here." When he said them this time, the words were more command than request and the younger man took them as such.

"All right, Nick. Just . . . be careful. You're a good man and nobody around here would want to see any trouble come to you."

Nick's only response to that was a slight nod. His mangled hands wrapped around the shovel's handle and drove the blade into the ground with enough force to dig another hole right next to the one he was filling.

After a moment or two, the younger man reached out to brush his fingers along one of the angels carved into the stone marker. He felt every feather of that wing before running his hand along the raised letters of his father's name.

"Our offer stands, Nick. Anything you need."

Once again, Nick nodded and kept right on digging.

Raymond's son walked out of the cemetery without looking back. Hearing the sound of Nick's shovel driving into the dirt followed by the splatter of dirt against wood was enough to keep him moving. He'd been through enough already and didn't want to spend any more time within the boundaries of the waist-high fence surrounding that hallowed ground.

TWO

Nick didn't have to look to know the figure was getting closer. Nick had plenty of shadows in his past and every so often one of them would pay him a visit. There wasn't much he could do about it now, so Nick just kept filling Raymond's grave until this most recent shadow got close enough to get a look at the finely carved marker.

"That's a hell of a job you did there," the figure said after coming to a stop on the opposite side of the hole from Nick. "You always were damn good with your hands. Either you've been practicing with the chisel or losing them fingers turned out to be a blessing."

Nick paused, but didn't look up at the man. Instead, he tightened his grip around the shovel and kept digging. "What is it you want, Kyle?"

The figure cocked his head like a dog trying to figure out the inner workings of a music box. Kyle Santos stood slightly taller than Nick with a thick frame that was wrapped in several layers of muscle. He moved in a purposeful way and without a hint of flourish. When he walked, his steps were strong and precise. Now that he was standing still, his feet seemed to have been nailed into the dirt.

"I watched you dig this grave last night," Kyle said. "Considering what you used to do for a living, it was a damn sorry sight."

"Is that why you came here? To give me grief about the job I do?"

"You know why I came here. That bounty they're offering for you is still valid."

"I suppose it always will be."

"Yeah. Right up until I cash it in."

Nick's shovel bit into the pile of dirt that had been getting smaller and smaller with every stroke. He held the blade over the grave, let out a breath, and then dropped the dirt onto the coffin. "How'd you know where I was?"

"After what you did to Skinner, did you really think you could just fade away?"

"Sure. Why not?"

"Because it don't work like that."

"Skinner was an animal and I put him down like an animal. You don't owe him anything."

"That's true enough, but he did flush you out and that was all that needed to happen before the folks you've been hiding from realized you were still alive and kicking."

The grave was over halfway filled by now and Nick still hadn't gotten more than a passing glimpse of Kyle's face. Instead, his eyes were focused on the other man's feet and where they were positioned in front of him. He also kept close watch on the Colt revolver strapped around Kyle's waist.

"So this is just about money?" Nick asked. "There's plenty of easier ways to get rich, you know."

"Yeah. I know. But there's more to it than money."

A smirk drifted across Nick's face. He nodded slowly and smoothed out the top layer of dirt he'd tossed into the grave. "There always is."

"You're getting soft, Nick. Time was that I never could have found you when you weren't heeled. Then again, it's not like you can fire for shit anymore."

"Really?" Nick said as he fixed his eyes upon Kyle and kept them there. "Maybe you should ask Skinner about that."

Kyle's sunken face twisted into a cruel smile. The scars on his cheeks were almost deep enough to bore straight through to his teeth and they formed an odd design as his smirk grew larger. "There's been plenty of stories going around about how you managed to drop Skinner. Think you could tell me what happened?"

"No."

Nick got back to his digging. The tips of his fingers itched in the same way that a soldier felt tickling in limbs that had been erased by a cannonball. Now, he felt the more pronounced absence of the gun belt that normally hung around his waist. He didn't like wearing his gun to funerals. The reason had to do with a simple matter of respect for the dead and grieving alike. Nick's job was a Mourner and part of his duties entailed comforting people in their time of loss.

Wearing a gun presented a problem when also trying to make folks feel comfortable.

Every so often, however, the lack of a gun was an even bigger problem.

Kyle looked around. The cemetery was empty except for the two of them. Any motion he saw that didn't come from himself or Nick was caused by the rustling of the wind. Every now and then, he would spot someone milling about outside the cemetery, but even from a distance Kyle was able to get them to quickly turn away with nothing more than a mean glare.

"I wish I could've known you in the old days, Nick. I really do. From everything I've heard, being there to see you in action would have been one hell of a show."

"You've been dogging my trail for long enough to have seen some blood," Nick said with no small amount of disgust. "Didn't that keep you satisfied?"

"I'm not talking about blood. There's more to it than that. Men like us aren't just killers or gun hands. We're craftsmen. We're a rare breed. That's why we seek each other out, just to get a look at another master working his trade."

Nodding toward the headstone, Nick said, "That's my trade now."

Kyle looked toward the sculpted stone and couldn't help but admire what he saw. "Like I said before. That's some damn fine work." Slowly, his eyes crept back over to Nick. Once again, Kyle's head shifted and cocked in another direction. He studied Nick's every motion, just as he'd been doing for the last several days. "How much have you been making digging graves and carving headstones? Was it more than the cash reward you got for handing in Skinner's carcass?"

Every word that came from Kyle's mouth

cinched the knot in Nick's stomach tighter and tighter. No matter how much he tried to lay low and keep to his own affairs, things had a way of coming back to him. The past was a dirty road and the more of that road he kept to his back, the better Nick felt about it. Listening to Kyle now was akin to being forced to stop, turn around, and stare at a particularly ugly ditch.

There would always be someone coming for him. That was the price Nick had to pay for living the life he'd lived.

His father had been a simple man who'd raised him throughout most of Nick's childhood. He'd taught Nick about several things that, while not so pretty to look at, were as natural as drawing the next breath.

Working with the dead, digging their graves, covering them up again; these were all natural things that happened every day. There was no way around death, but a man did have a bit of say in the road he took to get there. Nick had certain choices a long time ago and some others had been made for him.

Giving good men like Raymond Hunt a proper resting place was one of the choices Nick had made for his life. Unfortunately, dealing with the likes of Kyle Santos fell into the latter category.

Nick dropped the last pile of dirt onto Raymond's grave and straightened up with the shovel in hand like a walking stick. When he pulled in a breath, he was the simple gravedigger that everyone in Switchback had come to know. When he let that same breath out again, he was the man Kyle Santos had been after.

"You want money?" Nick asked. "I'll pay you money."

"Now that wasn't something I was expecting. Not from the likes of you. Then again, you'd probably be singing a different tune if you had that gun of yours right about now."

And there it was.

There was a shift in a killer's voice when he changed from the man that his mother would have liked into the man he truly was. It was something that couldn't be seen in the eyes of every person who'd taken another's life, but it was there inside those who'd enjoyed the act.

That cold spark was like the flash that came just before a match caught fire. Nick knew all too well how to find that spark. He'd seen it plenty of times and had felt it enough to be immune to the reflex that made most God-fearing souls look the other way.

"I wouldn't be paying you to save my own

skin," Nick said. "You'd get the money for leaving this place and forgetting anything that had to do with me or mine. I can offer you more than the price on my head and I'll only be making the offer one time."

The spark had burned away and Kyle's eyes still had an eerie quality that left them cold and lifeless. "That's not how it works. That's not why I came."

"You wanted to fight or was it just bragging rights you were after?" Nick asked, holding out both arms as if to drive the point home that the shovel was all he had. "Whichever it was, you won't get it. I'm not that man any more."

"No? Well, I'm still going to have to go through with this."

"Yeah," Nick said regretfully. "I know."

"It really is a shame, though," Kyle said as his hand dropped down to hang over his holster. "After everything I've heard about you, I would have loved to face you down to see what you're really made of."

Nick watched the other man closely, studying his every move with expert scrutiny.

Letting out a breath that was just big enough to flare his nostrils, Kyle narrowed his eyes and nodded as if sealing a deal within his own mind. "I guess this'll just have to do."

With that said, both men fell completely silent.

It wasn't the kind of silence they might have had if Nick had been armed. In that case, Kyle would have weighed each second more carefully since it very well could have been his last. Instead, Kyle was picking the spot where he wanted to place his shot and giving pause to the moment that he was about to commit a mortal sin.

For Nick, the moment was equally powerful. He was unarmed and about to stare down the wrong end of a pistol. He could tell Kyle's arm was twitching slightly beneath the skin, waiting for the moment when he would draw his gun and fire. To be honest, Nick was surprised that the man hadn't drawn just yet. Perhaps that was because Kyle knew better than to assume Nick was helpless even though his gun wasn't in plain sight. If that was the case, then at least Kyle wasn't stupid.

Only a precious few seconds ticked away before Kyle made his move. It still didn't sit too well with him that he was about to gun down an unarmed man, but he knew those regrets would fade soon enough once he cashed in the reward being offered for Nick's dead body.

In a smooth, fluid motion, Kyle reached for his gun.

The instant he saw the first trace of that motion, Nick clenched both hands around the shovel's handle and swung the blade toward Kyle's shoulder. Connecting with the edge of the shovel's blade, Nick could feel the impact as iron met bone.

Kyle's entire upper body twisted to one side, partly to try to get away from the shovel and partly to roll with the blow he'd been dealt. His lips curled back to display a toothy snarl as the sound of cracking bone rode through the air. The fingers of that hand straightened out and twitched reflexively as his arm dropped and hung limply from its socket.

Even with daggers of pain shooting through his arm and shoulder, Kyle wasn't about to give up so easily. The bones in his gun arm may have been splintered, but that didn't drain all the fight out of him just yet. In a genuinely impressive show of speed, he crossed his left hand over his body and reached for the gun that still sat in its holster. What he hadn't counted on was Nick's own speed with his improvised weapon.

Turning the shovel in a quick half-circle, Nick spun it around so the blade sliced through the air behind him on an arc headed toward Kyle's right shin. Rather than crack another set of bones, he turned the blade flat side up and brought it underneath Kyle's holster. From there, the blade of the shovel smacked against the barrel of Kyle's gun, which stuck out from the bottom of its holster.

Metal clanged against metal. The pistol popped up from its resting place and jumped into the air, only to be snatched away by a gnarled, yet lightning-fast hand. By the time the shovel dropped to the ground, the tables were turned and it was Nick who now sighted down the barrel of Kyle's gun.

Kyle couldn't believe it. After all his preparation, all the scouting and all the watching, he'd somehow wound up on the losing end of the deal. The very notion pushed aside the pain that tore through his body as the splintered bones of his right arm grated against each other. The pain made him feel light-headed, adding to the sensation that he was in the middle of a bad dream.

Nick's eyes were cold and his hand was steady. Tightening around the pistol's grip, his fingers slid uncomfortably where any other man's would have fit right in. He could feel the weapon turning in his hand as his mangled fingers shifted awkwardly around the grip.

Nick kept his face passive. He pointed the gun back toward Kyle's forehead, hoping the other man hadn't noticed the momentary lapse in aim caused by his handicap.

"I'll be . . . damned," Kyle said as his eyes traced the path of movement starting from the edge of the grave to where the shovel now lay discarded in the dirt. Waves of agony mixed with nausea made it difficult for him to speak. "Maybe I'll take that . . . money . . . after all."

Nick shook his head. "I told you my offer was only good once."

Squirming under the close scrutiny of Nick's glare and the pain of his fractured bones, Kyle said, "Then maybe you could just let me go. Nobody needs to know I found you."

"You'll know," Nick said, staring into the other man's eyes and seeing straight through the line of bullshit he was being fed. "Just like I know that you've got another gun hidden under that jacket."

For a moment, the expression on Kyle's face froze. He tried to preserve that half-smirk just like a kid who knew he'd been caught breaking a plate. Slowly, that smirk faded and he was faced with the hardest decision he would ever have to make.

Having already snuck his left hand up underneath his jacket, Kyle grabbed the holdout pistol secreted there and brought it out to take aim at his target.

Nick was ready to answer in kind and snapped his gun hand forward to put the pistol's muzzle less than half an inch from Kyle's face. Not even a blind man could miss from that distance, but the holdout gun was still in Kyle's hand. That left nothing else for Nick to do besides pull his trigger and show Kyle's brains the light of day.

Blood, pulp, and chips of bone sprayed out in a mist as a muffled gunshot rolled through the air. Smoke billowed out from Nick's barrel, spewing over the surprised expression that would become Kyle's death mask.

For a moment, Nick stood with gun in hand while staring into suddenly vacant eyes. Kyle's legs wobbled and finally gave out, dropping him back onto the ground like a load that had been tossed from the back of a cart.

It was a moment that Nick had been hoping to avoid, yet was as inevitable as the dawn.

In that moment, Nick knew his life in Switchback was over.

THREE

Samuel James was a short man with a build more suited to someone who split rails for a living. Instead, he was the undertaker in Switchback and was also the man who fretfully wrung his hands while pacing back and forth outside his parlor.

"Are you sure you have to go?" Samuel asked.

Nick was busy loading up a small wagon hitched to two mismatched horses. He nodded while tossing one of his bags into the wagon's bed. The gun belt he now wore had been strapped around his waist beneath his jacket from the moment he'd gotten back from the cemetery. The weight at his side was familiar enough, yet somehow not very comforting. "Yeah. I'm sure."

"But folks appreciate what you've done around here. They know what kind of man you are." At that moment, his eyes drifted to the gun belt around Nick's waist. Although it wasn't an uncommon sight, it seemed especially forbidding just then.

Turning to look at Samuel directly, Nick asked, "Do you think anyone around here missed what happened up at that cemetery? Or do you think nobody'll ask any questions about the fresh, unmarked grave outside of town?"

The undertaker shrugged his shoulders and tried to look casual. "Maybe nobody saw what happened."

"Maybe. Maybe not. But there's plenty of talk, I'm sure."

"I heard that the sheriff ain't too concerned."

"You know something? That troubles me even more."

Taking a moment to figure out what to say next, Samuel watched as Nick completed loading his wagon. "This is the best my business has done in years, Nick. I even heard that folks in other towns are starting to take notice and ask for us special. You remember that funeral last month? The Wickermeyer boy? That was from Rogan's Bluff and that's a day's ride from here!"

"You'll do fine, Sam."

"Yeah, but that's because of what you done for me. Hell, I learned more from watching you than I ever did from when I was an apprentice and you never even unpacked them fancy tools you've got in that wagon."

Hearing that brought Nick's eye to his gear, which was wrapped up and stored at the bottom of his wagon. After his last ride through Nebraska, he'd managed to pull together enough money to upgrade his tools and get a few things that would have made his father jealous. Of course, he hadn't made all that money in his duties as a Mourner, but that was another story.

Shaking his head, Nick walked around to the other side of his wagon to make sure the tarp covering his belongings was tied down properly. Seconds later, he heard the scuttling sounds of Samuel's boots shuffling over the dirt.

"I did hear some things," Samuel said as he rushed over to stand on Nick's side of the wagon. "The sheriff himself said that whatever happened in that cemetery stays there. Everything he heard tells him what you done was in self-defense and there's nobody that's gonna say otherwise. You weren't even armed!"

"Maybe I don't like being somewhere that I get ambushed. You ever think of that?"

For a second, Samuel looked Nick over as if he were taking stock of the man. Nick moved as he always did, every motion precise and showing an underlying strength. It didn't matter if he was nailing a coffin together, digging a grave, or tossing away a busted flush when playing cards at the saloon, Nick always looked as though he was in control of a situation. This time was no different.

"I don't believe that," Samuel finally said with a shake of his head.

"Oh, so I guess I enjoy getting shot at?"

"That's not what I mean."

"Then what do you mean?" Nick asked with a sudden harshness. "You're worried about losing a good worker who did his job for a pittance of a fee. Is that it? You're worried that you might not be able to handle the business that's coming your way unless I'm here to take you by the hand?"

Samuel stood almost a foot shorter than Nick, but when he straightened up he did a good job of almost closing that gap. His face set into a solid, neutral expression when he said, "I'm not worried about my business. I just don't want to see you go like this. Men like us, in our line of work, we don't get a whole lot of folks wanting to be our friends. We don't get to talk to many others without seeing them turn away and find somewhere else to be.

"Plenty of folks heard that shot and not one of them was surprised to see you walk away, dragging that killer's worthless hide behind you."

Nick winced slightly at that. He'd figured people had heard the scuffle and might have seen a thing or two, but he didn't think they would have seen so much.

"Whatever that fight was about," Samuel went on to say, "it don't need to be the reason for you to leave. You can stay here, Nick. Something tells me you could use a good place to hang your hat for a while longer."

For all the months Nick had worked there, he'd never thought it would be so hard to pick up and leave. Samuel could be a true pain in the ass, following him around and flapping his gums. The work was hard, the hours were long, and the pay was just shy of pathetic, but it was still one of the best stretches of employment Nick had had for some time.

After leaving Nebraska, he didn't think he'd be able to find someone to match the friend he'd made in his last employer, but Samuel was actually pretty close.

"Do me a favor, Sam."

For a second, the undertaker's face lit up. "Name it."

"Give my best to everyone at the poker game tonight. And do the same for Jen and Sara down at the steakhouse."

"I'm tellin' ya, there's nobody around here who'll give one more thought about what happened today."

Leaning in a bit closer, Nick made sure that he could stare directly into the man's eyes as he spoke. "You know what a boot hill is?"

"Yeah," Samuel responded, obviously confused by the question. "It's where they bury gunfighters."

"It's where they plant people who can't afford or don't deserve a funeral like the one thrown for ol' Raymond Hunt. Have you ever seen one?"

Samuel shook his head.

"The graves are so shallow," Nick explained, "that their boots stick up from the ground after a few windy days or one too many animals come by. Boot hills are ugly as death and the reason you've never seen one is because there never was one in Switchback. Well, guess what. You've got one now and it's because of me. If I stay, there'll just be more boots sticking out of the ground next to the ones I planted today. Eventually, two of those boots will be mine."

Samuel shook his head again, but stopped

himself. Soon, the expression on his face shifted from regret to acceptance. Finally, he began to nod. "So where are you headed?"

"I don't rightly know just yet."

"Think you might come back this way?"

Although Nick's first response was to answer in the negative, he paused and allowed a genuine smile to slip onto his face. "Yeah. Actually, I would like to come back here once I get some things straightened out."

"Things?" Samuel asked in a tone shifting back to the conversational. "What things?"

That brought Nick right back to where he was when he'd first begun loading the wagon. "Just some old debts that need to get paid."

Samuel may not have been the best hand at poker, but he could read a man's face well enough to know that Nick was firmly set in the path he'd chosen. Accepting that fact grudgingly, he nodded once and extended his hand. "Well, take care of yourself, Nick."

Reaching out to shake Samuel's hand, Nick instead saw the other man pull it back and slap something else into his palm. "What's this?" he asked, twisting his hand to get a look at what Samuel had given him.

It was a folded wad of dollar bills.

"It's not much," Samuel explained, "but it's the least I can give you after all the work you done."

"You already paid me. Keep it."

"No, no. I insist. Besides, I do still owe you about twice as much as that from all the times you beat me at poker."

"Since you put it that way . . ." Nick closed his grip around the money and stashed it into his pocket. From there, he climbed into the driver's seat of his wagon and gathered up the reins. The two horses, Rasa and Kazys, were shifting and scraping their hooves against the ground. It had been a while since they'd been hitched up and were anxious to get moving.

Without another word or one more delay, Nick snapped the reins and got the wagon rolling. The wheels creaked and groaned beneath him, making almost as much noise as the horses pulling them. But, much like those animals, the wagon held together and quickly settled into a bumpy, swaying rhythm.

Samuel watched him go, waving slowly to Nick's back even though he was certain the gesture would go unseen. Just after the wagon pulled onto the street and just before it turned a corner, Nick lifted his hand and tossed a wave over his shoulder. Samuel smiled, hoping that it wasn't the last time he might see those two worn-out horses and their driver.

Before leaving town, Nick headed for the largest building on the edge of the saloon district. It was a garishly decorated place with banners and painted signs all displaying the words GILSOM'S GAMING EMPORIUM in every direction. Throughout his entire stay in Switchback, the only place he'd frequented more than Samuel's parlor or the steakhouse was Gilsom's.

Nick still came to a stop outside of the two-level structure that was already starting to see its nightly bunch of regulars step through the doors. Remaining in his seat, Nick knew he wouldn't have to wait long before a familiar man wearing a gray suit stepped outside. In fact, Gilsom was walking out to meet him before Nick had a chance to set his brake.

Everything about the man, from his fancy clothes to the cocky smile on his face, marked him as a gambler. "I was wondering if I'd be seeing you tonight," Gilsom said. "Where you headed?"

"That way," Nick said, pointing a finger down the street and to the open trail beyond. "Just thought I'd stop by and see if you heard anything about any business I might have with the sheriff."

"You mean concerning that man who tried to gun you down after Ray's funeral? If you killed him, you saved the sheriff a length of rope to do the same job. If you ran that bastard off, then you saved the law some trouble there as well. Other than that, there's nothing to tell. At least, not that I know of."

"Good," Nick said with a nod. "Then I'll just collect what you owe me and I'll be going."

Suddenly, Gilsom took a few steps back and raised his hands as if he was being robbed. "Hold on now. I don't have that much on me."

"That's a shame," Nick replied, slipping in just enough menace to add an edge to his voice.

"I do have something else for you, though. Remember that matter you were asking about a month or two ago?"

"Yeah."

"Bitter Creek," Gilsom said as if that was all anyone would need. Seeing the confused look on Nick's face, he went on to say, "You asked me to keep an ear open for any unsavory types asking about you and I heard just that."

"Who was it?"

"I don't know. One of my girls put a smile on the face of some fella from Bitter Creek and he mentioned you and some business in Nebraska concerning a mad dog killer. You're lucky she was a bit sweet on you by then or she might have told him where you were working. She mentioned it to me the other night and I figured I'd tell you at your poker game this evening."

"Tonight or some other time when you could trade that instead of money."

Unable to refute the accusation, Gilsom shrugged. "It wasn't much, but you asked me to keep my ears open for anyone coming around asking about you and that's what I did."

"Bitter Creek, huh?"

"Yessir. It's a few days' ride north of here. Then again," he added, taking a long look at the mismatched horses pulling Nick's wagon. "It might just take you a bit longer to get there."

"You keep talking like that about my horses, and I might just hold you to those debts after all."

"You mean you could let them slide?" Gilsom asked hopefully. "At least, for the time being?"

"As long as you swear that information you gave me is correct."

"It is! I swear it is. If not, then feel free to come back and get your money with interest. I don't lie when it comes to important matters. Cards and women are different, but men like us need to stick together when it counts. She said the man was from Bitter Creek, so you'd do well to steer clear of that place."

Nick studied the gambler carefully and couldn't rightly say if Gilsom was being forthright or not. A man like that didn't get a place like the Gaming Emporium by being easy to read, but Gilsom didn't really have much of a reason to lie either. Paying Nick back was a simple matter of stepping inside and shaving a bit off the top of what was in Gilsom's safe. There was more for him to lose by being known as a liar and cheat to other gamblers Nick might meet along the way.

"Is this fella after you like that poor bastard who crossed your path at the cemetery?" Gilsom asked.

"How should I know? I don't even have a name to go by."

"Sorry," Gilsom said with a shrug. "She never mentioned a name. So is that what you were after? I mean, I know it's not much, but does that fit the bill?"

"Sure it does. Thanks for letting me know."

"Anytime, Nick. You got time for a few quick hands and a drink before you go?"

"No. Sorry."

"Then hold on. Wait right there." Before he got an answer, Gilsom rushed back inside and came out again less than a minute later. In his hand was a bottle half full of a clear liquid. Standing at the edge of the boardwalk in front of his place, he tossed the bottle over to Nick who caught it in one hand.

"It's that vodka you like so much," Gilsom said.

"You sure you want to part with this? I know it's hard to come by."

"Eh, take it. You're the only one who drinks that piss anyway."

Stowing the bottle in a safe place beneath his seat, Nick tipped his hat and snapped the reins.

FOUR

It only took a few minutes before Nick was outside of Switchback's limits. He'd spotted more than a few familiar faces as he left and returned plenty of waves, but he didn't offer any explanations. Between Samuel and Gilsom, Nick figured the news of his departure would be spread sure enough.

After leaving his first home, picking up and moving on had only gotten simpler with practice.

The first home Nick remembered was a farmhouse in the middle of a little-known European field. Every time he thought back to that place, the grass always sprouted taller and each blade was a little greener. The breezes even cooled and became more fragrant with each recollection. Of course, he was more than a little biased.

Having been taken from that farmhouse by his parents when he was still a small boy, his recollections of that field and farmhouse were more like dreams. He remembered his mother's face and the way his father would smile when he looked at his small family. He remembered the flowing, almost lyrical sound of his native tongue when spoken in a constant, daily flow.

That flow became more of a trickle once he and his parents climbed aboard a ship bound for Boston Harbor. Part of that was because his parents wanted to get him used to speaking English before they arrived. Another part wasn't so practical and stemmed from the hardships of the voyage itself.

Stasys would look down at his little boy, ruffle his hair, and start to talk but the words just wouldn't come. Thinking back to one particular day, every last detail filled Nick's mind like raw swamp water. Unlike his fonder memories, these were so intricate that if he let himself wallow in them for too long, he could feel the sorrow sinking straight into him like a knife being slowly pushed through his chest.

She'd been sick for a while, but practically everyone on that boat had gotten sick at one time or another. The only difference in his mother's case was that she never got any better. The infection robbed her of every-thing she was. It took away her smile, her voice, even the color in her cheeks. Finally, it closed up her throat and took her away altogether.

Nick lowered his eyes and took a deep breath as the memories washed over him. It was no good trying to fight them, no matter how much he wished he could. . . .

"Motina?" Nick had said all those years ago, still using the word for mother in his native tongue. *"Motina,* wake up!"

Most of the sailors treated their immigrant passengers no different than the other cargo they were hauling. There were a few exceptions to the rule, but even they just pushed the travelers with a bit less roughness than the rest. Unfortunately, the ones that came into the room where his mother had passed away weren't one of the exceptions.

The sailors had been kicking in every door in the hold until they got to the one occupied by Stasys's family and a few others. When they saw the dead woman staring blankly up at the ceiling, the sailors stomped straight for her.

Stasys protested in his native language and was ignored by the seamen, so he did his best to snarl in English, which was a language everyone on board at least tried to learn. "No!" he growled, throwing himself in front of the sailor. "You leave her!"

"Shut your mouth," the biggest of the sailors grunted as he tried to push Stasys aside. "You live down here like animals, but we can't have dead carcasses on board. It's bad luck."

Stasys's face twisted as though he didn't understand. Then, the anger shone through like a fire burning just beneath his surface. "Bad luck? You talk to my dead wife and say bad luck?!"

From there, all Nick could remember was a tangle of punches being thrown, blood spraying through the air and a chaotic jumble of violence contained in the confines of that room. When it was over, Stasys and most of the sailors were battered and bruised but the main reason for all the anguish was still there.

His mother was still dead and her body was still lying on the floor.

The sailors had a job to do and they did it. After the fight, however, they did their job quickly and respectfully. They picked up Nick's mother by the arms and legs to carry her out of the room and onto the upper deck. Nick followed as quickly as his little legs would carry him, trying the whole time to get one more look at her face or one more touch of her hand.

His fingers brushed against her temple for the briefest of moments, but it was a moment that would stick with him for his entire life. It was one of the most tranquil moments he would ever experience.

As her body was hefted over the side of the ship and dropped into the ocean, Nick felt a strong hand drop onto his shoulder. He didn't need to look to know whose hand that was.

"Tevai," he said, using the word for father from his native language. It wasn't a question or a statement, but more of a way for the boy to make sure that he had at least one person that would hear him.

After she died in the dark hold of that leaking ship, Nick and his father didn't speak much until they were approaching the eastern shores of their adopted country. All that time, Nick knew his father was there, but felt the absence of his mother even more. He and Stasys grew closer, but the remainder of that quiet voyage taught Nick a valuable lesson.

If necessary, he could survive on his own.

The only person he could fully count on was himself. With that knowledge in place, a whole world was opened to young Nicolai just as he was about to set foot upon unfamiliar soil. He took that bit of knowledge to heart, since it would eventually free him up to take roads most people would never consider. . . .

Nick snapped the reins and looked up at the cloudy sky overhead. The trail was fairly straight, but the terrain was just tricky enough to shift the things in his wagon from one side to another like the cargo in that boat from his memories. Pulling in a generous helping of fresh air, Nick smiled slightly as he surveyed the road he was currently on.

Ever since that voyage was over, Nick had hated the sea. His father must have felt some of that as well since he didn't seem to have any trouble promising to find a home far away from it.

The Badlands stretched out in the distance, but that wasn't where Nick was headed. The mountains weren't too far off either, but he wouldn't be going in that direction just yet. His eyes settled in the direction he knew those mountains to be and he stared at them as if making a silent promise. He would be there soon enough. First, there was some other business to attend to.

Rasa and Kazys were getting up in years. They could pull the wagon well enough and even ride on their own pretty well, but they weren't exactly able racehorses. Their pace gave Nick plenty of time to think, which usually was a good thing. Sometimes, however, it was something else.

Nick could still hear the distant, plunking sound of his mother's body dropping into the ocean. At the time, it had sounded like a penny being pitched into a bucket of water. It was actually the final nail being driven into his childhood. It was the moment when he'd truly become a Mourner.

FIVE

Although Nick had a good idea of where he was headed, he still thought he might have missed the town of Bitter Creek altogether. The land had become more rugged and the path he rode took on a lot more twists and turns. He knew which way he needed to go, and had been headed there for a few days. Even so, he was starting to wonder if he might have taken a wrong turn.

Just when he was truly starting to get concerned, he spotted the first trace of civilization. As always, the first glimpse of a town wasn't much. Usually, it wasn't more than a cluster of shacks or the curls of smoke rising through the air that tipped it off. But to eyes that had had nothing else to focus on apart from grass and sky for days on end, those simple things were like a gift from above.

Nick was no stranger to living off the land. He'd spent years of his youth holed up in caves or huddling over a sputtering fire and truly enjoyed a good portion of it. But a man had a tendency to get accustomed to certain things like the feel of something softer than a rock under his head at night or a blanket that didn't smell like horse.

When he got that first look at the town, Nick felt a smile come over him that cracked the dirt that had collected in layers upon his face. A few minutes later and he could smell food being cooked. A little while after that, he could hear voices as folks went about their daily lives.

It hadn't been too long since he'd been in Switchback, but leaving that place hadn't exactly been Nick's first choice. It had been a necessity and a damn hard one at that. For that reason alone, the ride to Bitter Creek seemed extra long. Now that he'd arrived, however, it was even better to be there.

"Kind of like pounding a rusty nail into yer foot," an acquaintance from Nick's past had once said. "The only reason to do it is because it feels so damn good when you stop."

Well, the ride hadn't been as difficult as all that, but it sure did feel good when Nick came to a stop.

Bitter Creek wasn't laid out in a straight

line or a square like most towns. In fact, it stuck a little too close to its namesake, winding in a crooked line along the banks of a slender flow of water. It wasn't much of a creek as far as Nick could see, but the sound of faster waters flowing crept in along with all the other sounds of civilized living.

There were folks talking, wheels turning, and doors slamming to wash away the more mundane sounds like wind blowing or grass swaying back and forth. Nick followed those sounds along the creek and through a stand of trees as he passed several rows of rickety houses and shacks that stretched out into the weeds.

Once he broke through another row of trees, Nick found that his wagon was suddenly upon a proper street and boardwalks now lined either side as if they'd sprouted up from the dirt. The street looked as if it had been planned by a drunk, but eventually straightened out before Nick reached the center of town. In fact, the town itself seemed to mature more the closer one got to its center. Clothing stores, a courthouse, and even a few churches sprouted up, these had been missing from the more twisted throughways.

As Nick kept riding down the street, he passed several corners and took a look down the roads branching off from the one he was following. Most of them seemed to become crooked again as they wound away from the main street. Saloons and gambling parlors dominated several of the farther corners. Nick spotted a few buildings in that direction with painted ladies lounging on the porches and waving to him invitingly as they did to any other man who came within their sight.

Nodding back to the working girls, Nick marked down every district he could pick out while keeping his eyes open for a comfortable-looking hotel. He'd spotted one place when he'd arrived, but knew better than to stop there before looking around first. There were bathhouses, a barber shop, and plenty more as Bitter Creek just seemed to keep on going and going.

By the time he reached the opposite end of town, Nick had to admit that he was impressed with the place. It was positioned strategically in a spot that was something akin to the crook of a giant arm. A man could ride past the place and not even see it if he was facing the wrong way. There were certainly plenty of places to get lost within the town's limits, but there was still a sort of comfort to it as well.

At that moment, Nick felt his stomach

clench and his teeth gnash. Without thinking about it, he pulled back on the reins and brought the wagon to a stop. Looking on either side of the street, he quickly spotted the restaurant that had brought about such an immediate response. He didn't even look at the name of the place before setting the brake and heading inside.

"Hello," came a bright, chirping voice even before Nick was all the way through the door. "Welcome to the Skillet. What can I get for you?"

Nick stood in the doorway of a narrow room that was lined with a few square tables and several old chairs. The girl who'd spoken to him stood about a foot and a half shorter than he and couldn't have been more than eighteen years old. Her face was bright and sunny, which was a fine match to the golden hair that flowed down over her shoulders.

Although she had the figure of a woman, she carried herself in a way that made it obvious she didn't know what effect such a shape could have on a man. Either that, or she wasn't aware of the problems such attentions could bring.

Nick couldn't help but notice how he immediately tended to be attracted to pretty serving girls. Perhaps it was the owner's intention to dress up his place with a pretty face. But Nick had enough years under his belt to keep from getting anxious at the mere sight of a sweet young girl in a pretty dress. It must have been the fact that pretty girls like this one were also about to bring him a heaping plate of hot food. Now, that was an unbeatable combination that appealed to two powerful instincts.

Suddenly, Nick couldn't help but feel older than his thirty-some years.

Standing on the balls of her feet with her hands clasped behind her and her back arched, she rolled her eyes at a gruff voice that grumbled at her from the next room.

"Dammit, I warned you about that." The voice was rough and almost as greasy as the curtains separating the dining room from the kitchen.

"Sorry." Then, lifting her voice so everyone in that room and the next could hear her, she said, "Welcome to *Norm*'s Skillet. My name's Sandy."

"And let me guess," Nick said, nodding toward the room behind the greasy curtains. "That's Norm."

Sandy smiled widely and started to laugh, but covered her mouth quickly with her hand. Instead, she nodded and took Nick by the sleeve so she could pull him toward the closest empty table. "Sit down right here and I'll get you something." She spun around and started to walk away, but stopped, spun back around and bent down to ask, "What do you want?"

Nick was no old man, but he'd put enough years behind him to feel like one when he got a longer look at Sandy. Her skin was smooth as silk and the curves of her firm body were on proud display beneath the low cut of her blouse. Knowing he was at least twice her age, Nick tried to keep his thoughts and hands to himself.

"Uhh, I'll just start off with some water," he said, doing his best to keep his eyes focused on hers and not the much more enticing view she was offering.

Smirking as she slowly straightened up again, the blonde nodded and patted him on the hand. "Be right back with that."

There was no mistaking it. Sandy wasn't only aware of what she was doing to Nick just then, but she was also very good at it. And while Nick wasn't about to ask her for anything but a meal, he was still plenty human and very much enjoyed the view of her hips swaying under the breezy flow of her skirts.

After Sandy had disappeared into the kitchen, Nick shook his head and realized that spending so much time trying to act respectably had had more of an effect on him than he would have guessed. Some things, however, never changed. Without him realizing it, Nick had still ended up with his back to a wall and had already picked out all the possible ways to leave the room. He looked around at the other folks sitting in the dining room. None of them seemed to have taken much notice of his arrival, but plenty of the men were still staring at the blonde just as Nick had been only moments ago.

Once the young woman was out of the room, the men in her wake got a chance to catch their breath. Of course, that was more of a problem for some than it was for others since a few of them had women of their own to deal with.

Nick winced as the women sitting with some of those men gave them everything from hushed brow-beatings to smacks on the back of the head in repayment for those lingering glances. As soon as those individual storms passed, the men glanced around at each other and shrugged. It didn't matter if they knew each other or not. At that moment, they'd all been caught with their hands in the same cookie jar.

Once they had gotten back to their meals,

Nick leaned back in his chair. He suddenly felt more comfortable just then, as if he'd looked out a strange window to find a very familiar view.

At that moment, Sandy entered the dining room as if she wanted to kick up the dust that had just got finished settling. None of the men were stupid enough to take the bait this time and they kept their noses pointed down toward their plates.

"Here you go, mister," she said, setting down a cup of water in front of Nick. Making sure she had his complete attention, she leaned in just a bit too much and asked, "Did you think of anything else you want?"

"I'd like a steak and some potatoes. Maybe even some greens if you've got them."

Sensing that she was losing her grip on him, she stood back up and shifted on her feet to give Nick alternating views of her backside and front. "We've got all of that and more if you like."

"That'll do just fine," Nick said evenly. "Maybe some dessert if I've still got room."

Once she saw that he was content to be off his feet and get some food in his belly rather than take whatever she was truly offering, she shrugged her shoulders and nodded.

"All right," she said. "I'll fetch you some biscuits. How'd that be?"

Nick smiled, keeping his expression friendly. "Just fine."

Sandy paused for a moment while she was in mid-turn to head back toward the kitchen. For a second, she looked a little confused. Very quickly, however, she shifted to a smile that wasn't only deeply genuine, but brought out a brighter light from inside of her. "I think we just got some honey in, too. You'll love that on those biscuits."

"That sounds great. Um . . . Sandy," Nick added before she could get away from him. "Just one more thing."

In a quick motion that sent the hem of her skirts sailing around her ankles, she spun back around and stepped closer. When she leaned in this time, she bent more at the knees than at the waist. "Yes?"

"You might want to watch how you handle yourself around these rascals," Nick told her, referring to the other men in a kidding manner. The tone in his naturally low and somewhat scratchy voice still let her know that there was a definite point to be made. "Best just give them their food or you'll get them all in a mess of trouble."

Sandy straightened up. For a split second, there was some embarrassment in her eyes.

That disappeared when she turned a stern glare to all the men who were still pretending to not drink in the sight of her young figure.

"You dogs should take a lesson from this one," Sandy said. "He's a gentleman."

Now, it was Nick's turn to roll his eyes. While he'd wanted to try and get his point across, he wasn't exactly wild on the idea of being announced to the entire room. In fact, that very moment was a prime example of why he normally found it was usually better to just keep his mouth shut.

"I'll be right back," Sandy said before making her rounds to all the other tables.

Although Nick would have preferred to have just walked in, had his food and walked out, he couldn't help but laugh when he saw the approving looks he got from all the wives in the room. Then again, some of the looks he got from the husbands weren't quite so friendly.

Sandy headed back into the kitchen. When she opened the door, she made a sudden move that caught Nick's eye. Judging by the way she hopped back, it was as though the door no longer opened into the kitchen, but straight into a brick wall. That brick wall was a man only an inch or so taller than she, but with at least another eighty pounds on the blonde.

The man reached out with one hand and took hold of Sandy's shoulder to move her into the kitchen. His eyes were set firmly on Nick and his other hand was wrapped around a huge butcher's knife.

"Just what the hell do you think you're doing gawking at my little girl?" the cook snarled.

"Jesus Christ," Nick muttered. "All I wanted was a damn steak."

SIX

"You've got it wrong, Daddy," Sandy pleaded. "He's just —"

"He's just like all the others!" the cook shouted as he stepped past the blonde and toward Nick's table. "He thinks you're some kind of whore."

Nick shook his head and held up both hands. "That's not true. I just want a meal. You're daughter was just . . ."

"Just what? Huh? Go on and say it."

There was a few things Nick wanted to say, but not much that would make the situation any better. It was definitely one of those instances where the fact that he spent most of his days without talking to live people truly showed.

"You've got the wrong idea, Norm." The person who'd said that wasn't Nick and it wasn't any of the other men in the dining room. The words came in a firm, yet soothing tone that only a woman could truly master.

Norm's eyes were wide and his nostrils flared as he shot a glance toward the woman who'd spoken up. "Sit down, Vera. This is just another stranger who thinks he can take advantage of my little girl."

Vera was an attractive woman with a solid build. Her straight black hair was gathered up in a braid that hung down almost to the small of her back. Keeping her hands on the edge of the table, she got to her feet and held her chin up high. "That's not true," she said to Norm. Turning to look at Sandy, she gave the girl a look that was loaded with meaning as well as a subtle reprimand. "Ask your daughter. She knows it's not so."

Norm's eyes flicked toward his girl, but he wasn't about to turn away from Nick to get a clear look at her. "What did he do, darlin'?"

"Nothing, Daddy."

"Aw, she could just be protectin' him. Especially since she knows what I'd do if I saw anything bad happening to my little angel!" As he said those words, Norm advanced on Nick while tightening his grip around the handle of his butcher's knife. His knuckles turned white and the intent in his eyes was clear enough to make Nick's hand start inching toward the holster buckled around his waist and under his jacket.

Most of the other customers in the place were scooting away from the two men, while also being sure to keep them both in sight so as not to miss the fireworks once the show began. Although Sandy was trying to talk to her father, Norm was no longer listening to her.

"I've heard what some folks say about my girl," Norm said. "And I'm not about to sit back and let this here stranger act on them rumors."

Suddenly, the man sitting at Vera's table smacked his fist against the wooden surface in front of him and spoke up in a tone that was more annoyed than anything else. "Go back and cook the man his meal, for Christ's sake."

The tension in the air was still mighty thick, but now Norm's attention seemed to be divided between Nick and the man who'd just thrown his own hat into the ring.

"This one here didn't do a damn thing besides order some food," the other man said. "Now put that knife away and stop acting like a damn fool."

Norm started to say something, but stopped himself. While lowering the knife, he jabbed a finger toward Nick and grumbled, "Just watch your step, mister." Norm spun back around and stomped into his kitchen. After that, the only sound that could be heard was the slap of raw meat against a pan and the sizzle of it being cooked.

Still perched on the edge of his chair, Nick looked around at everyone else in the room. Most folks seemed to be getting back to their meals and picking up on their conversations. Nick's hand slid from his gun. It had been so close to the grip that his fingers were already tensing in anticipation. After another moment, he let out the breath he'd been holding and put both hands flat upon the table. He could hear footsteps approaching and when he looked up, he saw Vera standing in front of him.

She smiled and let out a small, nervous laugh. "Don't let Norm get to you. He doesn't exactly have a grasp of how to handle his Sandy growing up so fast."

"Yeah?" Nick replied. "Well, he seemed to have a good enough grasp on that knife of his."

Glancing around, Vera leaned in a little closer so only Nick could hear when she whispered, "If you ask me, that girl needs a mother around to teach her a thing or two before she gets hurt. If it wasn't for Norm,

I know she would have been in a lot worse situations with the way she turns men's heads." Standing up again, she patted Nick on the shoulder. "Why don't you come join my husband and me at our table?"

"Oh, I shouldn't."

But Vera had already grabbed Nick's water cup and was pulling him to his feet. "I insist. It's the least I can do to make up for the way you were treated."

Instead of arguing with the lady, Nick allowed himself to be pulled over to her table where the only other person to come to his aid was gnawing on a buttered roll. Nick didn't exactly know how to act when he situated himself at the table and it showed.

Just when it looked as if Nick couldn't be more uncomfortable, the other man at the table wiped his hand on the napkin hanging from his neck and extended it toward Nick. "Name's Matt Coswell. This here's my wife, Vera."

Nick's first impulse was to refuse to shake the other man's hand. Normally, that worked out better than watching the look come onto people's faces when they saw the mangled remains of his fingers. This time, he opted for politeness and reached out to shake the hand he was offered.

"I'm Nicolai Graves," he said, grasping

the other's hand with a strength that would have been impressive for any man.

Matt flinched a little in response to the sight of Nick's missing fingers, but shook his hand all the same. "You a miner?" he asked. "Plenty of miners get hurt a lot worse than that with all that dynamite they toss around."

"No," Nick said with a smirk. "It's nothing like that."

Shrugging, Matt turned his attention back to his food. He did, however, shoot Nick a sly look when he said, "That Sandy's quite a looker, huh?"

"Oh, Matt," Vera snapped while smacking his arm with the back of her hand. "She's a good girl."

"Yeah, that's what I've heard."

Shaking her head, Vera regarded her husband as a lost cause and focused on Nick. "I saw you tell her something that seemed to make her compose herself a bit. What was it?"

"Aw, who cares?" Matt cut in. Looking to Nick, he said, "You'll have to excuse my wife. Not only is she on the town's Welcoming Committee, but she's more than happy to stick her nose in where it don't belong. Perhaps that helps explain why you got yourself dragged over here instead of sitting back there where you can eat your meal in peace."

Vera rapped Matt on the arm once again, the impact of which was barely enough to rumple his sleeve. "Don't be silly. Anyone would rather share some time with good company instead of . . . oh lord. You don't mind that I brought you over here, do you?"

Nick had to laugh while shaking his head. "Not at all. This is probably some of the best conversation I've had in a while."

"Conversation?" Matt scoffed. "Entertainment is more like it."

"My husband is correct in some respects, though. I am on the town's Welcoming Committee. So, on behalf of that committee, welcome to Bitter Creek."

"Thanks. I appreciate it. And I do appreciate the company as well. It's been . . . well . . . a while since I've had a welcome as warm as this."

Matt started to laugh at that as well, but was silenced by yet another smack on the arm from his wife.

"So what brings you to town?" Vera asked. "Are you passing through or staying a while?"

"I'll be staying for a little while. Actually, I was hoping to find some work."

"I might be able to help there. What kind

of work do you do?"

Nick paused before giving the real answer to that question. Most folks just didn't really want to think about the skills that were practiced upon the dead.

For those reasons, Nick simply said, "I'm a gravedigger."

Although Vera seemed a bit put off by that, she kept herself from showing it too obviously. "Oh. Well, that's unusual. The undertaker has a place over on Cobbler's Avenue. I can't recall the name of the man who runs it, but he might have some work for you."

One thing that Nick had noticed ever since he'd observed his own father plying his trade was that people not only didn't want to think about those who worked with the dead, they tended to overlook them completely. They knew well enough who did what job in town, but when they saw an undertaker coming their way, the first reaction was to find somewhere else to be.

Stasys had been a simple gravedigger and coffin maker, but he was treated like a ghoul by some and ignored by most everyone else. That had suited his father just fine since he was a quiet man anyhow. It suited Nick just as well, but for a much different set of reasons.

"I'll go see him," Nick said. "Thanks for pointing me in the right direction."

"It's nothing. That's what the committee is here for."

Just then, Nick noticed something peculiar about Matt. The man seemed to be watching him more closely with every passing second. As he ate, he kept glancing over to Nick as if he was sizing him up. Eventually, he saw that Matt's eyes were actually wandering toward the gun strapped around Nick's waist which had become visible once his jacket had fallen open.

Nick closed his jacket to cover his pistol. At that moment, the door to the kitchen swung open and Sandy came hustling out with her hands full of plates. She made a line straight for the table where Nick had been and then stopped short as if someone had rapped her between the eyes.

Blinking in confusion, the girl glanced around until she finally spotted Nick's new seat. "There you are," she said. Reaching over Nick's shoulder, she placed two plates in front of him and then reached into the pocket of her apron to set a small jar of honey down as well. "I'm sorry if the steak is a little bloody, but my Daddy didn't want to cook it anymore. He said he wanted you to . . . well . . . just that he didn't want to cook it anymore."

"That's perfectly fine," Nick said, poking the cut of meat with his fork. "I like my steaks rare."

Sandy looked down at him with a widening smile and wide, sparkling eyes. "So do I. We have so much in c—"

"Sandy," Vera interrupted. "Could you get us some more to drink?"

Matt let out a short, snort of a laugh. "Yeah, before your pa decides you've spent too much time over here."

After being cut short in the middle of her flirtations, Sandy spun around and huffed from the room.

"I swear that girl won't be happy until she gets someone to trip all over themselves," Matt said.

This time, Vera was the one to laugh cynically. "With the way you men act, she'll never have to wait long for that. It's like you've never seen a pretty face before."

"It's not the face we're . . ." Matt stopped himself before he got every man in the room into hot water. "You're right, darlin'."

Nick was already tearing into his food. After swallowing his first couple of bites, he looked up and said, "I've got to give the man credit. Even though he wanted to gut

me not too long ago, Norm cooked me one
hell of a steak."

SEVEN

Walking out of Norm's Skillet, Nick was accompanied by Vera and Matt.

"Well, it's been a hoot an' all," Matt said, "but I gotta get back to work." Saying that, he kissed his wife and then reached into his pocket to remove a little tin star that he pinned to his lapel. Once the badge was in place, Matt reached out to shake Nick's hand once more. "Glad to meet you, Nick. I'm sure we'll be seeing each other soon."

Nick's poker face was put to the test and it held up. No matter what kind of knots his stomach was being tied into, all he did was nod amiably and shake Matt's hand. "I'm sure we will. Perhaps I can buy a round of drinks sometime."

"Don't think I won't take you up on that."

Vera watched him leave and then said, "I've got to be going as well, Nick. It was nice meeting you. If there's anything else you need, the Welcoming Committee's office is right down the street that way."

Although Vera pointed out the building carefully and even gave directions, Nick wasn't really paying attention. Instead, he was too busy kicking himself for sitting down and having a meal with the exact person he normally tried to avoid when entering a new town. No matter how many changes he'd forced into his life, Nick still was a long way from being able to socialize with the law.

"Guess I should be going," Vera said. "Be sure to let me know how things go with finding some work. If you'd like, I can introduce you to the town's undertaker. You remember where to find him?"

"Cobbler's Avenue."

"That's the place."

"I won't need an introduction, but thanks." After learning that he'd sat down and eaten with the law and his wife, Nick was in a hurry to get moving.

"Are these your horses?" she asked.

Nick stopped after having only made it a few paces away. "They sure are."

"If you need to put them up for the night, I can recommend a good stable."

No matter how much his instincts were screaming at him to leave Vera and leave her quickly, Nick couldn't bring himself to just cut the kindly woman off so rudely. "Actually, I could use some directions to a stable. This town is kind of hard to navigate."

She laughed and gave the directions before walking down the street toward her home.

The livery was just down the street and along the way, Nick even managed to spot a few comfortable-looking hotels. Rasa and Kazys were unhitched and put into clean stalls before the liveryman could leave to get some supper. That worked out even better because the man was in such a hurry to get the horses squared away that he hardly seemed to take a look at Nick's face.

"I'll need payment in advance," the liveryman said in a rush.

"Here," Nick said, flipping a silver dollar into the air rather than handing it over. "This should cover me for a while."

The liveryman snatched the money from the air and pocketed it. "It'll do well enough. Just come by in a few days and we can settle up from there. If'n you need me to brush them down or make any repairs to your wagon I can do that, but it'll be extra."

"I'll get back to you on that," Nick replied while already heading for the door. Even before he got out of the stable, he could hear the liveryman locking up the stalls and preparing to close up for the night.

By the time Nick was across the street, he heard the door to the stable open and slam shut again. He glanced over his shoulder and saw the liveryman hang a sign on the door telling other prospective customers where to find him if they needed a stall. From there, the liveryman made a line straight for the restaurants in the vicinity where Nick had been not too long ago.

Nick stuffed his hands into his pockets, kept his head low, and started walking down the street toward the hotels he'd spotted earlier. A town was always different when a man saw it on foot as opposed to riding on horseback or in a wagon. He never waited long after settling into a place before walking its streets for himself. Part of that was a holdover from his rowdier days and part of it was something acquired through age and experience.

For a man who lived or died by knowing who or what he was dealing with, a walk like the one he was taking was pretty damn important. But there was more to be seen than escape routes and ambush spots. As he walked along the meandering streets of Bitter Creek, Nick saw the town as a tough breed of animal that had been born in a bad spot and was forced to either nestle in and survive or be picked apart by the countless scavengers that would come along.

It was surprising just how much a man could learn about a place by soaking some of it up through the soles of his boots. It was just as surprising that such a simple thing could be so good for Nick's spirits. For him, one of the essential luxuries a town could give a man was the ability to stretch his legs without too much worry. Taking walks alone when camping in the middle of nowhere wasn't just a bad idea, it was an awful one.

Staying in town meant being able to stroll. It was a simple pleasure for Nick, but still a pleasure all the same.

Of course, that didn't mean there weren't snakes lurking in the shadows. In town, they were usually of the two-legged variety.

Nick picked up the first trace of one such predator as he'd turned a corner and put his back to what appeared to be the saloon district. The sounds of off-key pianos and equally bad singers filled the air to one side, only to be overpowered by the bawdy laughter coming from the other. In between those choruses, there had been the sound of approaching footsteps, which caught Nick's attention a hell of a lot more than any out-of-tune piano.

At best, those footsteps could just be someone passing by.

At worst, they could have been the steps of the Reaper himself.

Knowing where he was without needing to know the name of the street, Nick followed the faint scent of bread and burning wood into what could only be a section of food stores and bakeries. At that time of night, the scents were faint but plenty noticeable to a well-trained nose.

The bread might have been cold and the smoke was all that remained of most of the baking fires, but that was only because the shopkeepers and bakers had headed home for the day. That left the streets bare, which was exactly what Nick had wanted.

Nick's hands were shoved into his pockets as always. As he walked along the empty street and stepped onto the boardwalk, Nick's hand shifted under his jacket until his fingers grazed against the handle of his gun.

He didn't draw the weapon or even take hold of it. Knowing that it was there and less than an inch away from his grasp was enough. The casual observer would have seen no difference in his motions or the pace of his steps. If he was being followed, however, the person behind him was no casual observer.

Just to test the waters, Nick slowed his steps slightly as he pretended to peer into a darkened window. He didn't actually see any of the wares on display behind that glass because his eyes were more focused on the glass itself. After a moment to adjust to the shadows, he started to see plenty of details reflected in the pane.

He could see the street behind him and then eventually the opposite row of buildings. When the moon peeked out from behind a passing cloud, he could see a bit more. It took the sharpness of a predator's eye, however, to catch the subtle shape formed by one shadow that didn't quite mesh with all the others.

Whoever was following him had come to a stop. Nick could pick out the wideness of frame that had to belong to a man. He could also see an almost perfect stillness that could only belong to one accustomed to hunting others in the dark.

No matter what went through his mind, Nick kept his outward appearance bland. It required the sort of control that separated a good poker player from a great one. Without a good poker face, all the skill, luck, or cheating in the world wouldn't help you.

And without being able to play possum convincingly, the predators would simply tear into you rather than pause to take a closer look.

Nick took a deep breath and rolled his head to both sides, wincing slightly as he worked out a few painful kinks. The kinks were real enough, even though he was playing up the winces just a bit. Sure, it was a bit of theater tossed into the mix, but that was all a part of the game.

Nick kept up the noise by clearing his throat and shuffling his feet as loudly as possible against the wooden planks beneath them. That, combined with a casual whistle, surrounded Nick with just enough noise to suit his purpose.

That purpose ran below everything he was doing, which was to make the man following him feel confident enough to come closer. Just a little bit closer and he would know whether he should just tip his hat and keep walking or draw his gun and put a round through the other man's gullet.

Keeping his steps casual and his face trained on the path in front of him, Nick only glanced a few times away from the boardwalk to catch a glimpse of the sky overhead. He was approaching a stretch of alleys and a dark corner, all of which would surely be inviting to anyone trying to get the drop on him.

He knew the other was still there. He could feel their eyes drilling through the back of his skull.

He kept walking past one alley, his eyes shifting toward the thick darkness and half-expecting to see another predator leap out at him. No hands reached out from that alley, however, so Nick kept on walking.

He was approaching the next alley, which was even bigger than the first. One of the problems that came from being a former predator himself was that Nick knew only too well how easy it was to overtake his prey. All it took was one good spot, the perfect moment, and the patience to wait for it.

He wanted to draw his pistol, but knew the other man was still back there and didn't want to light his fuse prematurely. Whoever it was, he was good enough to keep quiet.

As far as outward appearances were concerned, Nick was still strolling along his way, clunking his feet against the boards, clearing his throat, and whistling his song.

Then, without the slightest bit of warning, Nick chose his own perfect moment to make a play.

All the sounds he'd been making came to a stop.

The moment his foot hit the boardwalk, he planted it.

Even the next breath he was about to take froze in his lungs.

Unable to stop quickly enough, Nick's follower couldn't help but let his foot drop noisily a few paces behind Nick's position. Although it may not have seemed like much at any other time, the subtle knock of heel against wood that came from behind Nick sounded like a clap of thunder in his ears, making the entire charade up to now worth the effort.

There was a tense moment of silence. Both men were aware of it, yet neither one was quite ready to make a leap. Tired of being the prey, Nick spun around on the balls of his feet and wrapped his fingers around the grip of his specially modified pistol. Even before he got a good look at who was behind him, Nick had his weapon halfway drawn. He waited before clearing leather, keeping the gun under cover to give him that last element of surprise by being able to aim without the barrel being watched.

Nick's brow furrowed in a scowl that was mean at first, but then showed a bit of surprise. The face that looked back at him was amused at best, while also being a little surprised himself.

"You always did like your evening strolls, Spud."

Before Nick could reply to that, he saw the man in front of him lift one hand and point a finger toward the alley at Nick's back.

Nick cursed himself for allowing himself to be distracted enough to let the sounds of heavy footsteps go by without checking on them. The thumping got closer, right along with the noisy, wheezing breaths that accompanied them. Crouching down low while spinning around on the balls of his feet, Nick was able to get a look at the man running up behind him while also dodging the hamlike fist being swung toward his head.

That fist sent a rush of air over Nick's face while clipping the top of his hat. Thankfully, the man trying to bushwhack Nick didn't feel the need to be any more original than going for a knockout blow with his first shot. Having ducked that first blow, Nick sent one of his own in return.

Nick's fist snapped out and up in a sharp hook, burying his knuckles deep into his attacker's gut. Only now was Nick able to get a look at the other man as he doubled over and crumpled around Nick's hand.

"Son . . . son of a b . . ." was all Norm could manage to say before taking a step back and sucking in some wind to fill his lungs.

For a moment, Nick couldn't believe that the restaurant owner had followed him this far. When he looked back at the first man he'd spotted, he saw that the darkly dressed figure was grinning from ear to ear.

"Looks like you still got a way of charming folks," the other man said.

Nick had plenty he wanted to say to the first man he'd spotted, but Norm wasn't quite through with him just yet. That fact became obvious enough when the big man straightened up and rushed toward Nick for a second time.

"Keep yer mangy ass away from my daughter," Norm grunted. He punctuated the command by pulling a kitchen knife from where he'd hidden it beneath his apron.

Nick spotted the blade and reflexively leapt into action. One hand snapped down into Norm's arm, followed by a quick upward thrust from his knee. Norm's entire arm went numb and the knife hit the ground. It didn't even have a chance to stop spinning before Nick kicked it away.

Stunned after being handled and disarmed with such speed and efficiency, Norm looked around with his mouth hanging open in a stupid expression. He then opened his arms and let out a loud snarl as he charged Nick outright.

Nick waited until the last moment before stepping aside. Norm stumbled right past him and into the other figure who'd been watching the entire scuffle. That figure was still grinning as he sidestepped and then sent Norm to the ground with a quick chop from the butt of his gun to the back of Norm's head.

"Enough fooling about," the other man said. "We've got business to discuss."

EIGHT

"Barrett?" That word sounded so familiar to Nick, yet it also felt somewhat odd. It might have been the way a superstitious man felt when he accidentally uttered a curse.

Nothing good could come of words like that, just like nothing good had ever really come from Barrett Cobb.

"Is that really you?"

The other man stepped forward like a shadowy reflection of Nick, himself. His hand was near his gun, yet refused to draw it. His steps were meticulously precise. His eyes were as sharp as two chiseled diamonds set deep within his skull.

Norm grunted and twitched on the ground. He was all but forgotten by the other two men in the alley.

Finally, the man nodded. "Yeah, Nick. It's me."

Barrett Cobb appeared to be slightly

shorter than Nick, but that was only because he was hunkered down a bit in expectation of making a quick, lunging move. With that possibility behind him, he straightened up again to reveal the fact that he was actually about Nick's height.

Cobb had a sturdy build and a solid frame coated in sinewy muscle. His skin was darkened from the sun, but not to the degree of one who favored the daylight hours. He had more of a gambler's complexion; not quite as tanned as it should be, thanks to so many hours spent cooped up inside a saloon at a card table. Rough without being leathery, his flesh was covered with scars that ranged from knife slashes to old bullet wounds.

Wearing a dark brown duster that appeared black in the shadows, Cobb blended almost seamlessly into the night. His dark hat and black trousers were only offset by the somewhat lighter shade of his gray shirt. The only thing to catch the eye more than the expression on Cobb's face was the glint of dim light off the buckle securing the holster around his waist. Much like Nick's weapon, the gun in Barrett's holster was kept out of view like a snake slinking back into its nest.

Although the two men approached each

other with a familiar ease, their hands remained close to their weapons. They stood in front of each other for another moment or two before one of them finally took his hand away so he could offer it to the other.

"It's been a long time, Nick," Barrett said as he extended his hand in greeting. "I was surprised to hear you made it out of Montana. After the stories that have been coming out of Nebraska, I'm a little shocked you're alive." Glancing down toward Norm, he added, "Especially considering these dangerous walks you insist on taking."

Nick nodded as his eyes flicked down to make sure that Norm was still out cold. He also checked to make sure that Barrett's hand was truly empty. It was nothing but pure reflex and he felt a little ashamed of himself when he saw that the hand he was being offered was holding nothing whatsoever.

Accepting Barrett's hand, Nick asked, "You heard about Nebraska?"

Barrett nodded. "All a man has to do is listen and he winds up hearing plenty."

"Well, you know more than me, as always."

"One thing I know is that it'd probably be best if that fella there wakes up by himself."

With that, both men put the alley behind them and started walking down the street.

The scuffle had been quick enough to go unnoticed for the most part. Nick had seen enough to figure that this probably wasn't the first time Norm had lost his temper in such a fashion.

"I wasn't even sure you'd made it out of Montana," Nick said.

"Just barely." Glancing down at Nick's hand, Barrett took another look at what remained of Nick's fingers. "I didn't get out without going through a bit of hell. Looks like that's something we've got in common."

"We've got plenty in common. Jesus, Barrett, we've got about five or ten years in common."

"At least." Barrett shook his head slowly as he took a step back in his mind. "Hell, if I try to think back that far it gives me a headache. I know you're not far off, so let's leave it at that."

Barrett and Nick kept smiling, but their hands drifted slowly back to their holsters. Each man regarded the other for a bit without committing himself to one course of action or another. This time, it was Nick who broke the silent tension by slipping his hands back into his jacket pockets.

"I knew I'd find you like this. You always did like to walk around a new town after you arrived," Barrett pointed out. "Still looking for ambush spots and escape routes?"

"Old habits die hard. You still lurk in the shadows and follow people until they get close to alleyways?"

"Alleys or an empty lot. Either one'll do." The menace in Barrett's eyes was unmistakable, but it only showed for another second or two before being outshone by a crooked smile that came across his face. "I had to make sure it was you before I showed myself, Nick. I'm not exactly the sociable type. Men like us can't really afford to introduce ourselves to every stranger we see."

"Yeah. I think you're the one who taught that to me."

"And Skinner was the one who taught it to me. Skinner was like that. Always full of good advice for bad men."

A lot went through Nick's mind at that point. He thought back to the last time he'd seen the man named Skinner in a town called Jessup, Nebraska. The town was a bit smaller than Bitter Creek, but it had been turned into a corner of hell thanks to the arrival of Skinner and Nick Graves.

When the two had collided, it was like tossing a match into a bucket of kerosene. Plenty of folks were burned in Jessup and, to some degree, Nick knew those flames would never go out. It had all started out so simply, in a way that the great battles often did. Innocents were slaughtered despite all of Nick's efforts to keep it otherwise. Nick had almost died himself, and it was all in the name of settling a debt.

So simple a thing, but plenty of deadly things in the world were simple. Knives were simple. Fire was simple. That didn't mean they couldn't do some serious damage. And when Nick thought about serious damage, there were plenty of demons inside of him to keep those thoughts going.

Only a second or two had passed since Skinner had been brought up, but Nick felt as if he'd been forced to relive a lifetime of pain.

"Skinner's dead," Nick announced in a voice colder than the grave itself.

Barrett studied Nick's face carefully. Finally, he nodded and said, "Yeah. I know."

"Nothing much ever did surprise you."

"I find I stay alive longer that way."

Glancing around, Barrett saw that they were still alone on the boardwalk. The sound of pianos being played and songs being sung came back into the air, even though they had never really left. In fact, the wind itself started to brush over them after a long, silent drought. It was almost as if the Almighty had been holding his breath to see what would happen when Barrett and Nick finally crossed paths.

"It's getting cold out here," Barrett said. "Let's get something to drink."

NINE

The Number Three Watering Hole was the name of the saloon where Nick and Barrett decided to have their drinks. Compared to the streets they'd left behind, the area around that saloon were positively brimming with people. Locals and strangers alike shared the street as they walked or stumbled from one of its accommodations to another. The Watering Hole wasn't the only place offering the promise of good times. Every carnal sin was represented, giving the air a distinctive odor that was a mix of liquor, perfume, smoke, and blood.

Needless to say, it was one of the most popular sections of town.

Barrett and Nick blended in perfectly. They kept their heads down and their steps quick so as not to draw any undue attention. For anyone who still wanted to approach the pair, the warning in their combined glares was more than enough to discourage that notion.

No matter how many drunks or pimps stepped aside and soon forgot about Nick and Barrett, there were two men on that street who would do no such thing.

Neither of the two men watching Nick and Barrett stood out in any particular way. They were both about average height and dressed in average clothes. They even walked in a way that made them resemble any of the others out for a night in the saloon district. Of course, those were the exact reasons why they were able to get close enough to Nick or Barrett without being spotted immediately.

"We haven't seen Cobb in a few days," one of the men said to the other. Of the two figures, he was slightly taller. It was much easier to tell them apart by the whiskers on their faces. The taller man sported a full beard while the shorter had a well-trimmed mustache and a small sprout of hair beneath the middle of his lower lip.

The bearded man's voice wasn't much more than a low grumble in the back of his throat. When he mentioned Cobb's name, the grumble shifted into something closer to a growl.

The man with the mustache nodded slowly while continuing to study the other two crossing the street. "He's not stupid. Cobb don't come out from wherever he's been hiding unless there's a good reason."

"You think that's one of the men he brought into town for the job he's got planned?"

"Could be. There's something different about the way they're talking, though. Cobb don't seem to be ordering this one around so much. He don't even look like he's talking about business."

"So what does that mean? You think this one might be running things?"

The man with the mustache shook his head without hesitation. "Men like Cobb don't take orders." Still keeping his eyes on Barrett, he added, "If anything this one here's a partner. Then again, he may not have anything to do with Cobb's business at all."

"Just passing through, huh?"

"Cobb's gotta have friends just like anyone else."

The bearded man let out a laugh that sounded more like he was spitting out sour milk. "But bastards like that tend to put their friends to work all the same."

"True enough. Still, why don't you head back to tell Sheriff Trayner what we found. He wants to be kept up on all the new developments, even if it is just a friend of Cobb's coming through town."

"You sure you want to trail those two on your own?"

"Yeah. Come back after you report back and I'll find you." Nodding toward the opposite side of the street, he watched as Barrett and Nick stepped through the seedy crowd to finally enter the Number Three Watering Hole through a set of double doors. "Looks like they're settling in for a while anyhow."

"Either that or they're meeting up with the others. This could be where they've been getting together. It'd be plenty easy for them to go unnoticed in a hole like that one. Most of the workers in there are a bunch of sneaky assholes that would lie for anyone with a few dollars to spare."

"Just go talk to the sheriff. I need a drink."

Without another word, the man with the mustache crossed the street and made a line straight for the saloon's front door. He sliced through the milling crowd in a manner very similar to the way Nick and Barrett had entered moments ago. The drunks and other lowlives even stepped aside the same way, as if sensing a similar kind of menace in him as they had in the previous pair.

Once his partner had disappeared into the

saloon, the bearded man turned and walked down the boardwalk. After taking less than a dozen steps, his entire manner had changed. Where before he was scowling and fierce, he was now actually friendly to the people who passed him by. They waved and nodded, so he waved and nodded back to them. His pace was always quick, however, and when he got to the building marked as the sheriff's office, he was all business once again.

The sheriff's office was slightly larger than an average house. Although there was no second floor, the two rooms it did have were wide open and only halfway filled with neatly arranged furniture. There were a few holding cells in the rear room, all of which were empty. Several racks of rifles hung from the walls with smaller guns and ammunition kept in a locked cabinet behind one of the smaller desks.

The sheriff was easy enough to find, simply because he sat behind the largest of the desks. His feet were propped up and he held a battered book in both hands. Rather than look up when the bearded man entered the room, he simply turned the page he'd been reading and acknowledged the new arrival with an upward nod.

"Where's Hyde?"

The bearded man waited until the door was shut behind him before answering. "We wound up at the Watering Hole."

"Which one?"

"Number Three. I left him there so I could come back here to report."

That got the lawman to put his book down, but only after he'd turned the page one more time. Carefully sliding a piece of paper between the pages to mark his spot, he closed the book and took a quick look at his deputy. "It don't look like you met up with any trouble, Dave, so what's to report?"

"Someone came into town to meet up with Cobb."

"Really?" the sheriff asked as his brow furrowed in thought. "Who?"

"I can't rightly say. Could be another gunman brought in for whatever Cobb's got planned. He looks like he might be the type."

"You don't sound too convinced."

Dave paused before he answered. "I don't know for certain. He just doesn't seem like the others that had been coming through here."

"How so?"

"Jesus, Sheriff, I told you I don't know. What else do you want me to say? We're supposed to let you know if something happens. This happened, so I'm letting you know about it."

Swinging his feet off his desk, the lawman got up from his chair. Now that he was standing, he could be seen for what he truly was. Sheriff George Trayner was a large, barrel-chested man who appeared to be in his early fifties. His hair was dark gray, as though it had only recently shifted from the black it had been throughout his earlier years. Although his face was friendly enough, there was a definite toughness about him that made others not want to talk back to him.

At the moment, an amused twinkle showed in his eyes as he walked around the desk to comfort his deputy with a good-natured pat on the shoulder. "No need to get your nose bent out of joint, Dave. I was just asking some questions, is all. Now, what did this other fella look like?"

Now that he was taken off the defensive, Dave leaned against the doorway and took a quick look out through the nearby window. He didn't see anyone passing by outside, which put the deputy even more at ease. Hooking his thumbs through his gun belt, Dave propped his coat open just enough to reveal the badge pinned to his shirt.

"He was about as tall as me," Dave said. "Thin. Seemed kinda pasty. He had eyes like Cobb's."

"What do you mean by that?" the sheriff asked, as if that was the first part of the description to genuinely catch his attention. "The same color?"

"No. They were . . ."

"Sharp," Sheriff Trayner said, filling in the gap as if he knew what was there all along.

Dave snapped his fingers and nodded. "That's it. They were sharp and always looking around like he knew he was being watched."

"Those are wanted-man's eyes."

"You think he's on the run?"

"Well, if he's meeting up with the likes of Barrett Cobb, I doubt he's got a clear conscience. Even if it is a social call, being Cobb's friend means this stranger must have traveled in some unsavory circles." Sheriff Trayner let his words trail off as he started tapping his chin thoughtfully. The way he stared at the window was almost the same way he'd been studying the pages of his book earlier.

After a while, Dave broke the silence. "You want us to bring him in?"

"No. Not yet," Trayner said as he made his way to the rack where his coat and hat were hanging. After he'd tossed them on, he paused while eyeing one of the shotguns on an adjacent rack. "I think I'll go have a look for myself."

"All right, then. I'll take you right to him."

"No," the sheriff replied as his hand reached out to take the shotgun he'd been eyeing. "You stay here in case someone comes by. We do have more to do in this town than just watch over one set of outlaws."

"But Hyde's waiting —"

"At the Number Three Watering Hole. I heard you the first time. It's not like he won't recognize me when I stop by. I'm the one who taught you boys how to follow someone, remember? I won't go storming in and point out where he's sitting." The annoyance in his voice had been building with every word. After taking a quick breath, however, Sheriff Trayner returned to the steadiness he'd had when Dave had first found him reading peacefully behind his desk.

"Look through the books while I'm gone," Trayner said, nodding toward a stack of papers and documents all bound in leather covers. "See if you can spot a familiar face or anything else that might tell you who our new friend is. Matt should be done with his rounds soon. Let him know where I went when he gets back."

"What're you going to do when you get over there?" Dave asked.

The sheriff paused with the shotgun hanging from one hand and the other hand on the door's handle. "That depends on how well this stranger's willing to act. If he is just some old friend of Cobb's, then there's no reason for me to interrupt their drinks."

"And if he isn't?"

"Then he'll just give me a good excuse to rid this town of Cobb and his piece of shit acquaintances before anyone who matters gets themselves hurt."

TEN

The Number Three Watering Hole was one of those places where time really didn't matter. Once he got inside, the only thing a man needed to keep track of was whether it was light or dark on the other side of the windows. To that end, the owners of the place did their best to keep the windows covered. After all, it wouldn't be good for business if they told their customers when they should head home.

With such cooperative hosts, the drinking went on until all hours. Card games ran for days on end and the only things that changed were the faces of the girls singing or kicking up their heels upon the small, half-circle stage. Fights were kept to a minimum thanks to the beefy men patrolling the main room. The few scuffles that did break out were eventually tossed outside and treated as just another form of entertainment by everyone else.

It was the kind of place that was as common a sight in most towns as grassy plains and open skies were outside of them. For men like Nick and Barrett, the Number Three felt so familiar that it almost felt like home.

Walking through the saloon to find a place to sit, Nick looked around and couldn't help but feel a bit nostalgic. He usually found his way to a saloon upon entering most towns, but there was something different about walking into one right behind Barrett. Alone, Nick was used to getting the sideways glances and occasional suspicious stare. Together, the pair demanded a different kind of respect along with something else lying beneath the surface of most of those glances.

Fear.

Although not outright scared of the two dark figures, the folks in the saloon gave them a bit more space due to an instinctual reaction to them. When a man caught Nick or Barrett looking straight at him, that person would quickly look away. It was a reaction that was familiar to Nick in an uncomfortable sort of way.

What made Nick even more uncomfortable was the feeling that he could easily get used to it once again.

Barrett, on the other hand, walked tall and proud.

As he circled around a small table toward the back of the room, Barrett reached out and grabbed hold of a serving girl as she tried to get past him. His fingers tightened around the loose material of her blouse, pulling her closer with just enough roughness to do the job. He didn't let go of her until she looked up at him and forced a shaky smile onto her face.

"What can I get for you two fellas?" she asked.

"Whiskey and a beer." When he saw that she was about to leave, Barrett pulled her back toward him. "That's for me. My friend here will have . . ." He paused for a moment and then smiled broadly. "Vodka. That's it. I remember. He'll have a vodka."

At first, the young woman maintained her smile. When she saw that Barrett was still staring at her, the smile started to betray a little more panic. She took a breath, still glancing between the two as if frantically hoping one of them would say something before she was forced to. Finally, she said, "I don't think we have any of that."

Barrett's expression froze. "What do you mean? This is a saloon, right? And saloons are supposed to serve drinks."

"I just . . . don't think I've ever heard of that one."

Nick snapped his head around to look at the young woman squirming like a worm on a hook. "That's fine. I'll just take a beer."

The relieved smile jumped onto her face as the young woman spun around and headed back to the bar as quickly as she could. Barrett watched her go without even trying to hide the amusement he got from her hurried steps.

"Vodka's hard to find," Nick said. "There was no need to scare her like that."

"Like what? All I did was ask for that fire water you like so much. It's not my fault if they don't have much of a selection."

Watching the flames dance behind Barrett's eyes brought back some more unwanted memories. Nick shook his head and said, "Jesus, were we always like this?"

"Yeah," Barrett replied, knowing exactly what Nick was referring to. "Only you were a hell of a lot worse."

"I was also a hell of a lot younger."

Barrett placed both hands flat upon the table and leaned forward. His eyes narrowed and he peered at Nick's face as though he was somehow able to take a gander at the other man's soul. "It don't matter how many wrinkles or gray hairs you get. Men like us don't lose our edge. We'd have to die for that to happen. I'll bet Skinner was even worse when you met him in Nebraska than when we all ran together like a pack of wolves."

Nick leaned back in his chair as the serving girl stopped by to drop off their drinks. She was there and gone in a flash, but Nick hardly seemed to notice her. He was lost in his own thoughts and knew better than to even try to fight them off.

The first thing that came to mind was Skinner's face. The big man sneered at him from the grave while slashing that blade of his through the air. He was a wicked bastard, that much was certain, and he'd killed anyone he could reach whenever the mood hit him. That mood had certainly hit him in Jessup, Nebraska, and it had left several dead bodies in its wake.

Nick hadn't exactly gotten out unscathed. In fact, as he thought about it some more, he recalled his pain so well that he could practically taste the blood in the back of his throat. Without thinking about it, he'd already grabbed his beer and was downing it. The bitter liquid didn't quite wash away the memories, but there was always the bottle of vodka in his wagon for that.

"So you found Skinner, huh?" Barrett

asked, intruding on Nick's thoughts. "That's no small thing. He was awfully damn hard to find when he wanted to be."

"I didn't find him, exactly. He found me."

Barrett nodded slowly and moved his hand toward his own set of drinks. Just then, his eyes took on a faraway quality as he was beset by his own memories. Nick watched the change come over the man's face, but the shadow passed in hardly any time at all.

Before, Barrett had been reaching more toward his beer. Now that he'd had a visit from a few of his own demons, he reached for the whiskey instead. He lifted it slowly to his mouth and tossed it back, swallowing as if his life depended on downing the liquor as quickly as possible. The breath he let out was slow and steady.

"He found you, huh?" Barrett said. "That sounds about right. Skinner knew how do to a whole lot of things. Finding folks was definitely one of them."

Nick found plenty of questions coming to mind, but held off before asking them. Instead, he took another sip of beer and set the mug down in front of him. It wasn't the first time he'd noticed that he was sitting with his back to the front portion of the saloon. Barrett had taken the seat against the wall and Nick had taken the only other one that remained.

The longer he stayed in that chair, the more Nick's skin started to crawl. Perhaps that was because of everything going on around him. Or perhaps his discomfort sprang from the company he was keeping.

Finally, Barrett broke the silence that had settled over the table by asking, "You remember the old gang?"

Nick nodded.

"We used to have some times, didn't we? There wasn't much that could touch us once we got rolling. Well," Barrett added as the shadow came over him one more time, "at least that's how it was for you and me. Those others . . . most of 'em weren't as good as us."

Laughing a bit under his breath, Nick said, "I never thought any of us were much good."

"That's where you're mistaken, friend. We were damn good at what we did."

"Yeah." In another sip or two, Nick's beer was gone. "So," he said, setting his empty mug onto the table, "what brings you into town?"

"Not a lot. Same old song and dance."

"You're here on a job?"

Barrett smirked a little wider and lifted

his glass. "Of course. And don't pretend that you didn't know I was here."

"You mean meeting up like this wasn't just a happy coincidence?"

"Coincidence?" Barrett asked. "Ain't no such thing and you know it. In fact, I'd wager everything I own that you got wind of all the questions I've been asking about you in every town within a hundred miles of this place. That's what brought you here," he added with confidence. "That is, unless you came to beg for work from the prick working in the undertaker's parlor."

Nick's first instinct was to cover his tracks. By this point, however, he didn't see much point in that. "Yeah, I heard. You must've been asking a whole lot of folks for it to get to me."

"Just the right ones. I know how you think, Nick. Hell, when it comes to certain things, whatever I didn't teach you, you taught to me. There ain't much for either one of us to hide from each other."

"Don't keep reminding me."

Barrett caught the serving girl's attention and motioned for her to bring a fresh round of drinks. She did so quickly and without saying a word. She was gone before Nick could even try to pay her.

Barrett took a sip from his beer and kept

his eyes on the man sitting across the table from him. "You look nervous, Nick. Is it because you're still on the run?"

"No. I've gotten used to that."

"Is it because you've got your back to the door and can't see who might be coming in after you?"

Nick's eyes narrowed slightly and he fought the impulse to turn around and glance over his shoulder. Barrett had always gotten a kick out of testing people and this was his way of testing him. Then again, there was the very real possibility that he was telling the truth. In the end, Nick guessed that his old partner was simply enjoying watching him squirm.

"You're a real prick, sometimes. You know that?" Nick asked.

"Yeah, I guess I am. Tell you the truth, I didn't really think I'd be seeing you. I put the word out after hearing about what happened with Skinner, but I just thought I'd get some answers from them folks that I asked. Either you've made some loyal friends digging them graves, or you've gotten real good at covering your tracks."

"Little bit of both, I guess. How did you know where to look for me?"

"That wasn't too hard. After I heard about Skinner being put underground and Red

Parks being run from one state to another like a dog with his tail between his legs, it didn't take much to figure you'd show up in there sooner or later. The rest was knowing what to listen for and waiting until I heard it. We've both got too many old habits to hide from each other for too long."

"Well," Nick said, raising his drink, "here's to old habits."

"May they die hard."

Barrett drained his whiskey to that toast and Nick swallowed about a quarter of his beer. After putting the mug down, Nick asked, "So what's this job you're talking about?"

"One of my better ones. But I probably shouldn't say much unless you want in."

Turning in his seat, Nick took a quick glance over his shoulder. There were a few rough-looking types standing by the front door that could have been the ones Barrett had been talking about a few moments ago. Then again, the saloon was full of rough-looking types. When he looked back to Barrett, Nick only saw a knowing smirk on the other man's face. "How should I know if I want in?"

"Because you know my jobs pay good enough to make up for whatever risk there may be."

"I also know you're a hell of a big talker and the risks are always pretty damn big," Nick replied.

Leaning back in his chair, Barrett shot back with, "I learned from the best, Spud. I learned from the best."

Nick cocked his head to one side as he felt the hackles rise on the back of his neck. "Spud? I haven't been called that for a long time."

"Bring back some memories?"

"A few. It also still makes me want to kick your ass up into your neck."

Once again, Barrett raised his glass. "Here's to old habits."

ELEVEN

Somewhere in southeastern Kansas
1862

A gunshot cracked through the air, followed by the hiss of lead speeding into empty space.

"Aw, fuck this piece of shit!" Nick's lips had curled around those words like he was singing in a choir. After joining up with the other boys that had become as much a gang as they'd become brothers, the opportunity to curse had been popping up pretty frequently.

There were five of them altogether. Besides Nick and Barrett, there was an ugly rod of a kid named Ned Peevely and the Cooley brothers. The Cooleys both had light hair and light complexions with a mean look that came naturally from their father's side of the family. They considered themselves a gang, but had yet to do more than steal a few bucks here and there and terrorize a few travelers. The War between the States had been raging for some time, but to the boys running on their own like a rambunctious pack of coyotes, the conflict may as well have been in another country.

Nick and his gang had better things to do and plenty of reasons to keep their noses out of the war. It was a part of their lives, but just not the focus of them. At the moment, Nick couldn't even see past the pistol he held in his hand and the old wagon wheel propped up about fifteen paces in front of him.

He was sixteen years old.

"Where the hell did you get these guns, Barrett?" Nick shouted.

Barrett was a short kid with a scalp covered with hair that looked more like dark bristles sprouting from his head. His eyes were sharp and his skin was covered with layers of freckles that made him look like Nick's younger brother even though both boys were about the same age.

"You know damn well where I got 'em," Barrett replied. "You were there when we stole 'em."

"Yeah, but you said they were good. These ain't nothin' but garbage."

Ned Peevely was the tallest of the bunch, but still looked as if he carried the least amount of weight. If a kid could be made up of nothing but skin, bone, and buck teeth, that kid would be Ned Peevely.

"Maybe," Peevely said in a drawl that came from never once stepping foot in a schoolhouse or coming near a book, "you just cain't shoot for a damn."

Those words were barely out of Peevely's mouth when Nick stepped up and sent the back of his hand so hard against the skinny kid's jaw that it rattled every one of his teeth. "You think I'm such a bad shot?" Nick snarled. "Then fucking try me, you son of a bitch." Pulling one of the several pistols he had tucked under his belt and tossing it to the ground in front of Peevely, he added, "Here. Take this and say that again, asshole."

Peevely's eyes darted to the gun lying in front of him. Every instinct inside of him told him to let that gun lie there, but he was too young to pay much attention to that kind of good sense. Looking around to see that the others in the gang were watching was enough to get Peevely to drop down and make a grab for the pistol Nick had tossed him.

Nick's reaction came swiftly and without a thought. His gun hand came up and his other hand snapped over to cock the hammer back. It was an unsteady, somewhat awkward motion, but it was still faster than anyone else in the gang could have managed.

The skinny kid froze where he was, squatting like a bony frog with his jaw hanging down in a mix of fear and surprise and his finger a mile from his trigger.

Nick paused for a moment, knowing that he was being watched carefully by the other three. An arrogant smirk eased across his lips as he steadied his aim and pulled his trigger.

Peevely felt everything in his stomach drop straight to the bottom, but was still too scared to do anything but clench his eyes shut as Nick's bullet came whipping toward him. The chunk of lead hissed less than an inch from his right ear and then kept right on going into the open range behind him.

"Y'see, Barrett?" Nick said. "I told you these guns weren't worth shit. I couldn't even hit ol' Peevely."

"That's probably because he was standin' sideways. He ain't any thicker than a newspaper when he's standin' sideways."

Nick and Barrett were the first to break into laughter. The Cooley brothers soon followed suit, but Peevely was still too rattled to do much more than toss a few halfhearted curses in Nick's direction.

Slapping Peevely on the shoulder, Nick walked back to where Barrett was sitting with his back against a boulder. Nick spun the gun around his index finger, which was a move he'd been practicing even before leaving his father and home behind.

"So them guns are really that bad?" Barrett asked.

Nick shrugged and plopped down next to the other boy. "They ain't too good, that's for sure."

"Can you fix 'em?"

"I could try. Maybe we should let Bobby take a look at them."

"Bob'd have more luck than some gravedigger's son, I guess," Barrett said in a taunting tone.

"Shut the fuck up."

"Watch that mouth of yours, Spud. Your pa would whip you something fierce if he heard you talk like that."

"My pa ain't here and don't call me that!"

"Call you what, Spud?"

"That!" Nick said, reaching over to swat Barrett on the back of the head. "I don't like that name."

"Well, if you didn't eat so many potatoes, maybe you wouldn't always smell like one."

Nick's other hand was already balled into

121

a fist and he cocked it all the way back next to his ear. "Call me that again and I'll knock yer damn teeth out."

Barrett could see the seriousness in Nick's eyes and knew he was awful close to eating that fist. It was a delicate balance, but one of the oldest struggles among any group of boys that age.

"All right, all right," Barrett said. "Just settle down so we can talk about our next move. I've got a plan. We might not need to fix those trash guns after all."

Letting out the breath that he'd been holding, Nick relaxed his fist and sat down next to Barrett. "You've got a plan? We don't even know where we are."

"What's that supposed to mean? I know right where we are."

"Oh yeah? Where?"

"We just crossed the Kansas border yesterday. That's where we hit them riders."

"And we had to chase them riders all over creation before getting the drop on them," Nick said. "Then you let Peevely lead us until nightfall before he let out that he didn't know where the hell he was going."

"That's all a part of being in a gang, Nick. If you don't like it, you can turn right around and head back to that backward-speaking pa of . . ." Barrett stopped himself before saying another word. "You can always go back home," he quickly corrected himself.

Nick started digging up little stones from the ground and pitching them through the air. "So, what do we do now?"

"We find a town. We can figure out where we're at and then move on from there. Joey," Barrett shouted out to one of the other boys nearby. "Come over here."

Of the two Cooleys, Joey was the youngest and most reserved. "Yeah, Bar," Joey said, shortening Barrett's name the way nobody else bothered to do. "What is it?"

"Tell Nick about that wagon."

Joey's natural response was to cower a bit under Nick's hard stare, but he managed to pull in enough breath to start talking. "I heard of a wagon coming through these parts on its way down to Pea Ridge."

"That's in Arkansas," Barrett explained.

"The Federals have been moving through there. That's what I heard from my uncle. He loads cannons for the —"

"Just skip to the important part," Nick interrupted.

Joey recoiled a bit, but nodded and then continued. "Last time when we were in town, I was at a saloon when I heard some fellas talking about a load of guns and ammunition being snuck to some Rebs about a day's ride north from there."

"You were in a saloon?" Nick asked.

Joey kept his chin up and even puffed out his chest a little. "I sure was, I swear." Letting his breath out a bit, he added, "I didn't have enough for no whiskey, but I stood at the bar with them gunmen."

Nick glanced between Joey and Barrett as the confusion on his face grew. "Where the hell was I?"

Barrett laughed and nudged Nick in the ribs. "We was getting on with them ladies in the house across the street. You should remember. It cost us enough."

Now it was Nick's turn to smile and puff out his own chest. "Oh yeah. I remember that lady."

"You do?" Barrett said with exaggerated surprise on his face. "But you were only in there for about a minute."

"Aw, go to hell," Nick grunted. "What about this wagon, Joey?"

Joey started to talk so fast that the words were like a current coming from his mouth. "I heard one of the men at the bar talking about it. I think he's a Reb because he was talking about doing his part in the war and putting guns in the hands that needs them and about giving the Federals hell.

"He said he was driving a wagon of guns, but that it was just a bunch of rifles and such that he and some neighbors could pull together. Some of the others were giving him a hard time, but he said there was enough in there to do some damage and that the Rebs needed whatever they could get."

"What's that got to do with us?" Nick asked.

Barrett leaned forward and started sketching a map in the dirt. "Joey told me where the wagon was coming from when he said the story before."

"Oh yeah," Joey said. "The fella was coming fr—"

"He's starting out here," Barrett interrupted, pointing toward an *X* he'd drawn on the crude map in the dirt. Moving his finger a ways down inside the map, he made a second *X* and said, "We're here, more or less. When did the fella say he was gonna be heading out, Joey?"

"The seventh or eighth of the month."

"That's a week from now," Barrett said with a glimmer in his eye. "If he's some half-assed Rebel lover, then he probably won't really get moving until the tenth."

"If he gets moving at all," Nick cut in. "There might not even be no wagon. Even if there is, we don't know which trail he's taking. Do we, Joey?"

Barrett dismissed the doubting talk with a few quick shakes of his head. "There's only one good road to take from there to here," he said, drawing a line from the first X to the spot marking where he thought they were. "With the horses we stole, we can scout out a place along the way and pick our spot to make an ambush."

By this time, all the others in the gang had gathered around and were listening intently. Joey was nodding furiously and squirming as though he was listening in on what he would get for Christmas. Even Peevely had forgotten about the earlier embarrassment and was staring at the map in the dirt while hanging on Barrett's every word.

"Ambush?" Nick asked. "What're you talking about? We're not —"

"We're a gang, ain't we? I say it's about time we started acting like one instead of just a bunch of big-talkers." Glancing around at the others, he asked, "Who's with me?"

All in the circle threw in their hands, nodded their heads, or did whatever else they could think of to signal their allegiance. All, that is, except for Nick.

"I don't know, Barrett," Nick said. "We may not catch that wagon, or we may not pick the right spot."

"If we miss it, who cares?" Barrett replied. "Either way, we don't lose nothing. But if we hit it, we can walk away with some real firepower and whatever else that pecker was gonna hand over to the Rebs. We also get a real score, Nick. Just think about it."

Nick was thinking about it, all right. He was thinking hard. And the more he thought, the more he smiled. "Let's do it. However it turns out, it beats the hell out of digging holes for my old man."

"And with your share of the money, you can buy all the spuds you can stuff in your face."

"Eat shit, Barrett."

TWELVE

"So what's this job that's got you smiling like a rooster in a henhouse?" Nick asked as he looked across the table at Barrett.

The Number Three Watering Hole was a long ways from that field in the middle of Kansas in many respects. Apart from the years that had passed, plenty had changed along the way for both of the boys who'd sat and plotted over a map scratched in the dirt. Still, when he saw that scheming look in Barrett's eye, Nick couldn't help but be reminded of that troublemaking youth from twenty years ago.

"It's a big job, Nick."

"Aren't they all?"

"This one's bigger than most. Maybe even the biggest one I've ever done."

"I don't know if you've heard," Nick said, "but I don't pull jobs like I used to. Big ones or small ones."

Barrett nodded slowly, easing back into

his chair, while looking at something over Nick's shoulder. "That's right. I heard once that you were taking up your father's trade. And here I thought you'd never go back to digging holes for dead men."

"I don't just dig holes."

"Really? So you've moved up in the world." Barrett paused for a moment when he saw that Nick's patience was wearing thin. Taking on a more amicable tone, he said, "So tell me what you do, Nick. I'd like to hear it."

Even though he knew Barrett was still building up to something, Nick decided to play along. Besides, he had to admit it felt good to catch up with an old friend over drinks like normal people might do. Of course, normal people didn't feel a growing discomfort thinking that someone was coming up behind them to collect a price that was on their head, but nobody was perfect.

"I carve headstones, build coffins, and arrange the showings."

Barrett winced. "Sounds gruesome."

"I help people when they need it the most. That's really what it comes down to. I take care of details they don't want to think about."

"Details. That's something I can relate to. Like what kind of details?"

"Like sending out announcements for funerals. I make sure that things go off like they should so the bereaved don't have to concern themselves. I even arrange the occasional hanging. From what I've heard, that's the part that you might become familiar with sooner rather than later."

"Oh, and what have you heard?"

"That you're still setting your sights a bit too high and getting the wrong people mad at you."

"Things have changed since we ran together, Nick. Now, I can back my own plays and if things go wrong, I can handle myself."

"If that's so, then why do you need me to sign on to whatever this job of yours is? I'm guessing you want me as a gun hand."

Barrett kept studying Nick's face in that certain way he'd done since they were both kids. Finally, he leaned forward with his elbows on the table and locked his eyes on Nick's face. "I don't need many gun hands, Nick. I need someone skilled who knows what they're doing if things get rough. Of course I need someone who knows their way around the steel, but what's more important is that they keep their head so things don't get that bad in the first place.

"We've covered a lot of ground together and I know you better than most anyone else. That's why I know you'd be perfect for this type of work and that's why I was asking around for you even when all I'd heard was rumor and hearsay that you were around these parts at all."

Nick's jaw clenched at the sound of that. "What have you heard about me?"

"Face it, Nick, even if folks want to cover for you, rumors about an undertaker with missing fingers who just happened to be around when lead started to fly are going to spread. Most of it's built up into a bunch of stories, but I recognized some things in them that made me think of my old friend Nicolai Graves."

Leaning back slightly, Barrett nodded with the knowledge that he'd definitely gotten his audience interested in what he was saying. "Don't worry too much, though. The rumors I heard have you pegged as anything from a bounty hunter to some farmer who'd gotten fed up and started gunning folks down. You know how rumors are. It takes a whole lot of sifting to get through the bullshit."

"All right," Nick said with a shrug. "You found me. I found you. Now what?"

"Now, you come with me for one last job and we both get so rich that we can pick our own spots to retire and never work another day in our lives."

That brought a smile to Nick's face. "I've heard that one before."

"But this time, it's true." Pausing for a moment, Barrett took some time to drain a bit more of his beer. As he did, he kept his eyes focused on the bottom of his mug as if whatever answers he was after were written there. He swirled the brew around, set the mug down, and then looked back up again.

"All right," Barrett said. "You want to know about the job? I'll tell you. But this is only because of all the history we've got. Otherwise, I wouldn't even bother unless I knew for certain you were in."

"Just spill it, for Christ's sake. I'm starting to remember why I swore so much when I was around you."

"All right. Here it is." He took one more breath and then lowered his voice as much as he could while still being heard over the background ruckus in the saloon. "There's a load of gems coming in to a jeweler who's setting up shop here in town. The owner is some fancy-pants who used to live in New York City before sending his son out this way to expand their interests. He's already got his place built and even had a safe driven in all the way from Texas that's made of iron thicker than ol' Peevely's skull."

If he were hearing this from anyone else, Nick would have wondered how someone could be so well informed. But from Barrett, the information sounded like the first drop in the bucket. "You still love your research, don't you?"

"Of course. I've been looking in on this company for years, on and off, back when I used to live out East. It's run by two fellas who came all the way over from England and they've made a fortune in shipping and selling everything from fancy wine to hand-crafted furniture."

"And jewelry," Nick added.

When Barrett nodded, he smirked in a way that made him look every bit the kid that had drawn that first map in the Kansas dirt. "And jewelry," he said. "They bring things over here, ship things back there and make a goddamn fortune on each side of the ocean. They've built it up to the point where they take special orders from rich folks and royalty until they're something close to royalty themselves."

"And you think you can steal from someone like this?" Nick asked. "I'd guess they've got plenty to spend on hired guns."

"They sure do, which is why we won't go after any of their bigger shipments. What we're after is something they might consider slightly bigger than average, but they also consider a town like this to be nothing to trouble themselves about compared to big bad cities like New York.

"You can see the shop for yourself. It's just a few streets down on Ashton Corner. It's a small place, but you can't miss it. It's called Finch's. Go take a look if you don't believe me."

"Oh I believe you. You've never lied about the facts regarding any of your plans."

The nodding smile on Barrett's face was full of confidence. "That's right. So that's how you know that coming in on this with me would be the smartest thing you've ever done."

"Save the snake oil pitch, Barrett. I'd be more interested in knowing how you found out all of your information."

"There's plenty of ways. You should remember that."

"Normally, I never knew what you were doing when you would check up on something. Half the time I was more concerned that all those people you were paying would either steal our money or turn us over to the law."

"Yeah? Well people like those are how I know so much. All it takes is a few favors or a few dollars and you find out all sorts of things. I got my hooks into a shipping clerk who works for Finch's in New York City and he's the one who let me know about this little purchase." Shaking his head, Barrett glanced over Nick's shoulder and then back to his face. "Why didn't you ever get back in touch with me? I know Montana was a bust, but that didn't have to be permanent."

"It was pretty damn permanent for most of the boys we were with," Nick replied in a deadly serious tone. "And just because I got out of there with my life, don't think for one moment that it wasn't permanent for me too."

"All right, then I'll just skip right to the bottom of what's going on here and now. The fella who runs the store here in town is the son of one of the men who started the whole company. He means to set this place up as a stopover for dealings with San Francisco, Dodge City, and such. It'll also be a fancy store in its own regard and all the place needs before opening its doors is its first load of inventory."

"And you got all this from a clerk in New York City?" Nick asked.

"That and by working for the store owner when the place down the street was being put together. Anyhow, the shipment is coming in a few days and there'll be plenty of goods running from clothes to some fancy spectacles. But all I'm thinking about is a few satchels holding some jewelry, watches, as well as a few uncut stones."

"What else?" As soon as he'd asked the question, Nick knew that he'd touched a nerve Barrett had been trying to keep covered. That nerve had been far from obvious, but Nick knew Barrett too damn well to miss it. In order to put the suspicion that was growing in Barrett's eyes to rest, Nick added, "There's always something else, Barrett."

Finally, Barrett started to nod and lowered his eyes so he was staring at the table. He stared down so intently, that Nick wouldn't have been surprised to see smoke start curling up from the wood in front of Barrett's mug.

"Remember that safe I told you about?" Barrett asked. When he saw Nick nod, he went on to say, "That safe's holding a good amount of gold and cash in it."

"How much gold and cash?"

"Enough to pay for this load of inventory, the jewelry, and possibly a few rough diamonds. That's how much."

"And you weren't going to tell me about that, were you?"

"I haven't told the others that're in on this

job, that's for damn sure," Barrett replied, gracefully sidestepping the original question. "But I'll cut you in on the whole lot as a bonus for old-times' sake. I know you're worth it."

Despite the fact that he hadn't taken part in a robbery for more years than he could remember off-hand, Nick's brain was already shifting into the old track after spending less than an hour with Barrett Cobb. One of the things he picked up on right away using that outlaw frame of mind was the fact that Barrett didn't say he'd split the gold and cash with him. The cut that was being offered could have been as low as 5 percent and Barrett wouldn't even consider it a deception on his part.

"So what's it going to be, Nick? Are you in?"

Nick hadn't come to town looking to throw his hand into a robbery. In fact, he'd been doing his best to bury that part of himself every time he dug a hole in the ground for some poor soul confined to a box. His road had taken him many places, but he knew better than to think he could figure out where the next twist would be. There was only one certainty and that was where his road would end.

The end wasn't in sight just yet, which

meant that Nick still had to decide for himself which way to turn when a fork presented itself.

On the other hand, just because it had been a while since his last job with Barrett didn't mean that Nick forgot what they were like. No matter how many laws were broken along the way, there was no denying the fact that Nick had spent some damn exciting years with Barrett and the rest of his gang.

Together, the boys forged themselves into a dangerous whole. They'd gotten good enough at their chosen trade to attract others who not only added to the gang, but sharpened each individual member as well. Nick sometimes thought it was like joining the army.

He learned to fight. He learned about death. He even saw his way into a woman's bed for the first time while traveling with his chosen regiment. But unlike any soldier, Nick hadn't been bound by any laws. He answered to nobody and the entire world was spread out before him like a whore eyeing the fat pouch of gold in his pocket.

He hated to admit it to anyone, especially himself, but Nick missed those old days almost as much as he regretted them. Sitting next to Barrett now made the alternative seem all the more dismal by comparison.

Digging holes for a living just didn't stack up to grabbing the world by the neck and squeezing until everything you wanted dropped from its pockets. No matter how many times he sat around thinking about what a better man he was compared to the man he used to be, the fact remained that he'd been that other man for a hell of a long time.

Nick had been working to pull himself out of the hole he'd dug for himself, but the scales weren't balanced just yet. He'd still taken more lives than he'd saved and that made him wonder if he wasn't just too far down that road to turn back now. There was always money to be made and jobs to pull. Barrett had taught him that much.

In the meantime, Nick had learned a few other things on his own. For one thing, he'd realized that Stasys may not have been so ignorant in the workings of a bad man's mind. If he didn't know any better, Nick would have sworn that his father had spent some time on the wrong side of the law himself.

The old man's words echoed through his brain like a constant chant, reminding him of the road that had been left behind. There was plenty to be said for familiarity, even if Nick had spent his youth becoming familiar with spilling blood and running for his life.

Of course, a Mourner only had to worry about burying the dead rather than being tormented by their faces every night as he slipped off into yet another night of liquor-induced unconsciousness. Since he'd stopped snuffing out lives like so many cheap candles, Nick felt those ghostly voices growing more and more distant with every night that passed.

His days of comfort seemed to be getting distant as well. Try as he might to live an honest life, Nick still had to pick up and leave whatever bridges he'd built and he still had to keep himself apart from any women who might want to share his bed for any reason besides the money in his pocket.

All of this went through Nick's mind in the blink of an eye and Barrett seemed to be able to see every last bit of it. Finally, Nick nodded solemnly and chose which road he was going to take.

"I'm in," Nick said.

Barrett actually looked a bit surprised as he reached across the table to shake Nick's hand. "Now there's the Nick Graves I remember!"

THIRTEEN

Kansas
1862

"I thought you said you were in!"

"That was when this whole thing started and before I spent a whole day lying with my belly in the dirt with the four of you so close that I can smell what you ate a week ago. I ain't in no more."

It had been a long couple of days since sixteen-year-old Nick Graves and the rest of his gang found their way to a rocky pass about three miles from where they'd hatched their plan in the first place. Actually, most of the plan was Barrett's, but Nick threw in enough of his own adjustments to make him feel that he was still in control.

Ned Peevely and the Cooley brothers were content enough to tag along for the ride. Although they would sound off a bit when the inevitable argument arose as to who was the leader of the gang, they didn't stake any sort of claim to that title. That particular fight would always boil down to Nick and Barrett. Mostly, Barrett would back off when Nick started getting rough, but that had started to change. That was evident enough when Nick got up from his spot overlooking a dusty trail and began to walk away.

"Get back here, Spud," Barrett snarled while twisting on the ground to look up at the other boy. "Or would you be more happy to just go back home and dig holes with your daddy?"

Nick stopped and looked at each of the boys in turn. Although Barrett was the only one challenging him, Nick gave the others a venomous glare just to keep them in their place.

"A million things could've gone different than what you said, Barrett," Nick said in a tone that was low yet quivering with anger. "That wagon could've taken another road. It might not have left yet. Hell, I bet that asshole in the saloon was just blowing smoke to look like a big man and you dumb shits bought it!"

"Get back down here," Joey Cooley whispered. "You'll give us away."

"Aw to hell with this," Nick snarled. "And to hell with all of you. There ain't even been anyone on this damn road since we got here. We've been laying around for days without a fire and without nothing else to eat but some moldy bread and a few strips of jerky. I'm going back to that town and get some hot food. Who's with me?"

Barrett got his feet beneath him and stood up. Even though he didn't come close to Nick's height, he drew himself up and stared the other boy down. "We don't got no more money, Nick."

"I'll steal some."

"We don't even have any guns that shoot for a damn."

"Then I'll get up close."

"We won't never be a gang if we just steal food and shoot men in the back. This is where we start living up to what we've been talking about and now you want to go home?"

Nick had been expecting to hear yet another batch of insults, but what he got was more earnest than that. It took a moment for the words to sink in, but when they did, they left him more than a little rattled. They made him realize that going home wasn't much of an option for him anymore.

Stasys had a way of looking at him that sent chills through Nick's bones. Throughout all of Nick's threats to leave, Stasys had responded with nothing more than a few words and that glare, which had been enough to squelch whatever rebellion had been brewing in the boy's heart. Thinking about returning home meant facing down the old man one more time and even though Stasys had never been cruel, Nick wasn't too anxious to find out what was waiting for him back home.

"No," Nick said after a few silent moments had passed. "I don't want to go back."

"Then we need to do this!" Barrett's voice had been insistent before, but now it was pumped full of steam. "Folks'll know our names if we give them a reason. They'll remember us forever if we stick together and take the rest of the world by the throat!"

Nick let out a grunting laugh and said, "Shit, even if we find this damn wagon, it's not like we'll be known men for turning it over."

"No, but we'll know what we done. After that, the next job won't seem so hard. And after a few more jobs, folks will start to hear about the jobs we pulled and then they'll start to hear about *us*." Looking around to the other boys lying on their stomachs in a row beside him, Barrett asked, "Or do you all just want to go back home when we've already come so far?"

Nick scowled when he heard that, knowing full well that their biggest real achievement was running away from home. But he could tell that Barrett's words were having their full effect on Peevely and the two brothers. They looked entranced at what Barrett was saying to them as they gobbled up every last word.

Just when Nick was about to storm off and put the other four behind him, he heard a distant rumble coming from over the rise they'd been watching. His mouth was frozen halfway open, the rude parting comments lodged in his throat like a hunk of stale biscuit.

Barrett's eyes widened and he twisted around so quickly that he wound up flopping onto his belly like a fish out of water. "You hear that?" he asked in a rushed whisper. "You hear that? Just listen to that!"

The Cooleys grabbed handfuls of dirt and pulled themselves closer to the edge where they were lying. Peevely used his feet to push himself in that same direction. The motion of his boots scrambling against the dirt kicked up almost as much dust as the wagon that was rolling on the trail below them.

Nick lowered himself to his knees and

then back down onto his stomach along with all the others. "I'll be Goddamned," he whispered.

"You see?" Barrett said, almost to himself as much as to anyone else. "I told you that wagon would come this way and there it is. You see?"

"Yeah, we see," Joey Cooley said. "What do we do now?"

For a moment, it seemed that Barrett didn't rightly know how to answer that question. His uncertainty didn't last long enough to keep his tongue in check. "We do just like we planned. Remember what we planned, Joey? Peevely? Bob?"

One by one, each of the boys nodded. Their breath was coming in quicker spurts now and their fingers were making fists in the dirt like birds afraid of getting blown off of their perch. One of the boys wasn't so quick to pledge himself to the cause, however. Unlike the rest of the gang, Nick had more going through his mind than what Barrett put there.

"That might not even be the one we're after," Nick said. "Give me that spyglass."

Bob dug around in the satchel slung over his shoulder and pulled out a dented telescope that barely held together when Nick lifted it to his eye. Peering through the chipped lenses, Nick squinted and concentrated through the glare until he finally managed to zero in on the sight he was after.

The wagon was approaching pretty quickly and following it only caused the image to jump more in Nick's eye. "Looks like one man driving. He's got a shotgun."

"What's in the wagon?" Barrett asked insistently. "How many guns does he got?"

"He's hauling something. It's under a tarp. I can't tell what it is."

The excitement was not only spreading among the other boys, but it was growing like wildfire in a dry cornfield.

Joey patted the ground with both hands. "It's the wagon with the guns," he whispered anxiously. "I know it."

Barrett reached up and swiped the spyglass from Nick. "Here, Joey. Take this and see if you recognize the fella driving as the one who was spouting off in that saloon."

Joey grabbed hold of the spyglass, put the wrong end to his eye and started nodding furiously. After getting swatted on the side of the head by Nick, he flipped the telescope around and looked through the narrower end. "That's the man," he said as though he could scarcely believe it. "I'd recognize him anywhere."

"All right then," Barrett replied. "Let's get

moving."

Nick looked at the path which sloped down about twenty to thirty feet. The wagon was coming around a bend in the path that would bring it directly beneath them in less than a minute. By the looks of it, the driver was pushing the team of three horses pretty close to their limits and didn't show any signs of slowing down.

"Get ready, Nick."

Hearing that from Barrett drew Nick's attention to the two pistols stuck beneath his belt. The guns jabbed into his hips like fat, iron fingers reminding him of what he was supposed to do.

Whatever was showing on Nick's face at the moment was lost to Barrett, who was too busy spurring the others to their appointed duties.

"Joey, Bob," Barrett said. "Go get the horses ready. Peevely . . ."

Nick got up even as Barrett started pulling him back down with a quick grab to his elbow. "Give me back that spyglass. We need to be sure before —"

But it was already too late. Peevely's job was to cover the gang using a hunting rifle that he'd brought from home. The intention was to start shooting once Nick had made his move, but the boy was so raring to go that he squeezed off his first shot before any of the others had headed over the side.

The shot rolled through the air like a living thing and smoke spewed out from the rifle's barrel. Peevely let out a holler as if he'd just put a bullet through the devil himself and quickly pushed another round into the breech.

For a second, Nick just took in what was happening around him. The Cooleys were already out of sight and rushing toward the horses they'd tied up not too far away. Barrett was in his moment of glory, scrambling for his own weapon and squirming as if he meant to slither straight down to the trail on his belly.

Nick then looked over to the wagon. Part of him wondered if the driver had even heard the shot over the rumbling of his wheels. Another part of him prayed for that driver to be deaf so he would just keep rolling until he was out of their sight. But the driver was already looking around, wildly searching for the source of the bullet that had just whipped past him.

Since the boys didn't know better, they marked their exact positions by standing up like sore thumbs atop the ridge. Nick could feel the driver's gaze sweep over him like a cold mist as the sound of the Cooleys and the horses grew louder in his ears. The driver turned the shotgun toward them and fired off a shot.

Nick wanted to curse. He wanted to swear at the top of his lungs. The words wouldn't come, however, since he could barely even breathe. All he could do was pull the guns from under his belt and start clambering down the ridge.

It was too late to do much else.

FOURTEEN

Grunting something under his breath, the driver twisted around in his seat to grab hold of his shotgun. Another rifle shot popped through the air, spurring him even more. Now that he had something to aim at, he brought up the shotgun and sighted at the first person he could see that was moving toward him.

That person just happened to be Nick skidding down the side of the ridge toward the speeding wagon. He had a gun in each hand, announcing his intentions more clearly than a sign around his neck.

Nick was jostling so much that it was difficult for him to see much of anything. But the man in front of him had a shotgun and was about to fire it in his direction. It would have taken more than some erratic movement to miss that sight. His stomach tightened into a knot and he ducked low out of pure reflex. That sudden motion caused him to slide along the sides of his boots, fold into a ball, and roll the rest of the way down to the path.

While that didn't do wonders for his body, the awkward fall got him out of the way as the shotgun belched out a plume of smoke and sent a wave of lead through the air. Nick was far enough away from the blast to avoid most of the pellets, but the shot had spread out enough to send a few chunks of lead raking over his shoulder and back. The pain was like a hand pushing Nick along as he continued to roll. When his back rolled over the ground, those same shallow wounds sent enough of a jolt through him to get the boy upright in a hurry.

When Nick sprang back to his feet, it was as if he'd been yanked up by an inexperienced puppeteer. Even so, he still wound up standing, if also more than a bit shocked that he was there at all. That shock was tripled when he saw he was standing in the path of the oncoming wagon and was about to get trampled into the dirt.

The horses were so close that Nick could see the crazed look in their eyes. Like most animals, they weren't exactly used to the sound of gunshots and shotgun blasts coming from directly behind them and they had been driven into a frenzy.

Nick doubted the team of horses even knew he was standing there, but he meant to fix that very quickly. The pistols were still in his hands, after all. He brought them up, thumbed the hammers back and pulled back the triggers in a motion that wasn't exactly lightning fast, but just fast enough.

He pointed the guns up and out as if he were just raising his arms. The pistols went off simultaneously, bucking against his palms while spitting their fiery cargo into the sky. Nick gritted his teeth and winced as the horses drew closer. The moment stretched out in his mind as if it was his last, but he still couldn't get himself to move. His ears filled with the thunder of stampeding hooves and his boots shook against the trembling ground.

Still rooted to the spot, Nick thumbed back the hammers even as he realized that he probably wouldn't live much longer after taking the next shot.

At that particular moment, he couldn't hear anything else. The world seemed to have held its breath, wiping away the beating of hooves, the rattle of wheels and even the scratchy voice of the driver as he shouted to his team and to his attackers. Suddenly, one sound managed to break through his mental fog.

It was the crack of Peevely's rifle followed by the distinctive hiss of lead rushing toward him.

Nick's heart slammed in his chest. That bullet came closer and finally lead slapped against the thick flesh of the lead horse's neck.

Flesh split open as the bullet came out the other side, spraying blood in both directions as the horse's eyes rolled up into its head. The horse twisted around to the edge of the road so sharply that it dumped the wagon onto its side while piling the remaining two horses into a flailing heap.

Nick stood by for a moment and watched in disbelief as the whole team and wagon turned away from him at the last possible second. The wagon came skidding over the dirt toward him like a slow-moving whip, but Nick had pulled himself together enough to hop out of the way and let it pass.

The wagon came to a halt after spilling its contents all over the ground. Nick wanted to get a look at the cargo, but caught sight of movement coming from the front of the cart. Not only had everything come rushing back to fill each of his senses, but Nick felt as though he could see clearer and hear more than ever before.

He could see every twitching muscle in

the dead or wounded horses as well as every last bit of dust settling over the wreck. He could hear every squeak of wheels turning in the air as well as every haggard breath taken by the driver as he struggled to get up from where he'd landed.

The Cooleys would be on their way with the gang's horses, but it would take them a while to ride all the way around the ridge and back to the wreck. Peevely was supposed to stay put, which only left Barrett for Nick to worry about. For the moment, however, he realized he needed to worry about himself more than anybody else.

The driver was a slovenly man sporting an unkempt mustache. His dirty face poked up over the side of the wagon and instantly focused upon Nick. Although it was tough to say just how bad he'd been hurt when the wagon had turned over, his scalp was bloody and a few of his teeth appeared to have been knocked out. One of his legs was curled beneath him in an unnatural angle, but he still fought to get to his feet. Snarling something unintelligible, he stretched out an arm to reach for the shotgun that had landed in the dirt nearby.

"Leave that gun where it is!" Nick shouted.

But the driver either didn't hear or wasn't

in the mood to obey because he kept right on grabbing for his shotgun.

Stretching out both arms so he could sight down the barrels of his pistols, Nick moved around the front of the wagon where the horses were still trying to get out of their harnesses and away from each other. Peevely was either a better shot than Nick had thought or was just plain lucky, because the horse he'd targeted was dead on the ground. The animal's body was still tied to the rest of the team, which kept them anchored to the ground.

Hearing the sound of the shotgun being reloaded and cocked, Nick ducked low and moved around the dead horse so he could cover the driver with his pistols. The moment he stuck his head around to see the man, Nick found himself staring down the wrong end of that shotgun. He snapped himself back behind the team a split second before the shotgun went off. Its thunderous roar deafened him and the storm of lead blew apart the head of one of the two surviving horses.

Covered in dirt and gore, Nick kept stumbling back while checking himself to make sure he wasn't shot as well. He looked around to see where the rest of his gang was and spotted Barrett limping toward the wagon with his left arm clamped over a bloody wound in his side. Apparently, the driver hadn't been aiming at Nick the entire time.

"You all right?" Nick asked.

Barrett tried to speak, but didn't have the breath for it so he nodded instead.

Nick was no doctor, but he didn't think Barrett's wound looked too bad. "Just stay put," he told the other boy. "I've got this one here."

Taking a deep breath and keeping his head down, Nick moved around the other side of the wagon. He paid close attention to every sound coming from the driver. As far as he could tell, the fat man wasn't able to get to his feet since every movement caused him to grunt in pain. Apart from the scraping of boots against the dirt, Nick could hear a steady stream of curses being spat in a wheezing tirade.

Suddenly, those curses stopped and Nick could hear the shotgun snapping shut and its hammers clicking back. Something heavy scraped against the opposite side of the wagon. Nick could hardly believe it, but the fat man seemed to have gotten himself moving. He nearly jumped out of his skin, however, when another shot from Peevely's rifle cracked through the air and hissed not too far from his head.

The shot was followed by the skinny kid's voice echoing down from the ridge. "I saw him stick his head out, Nick! Be careful!"

Taking a deep breath, Nick prayed that Peevely truly was a damn good shot with that rifle and hadn't missed him twice now out of luck. Keeping his head down even lower, he scuttled around the wagon as quickly as he could.

Every breath he took was an effort. His hands were on the verge of shaking and it seemed a miracle that he was still alive. Even with all of that, however, there was no denying one simple fact: Nick had never felt so alive.

He'd gotten into fights and even gotten into a few dangerous predicaments, but none of them had been like this. He was gambling not only with his life, but with his future as well. If he somehow managed to get away from that wagon alive, then perhaps Barrett would be right. Perhaps they would be on their way to becoming bad men.

At the very least, Nick could see that Barrett had been right about one thing. When the wagon tipped over, it had spilled its contents onto the ground and firearms of all kinds were splayed out in the dirt.

There weren't more than a few dozen in all, but there were some fine pieces in the collection along with plenty of ammunition.

Nick didn't want to start taking inventory just yet, however. There was one slight detail that had yet to be squared away.

"Come on, you bastard kid!" the driver shouted. "Stick yer head around that corner!" He punctuated his request with a blast from his shotgun.

Lead pounded into the side of the wagon. It sent a curtain of splinters and smoke into the air and got one of the overturned wheels spinning as well. None of the pellets came close to hitting Nick, but they did cause him to squat down so low that he was practically crawling as he approached the back end of the wagon.

Realigning himself so that he was crouching with his back to the wagon, Nick sucked in a deep breath and dug the toe of his boot under a piece of timber that had been broken off the back gate. With a snap of his knee, he sent the chunk of wood over the ground where it landed less than three feet away. It knocked against the ground when it landed and the sound was enough to get the driver to twitch just as Nick had hoped.

The shotgun obliterated the piece of wood into too many pieces to count. With the echo of the blast still ringing through his ears, Nick tightened his grip on his pistols and jumped around the end of the wagon. He was still crouched down low when he came face-to-face with the driver.

Smoke curled from the shotgun's barrel as it was pointed straight at Nick's head. A nasty smile curled the driver's lips, exposing the jagged, bloody gaps in his teeth.

Every bit of color drained from Nick's face, leaving his skin cold and clammy. The bottom dropped out of his stomach and he felt as though the ground itself was being tilted beneath his boots. It was a moment that was frozen forever in his mind like the photographs of dead soldiers that showed up in newspapers during the war.

The moment ended when the driver spat, "Fuck you, kid," and then pulled his trigger.

The hammer dropped and smacked against the back of a spent shell.

Nick blinked a few times and let out the breath he'd been holding. Even though he knew the driver had emptied both his barrels, it was still one hell of a feeling to test the theory with his life on the line.

As Nick walked forward, he still felt the same clamminess on his skin and shakiness in his step. The driver clenched what was left of his teeth while cocking back his hammers and squeezing his triggers again and again. Rage showed on the man's bloody face, only to be replaced by a growing desperation.

Before the driver could pull the trigger one more time, Nick had walked up to him to kick the shotgun from his hands. The driver was hanging on too tight, however, and he kept hold of it even as the shotgun knocked flat against the ground. Nick stepped down upon the man's wrist, pinning both his arm and the weapon to the dirt.

"So what now, kid?" the driver asked. "You gonna kill me?"

Nick stared down into the driver's eyes. His breaths were coming slower now, but that didn't seem to help ease the cold fist clenching around his innards.

The driver squinted and took a longer look. "You ever killed a man before?"

Although he didn't really know why, Nick answered with a grunted, "No."

The driver studied Nick's face and seemed to find something in the boy's eyes that gave him hope. Perhaps it was the paleness of his skin or the way both of Nick's pistols were starting to tremble slightly despite the lack of wind. "Go on and take the wagon, but

I'll be seeing you again, kid. You and your buddies run all you like. You started this mess and I'll finish it, by God."

"Nick?" came Barrett's voice from the other side of the wagon. "What's going on? You need any help?"

"What's happening?" Peevely shouted.

Now that the shots had died off, the sound of approaching horses drew closer. At least the Cooleys were doing their part and hadn't been scared off.

The driver winced as Nick pressed his boot down harder against his wrist, but he wasn't about to let go of his shotgun. Finally, he smirked even wider.

Nick couldn't think of what the driver could be so happy about until he saw the man's other hand reaching for one of the guns that had spilled out from the overturned wagon. There was a moment of worry, but it quickly faded once Nick saw that there was no way in hell the driver could stretch his arm far enough to reach the gun. That didn't keep the driver from trying, though. Nick had to give the guy credit for that much.

"Come on, Nick," Barrett said as he came around the wagon, his eyes wide with the sight of all those guns. "Let's finish this up before someone else comes along."

162

Nick's eyes drifted over the driver's legs. One was still twisted at an unnatural angle. The other was straighter, but had a hunk of bone jutting out from just beneath the knee.

Using up every last bit of his strength, the driver snapped out with his hand to make one last grab for the gun. He actually managed to reach about twice as far as Nick expected and might have even made it to the gun if Nick hadn't carved two messy tunnels through the driver's face with a quick pull of his triggers.

FIFTEEN

*Outside the Number Three Watering Hole
1882*

The sound of those two guns echoed in the back of Nick's mind like a storm that had already passed, but was still wreaking havoc somewhere else. His fingers curled reflexively as though he could still feel the pistols bucking against his palms. It was true that a man never forgot his first time. Unfortunately, some first times were more pleasant than others.

Barrett had gone to meet up with some of the others he'd pulled together for this job of his, leaving Nick to face the men that had been creeping up on them all night. He'd given a warning before leaving, but it was hardly necessary. Even though he'd been forced to put his back to the door, he could feel the others drawing closer the entire night. They'd let him pass when Barrett and he had gotten up and paid for their drinks, but were now following without making much of a secret out of it.

After he'd walked about halfway down the street, Nick stopped and spun around so quickly that two of the men behind him twitched back a step.

"I haven't done anything wrong," Nick said. "So there's no reason to follow me and there's no reason to arrest me."

The one man who hadn't flinched when Nick turned around was built like a grizzly. His shoulders were wide and his arms were muscular, yet his face still retained a somewhat friendly cast. When he looked at Nick, he regarded him carefully, but without doing anything to cause any sparks to fly.

"Arrest you?" the big man asked. "What makes you think we'd do that?"

"You're lawmen aren't you?" Nick pointed out, even though none of the men were displaying badges.

After a pause, the big man nodded once.

"And you strike me as honest lawmen to boot."

A smirk crept onto the big man's face, but there wasn't much humor in that expression. "I'm Sheriff Trayner. Or did you already know that too?"

Nick shook his head.

"You seem to know plenty, though,"

Trayner said, holding his ground while the other two men took up positions beside him. "Did you learn the rest from that no-good friend of yours?"

"Nope. If all you wanted was trouble, you would have done something in the saloon or right outside of it. Usually lawmen are the ones who hang back that far for that long like they've got all the time in the world."

"All right, then. And how would you know I'm honest?"

"Just a guess."

"Well, I don't like guessing," Trayner said. "Especially about certain things. For instance, what business would a man like you have with a man like Barrett Cobb?"

"You were watching the whole time. All we did was have some drinks."

"You're old friends?"

"Is that against the law?"

Trayner nodded as he stepped forward. Placing his hands on his hips not only exposed the badge he wore, but the double-rig holster as well. For most men, sporting two guns made them look either paranoid or inexperienced. With Trayner's bulk, however, the guns seemed to fit him just fine.

"You were right when you said I was the

law around here," Trayner said in a tone that was like a fist wrapped in a velvet glove. "And as such, I don't much care for being talked to like I was just some bartender. Now what was your business with Cobb?"

Perhaps it was part of his younger self coming through, but Nick felt the urge to knock Trayner on his ass. "We had drinks," Nick replied evenly.

"Why are you in town?"

"I'm looking for work."

"What do you do?"

"I'm a Mourner."

Nick was used to the confused look that that answer typically received. Rather than clear it up, he let Trayner wallow for a few moments in his confusion. Surprisingly enough, the lawman actually got closer to the mark than most others.

"Is that some kind of undertaker?" Trayner asked.

"Something like that."

"Well, I'll tell you what. Since we don't take to no outlaws or transients cluttering up these streets, you'd best make sure you get yourself some gainful employment. If I see you next time and you're drinking with known men without some other kind of job, I'll run you out of this town. You heeled, boy?"

Hearing himself called that set Nick's eyebrow to twitching, but Nick swallowed his anger and nodded.

"Let's see what you got," Trayner said in a way that was part challenge and part command. The deputies behind him prepared for the worst, but the sheriff held his ground while only shifting one of his hands closer to his holster.

Slowly, Nick peeled back his coat to reveal the gun strapped around his waist. When the lawmen saw it, they didn't even try to hide their reactions. There were a few snickers, but Trayner himself looked mildly amused without being so blunt.

"What the hell is that?" Trayner asked, nodding toward the gnarled handle of the gun.

Nick allowed the sheriff to take the gun from him and examine it. The pistol's handle appeared to have been whittled down to half its regular size and the trigger was equally stunted. Even the barrel was mangled as though it had been heated and twisted until deep grooves formed in the steel.

Trayner's eyes focused on Nick's fingers and he nodded. "I guess maybe you wouldn't need to invest in quality iron." Handing over the gun, he added, "Maybe I had the wrong idea after all about you being a gunman. But don't think I'm kidding about what we talked about, you hear?" Motioning to his deputies, he turned his back on Nick with full confidence that his men would cover him. "And don't forget about that job I mentioned," he said over his shoulder.

Nick dropped the gun in his holster and pulled his coat back around him. The deputies stepped away and didn't turn their backs on him until Trayner was almost inside the Watering Hole. Once the other lawmen turned, they started joking among themselves and glancing back toward Nick.

There had been a few hotels Nick had passed on his way to the saloon. Barrett had even recommended a few of them, but Nick avoided those like the plague and kept walking until he reached a quieter portion of town. Renting a room nearby would mean that one of the lawmen would probably spot where he was and know where to find him. Going to one of the places Barrett had mentioned would give him an edge in tracking Nick down. For those reasons, Nick kept on walking until he turned onto a street he didn't even recognize.

Although he'd only been in town for a

matter of hours, it felt as if he'd been there for months. Other places like Bitter Creek seemed to blend together in his mind and having Barrett around again only made things muddier. Besides that, Nick was dead tired and had so much swimming around in his head that he knew it was going to be difficult getting to sleep.

At that moment, dropping off the earth completely sounded mighty appealing. Since he couldn't arrange that, he would settle for a night's sleep in a bed that wasn't under someone else's nose. The place he found that fit the bill was tucked away so well that Nick himself had almost walked right by it. There was nobody around to see him enter the building and nothing more than a faint flicker of light coming from inside. The only sign was a small shingle propped up inside the front window that read, CLARKSON HOTEL.

Nick walked in and had to slam the door to wake up the bespectacled old man sleeping facedown behind a tall desk.

The man awoke with a snort and looked around as though he didn't see that Nick was standing directly in front of him.

"You smell like a goddamn saloon," the old man snapped.

By this point, Nick was too tired to get

mad at the codger. "Good evening to you, too. I'd like a room."

"I don't allow no whores in here."

Keeping a straight face, Nick replied, "I'm not a whore. I don't have the body for it."

That brought a glimmer of a smirk to the old man's face, but when he wiped his hands flat over his face, he seemed to have wiped the grin away as well. "You know what I meant. I'll need two dollars up front to cover the first night's stay."

Nick took the money from his pocket, dropped it onto the desk and took the key the clerk handed to him. There was a tag tied to the key with a frayed bit of string. On the tag was the number one scrawled by a shaky hand.

"And no drinking in there," the man shouted as Nick started walking toward the door marked with a One a little way down a hall. "If you start any trouble, I'll call the sheriff."

Nick rolled his eyes as he went into his room. He could hear the old man snoring before he closed the door.

The room was about what he would have expected. The bed was a thin mattress covered by threadbare sheets setting on a rickety frame. One table. One empty wash-basin. One curtain hanging from a rod over a dirty window. None of that mattered, however, since Nick was only interested in the very first thing he'd spotted upon entering the room.

The bed creaked under Nick's weight, but was still a hell of a lot better than sleeping on the ground. Ironically enough, the room stank of whiskey and when he closed his eyes, he could hear the muffled groans of a couple in another room having their fun for the night. He had to laugh when he heard a door open and light footsteps tap down the hall moments after the nearby moaning came to a stop.

Apparently, the old man's rules only applied to Nick.

Perhaps things would take a turn for the better once he got his sleeves rolled up and put in an honest day's work. Before that, Nick decided to put everything else to the back of his mind so he could indulge in a full day's rest.

He wound up taking two days.

Sixteen

When Nick came out of his room after his rest, he felt like a completely new man. He looked like a new man as well, complete with clear eyes and a spring in his step. After getting caught up on his sleep, the whole town seemed to have taken on a better slant. There wasn't much that could help the Clarkson Hotel, however. The floors were still dirty and the place still reeked of booze. At least the old man who seemed to live behind the front desk had lightened up a bit.

"Mornin', Nick," the old man said from his post.

Nick tossed a friendly wave toward the desk as he walked by. "Morning, Clark." He wasn't sure if that was the man's name or not. Nick decided to call him that because of the name of the hotel and had yet to be corrected.

"You headin' out for somethin' to eat?"

"Yeah," Nick said, stopping at the front door. "But there was something else. Could you direct me to the undertaker?"

"The undertaker? What do ya want with him?" Suddenly, the old man stopped himself short and winced as if he'd just been rapped on the nose. "Did someone die? I didn't mean to be harsh."

"No," Nick said reassuringly. "Nobody died. Well, nobody I know. I'm looking for work."

"Ain't there better jobs to be had? I could set you up helping out around here if you'd like."

"No, just directions to the undertaker will be fine. That's what I do."

While most folks didn't look outright disgusted when they found out what Nick did for a living, they never seemed too thrilled about it either. The man behind the desk was no exception and he did his best to keep his shudder to himself. The directions he gave were quick and to the point, being only slightly more detailed than the ones Nick had gotten from Vera.

"Much obliged," Nick said, tipping his hat. And with that, he was out the door.

It was amazing how different everything looked after a healthy dose of sleep. Stepping outside, Nick was almost overtaken by the sunlight that caught him in the face. The wind seemed especially fragrant, filling his nose with scents ranging from horses and straw to burning wood and food being cooked. Following the latter of those scents, Nick decided to try out a restaurant that he hadn't frequented during his self-imposed sequester.

He wound up at a nice place within eyeshot of Cobbler's Avenue. The moment he stepped inside, he smiled while pulling in a lungful of air filled with the scents of griddle cakes and hot coffee. By the time he sat down, his mouth was watering. That condition only grew worse when he found out that the place had just gotten in a fresh batch of maple syrup to go along with the cakes.

After a breakfast like that, Nick felt practically at home in Bitter Creek. The events surrounding his arrival seemed like a distant memory and he hadn't seen one glimpse of either the sheriff or Barrett Cobb. Deciding not to trifle with his luck, Nick paid for his meal and left the restaurant with a full belly. He knew he would be hearing from one or both of those men soon enough.

The sheriff seemed like a good enough sort. A little heavy-handed, perhaps, but not a bad man. With the life he'd led before becoming a Mourner, Nick's very existence hinged upon judging certain characters. Some lawmen could become an outlaw's best friend or doormat. Others could be the death of him. As long as he kept his own nose clean, Nick didn't foresee having any trouble from Trayner.

As for Barrett, Nick knew better than to try and judge that one. When Gilsom had told him that someone was asking for him, Nick had several candidates in mind. That list included men on both sides of the law and he had accounts to settle with each of them. Barrett, on the other hand, was a different story.

Of all the men Nick knew in those years of his reckless youth, Barrett was the one who fit into the grayest area of Nick's mind. Barrett had been his best friend and worst influence. Of course, Nick had done his part to get Barrett into some nasty scrapes as well, so he couldn't look back on things too self-righteously. Mostly, Barrett was the one who'd talked Nick into making the biggest change of his life by leaving his home and his father behind.

Barrett showed Nick that freedom, money, and even women were all out there for anyone with the stones to grab it. When Nick had become a Mourner, he knew for certain that Barrett would have been the first one to try to talk him out of it. And on the days when he was digging under a hot sun to bury a box full of dead, rotting meat, Nick could hear Barrett laughing at him from the back of his mind.

What bothered Nick the most was knowing that if he wanted to take his old life back and throw caution to the wind, all he needed to do was track Barrett down and he'd have a partner. Barrett had saved Nick's life almost as much as Nick had saved his. And now that Barrett had tracked him down, Nick honestly didn't know what to do.

Although his feet still took him toward the undertaker's parlor to look for work, Nick's thoughts were wandering back out onto the open trail. His ears were ringing with gunshots and his blood was moving quicker through his veins at the thought of going out and grabbing a life for himself that didn't involve a shovel and a bible.

Of course, there was a reason that he and Barrett had parted company. Living by the gun was a hell of a way to squander a man's youth. Nick often wondered if he might have found himself a good wife if he hadn't been buried in a life that only introduced him to whores. And there was always the very instant when Barrett had shown his true colors.

Barrett was awfully good at disappearing when the need arose and that need had certainly arisen in Montana. Just when he'd needed his friend the most, Nick found himself surrounded by dead men and traitors. Neither of those was much help once the vigilantes had closed in and offered him one of the most painful decisions in his life.

And that was when Nick felt himself brought right back to where he'd started: walking alone toward the undertaker's parlor. His road, as always, brought him back to boot hill and for the moment, he decided to keep it that way. The temptation to stray would always be there as it was for every man. For the moment, Nick figured he'd keep an eye on his old friend and see what came next.

Things might just turn out fine and the friends could part ways amicably.

Things might just go straight to hell on a shutter.

Then there was the matter of the job Barrett was planning. As soon as he thought about that, Nick felt his head start to ache and all the progress that had been made from resting up began to unravel. The fact of the matter was that Nick had always been more comfortable living in the moment and dealing with the next few steps in front of him.

Barrett was the planner. Now that Nick was in the picture, that meant he was bound for a change whether he liked it or not.

That thought settled in the back of Nick's mind right along with the rest of what nagged at him.

While thinking about all of this, Nick's feet had kept moving him along down Cobbler's Avenue. When he finally snapped to and started paying attention to where he was, Nick was comforted by what he saw.

Cobbler's Avenue was pretty much what he'd become accustomed to throughout all his years in working with the dead. Undertaker's parlors were usually kept in the quieter portion of town, sometimes stuck out all by themselves. Usually, it was the owner who wanted to keep his shop in a location suited to dealing with the bereaved. Most town folk didn't want to look into the face of death when they went to buy their sugar and clothing.

To Nick, spots like Cobbler's Avenue were quiet, peaceful, and inviting. He'd grown up digging holes for the dead, carving their markers, and even bowing his head to honor folks he never even knew. Being back in the quiet part of town was something of a homecoming to him.

Once Nick got close enough to see the beginning of the trail leading to Bitter Creek's cemetery, he felt as if he'd settled into a familiar rut. When he stepped into the undertaker's parlor, there was even a faint trace of a smile upon his face.

"What the hell do you want?" came a gruff Italian voice to greet Nick before the door had swung all the way open.

Before Nick even got much of a look at the parlor itself, he was forced to deal with the olive-skinned man who came at him head-on. The other man was balding, but what hair he did have formed a dark black ring around the back and sides of his head. By contrast, the top portion of his scalp looked as though it had been polished to a near-perfect gleam.

His mustache resembled a thin caterpillar that had crawled onto his upper lip and stayed there. The man wasn't exactly fat, but he sported a gut that bulged out over his belt in a way that made his otherwise slender body seem downright strange.

Come to think of it, Nick decided that "strange" was the best word to describe the man who now stood in front of him with both hands propped upon his hips.

"I came to see about getting a job," Nick said, trying not to smile when the other man was trying so hard to assert himself.

"Job? What job? There's no job. Where'd you hear about a job?"

The questions came out of the Italian's mouth in a flood. His voice was smooth and strong, with just enough of an accent beneath the surface for Nick to feel a bit of kinship with him. There was also a confident strength in the man that reminded Nick of so many immigrants forced to fend for themselves in a strange land. Even though the undertaker was a good deal shorter than Nick, he carried himself like a giant.

"I don't need much of a salary," Nick said, maneuvering straight through all of the other man's protests. "I can do plenty of work around here. Surely you could use an extra set of hands."

Although the undertaker's head was already starting to shake, he stopped and gave Nick a closer inspection. "Who sent you here?"

"Nobody sent me."

"Then why did you come? And don't tell me it's to work. There's plenty of other places to work in town that will keep your hands cleaner than if you work here." Before Nick had a chance to respond, the undertaker squinted his eyes and cocked his head slightly to one side. "You trying to stay away from the law? You not want to run into the sheriff? Is that why you want to be here, because you think nobody comes around here too much?"

"I've already met Sheriff Trayner. The reason I came here was because this is what I do," Nick said, extending his arms toward the entire parlor and everything inside of it.

The undertaker caught sight of Nick's hands and said, "You don't look like you do this for a living. You look more like a carpenter or maybe work on the railroad."

"Most people confuse me for a miner."

The Italian laughed and shook his head. "I know miners. I see what happens when they don't know how to use the dynamite. If that was you," he said, waving his hand as though he was erasing a blackboard, "you wouldn't have that much left of your hand."

"True enough."

Nodding as he continued looking Nick over, the undertaker rubbed his hands together and finally took on a somewhat lighter tone. "All right. So what can you do? Dig a hole?"

"I've dug plenty of holes. I can build coffins and can even carve wood or stone. Lately, I've been a Mourner."

"Mourner?" The Italian actually laughed at that one. "We have not so many big funerals here and even so, there's usually plenty who come to fill this place."

Nick looked at what the other man was referring to and saw that Bitter Creek's parlor was less than half the size of the ones Nick usually saw. There wasn't a separate room for displaying stones and coffins, but there was a door at the back of the room that Nick presumed led to a workshop. The front area was only slightly bigger than a modest living room with a rectangular table up front and only two rows of seats facing it.

Part of a Mourner's job was to make sure wakes were well attended and this parlor was small enough to be filled by a few immediate family members.

Shrugging, Nick looked away from the small viewing room and back into the face of the undertaker. "If you need someone to dig, I can dig. If you need someone to sweep, I can do that too."

"If you're a real Mourner, than you can do plenty more than that, I bet."

"Yeah," Nick said, hoping the man hadn't noticed the gun belt under his coat. "I can do plenty more if the need arises."

The undertaker thought for a moment

while fussing with the whiskers on his lip. He turned on the balls of his feet and started pacing away from Nick before stopping and glancing back at him over his shoulder. Just when it seemed he was about to say something, he would stop, shake his head, and walk away again. Finally, he stomped toward a side door and motioned for Nick to follow. Once they were outside, the undertaker walked to a small shed and began rummaging inside it.

"I'll hire you, but it's only temporary. I could use some time to spend with my family and you can take up some of the slack. But I won't pay much. You take it or leave."

"Sounds good to me," Nick said. "When do I start?"

"You start now."

"Great. By the way, my name's Nick Gr—"

"Here you go, Nick," the undertaker said while tossing a shovel toward Nick. "I'm Carmine Minneo. Now bury those coffins in that hill over there. You want me, I'll be inside."

Nick looked at where Carmine had been pointing. The hill looked to be just under fifty yards away. The coffins were stacked against the building's rear wall and it looked as though he was going to have to drag them up the hill all by himself. Even though he'd been hoping to land an honest job, Nick realized he might have gotten a bit more than he'd bargained for.

"Well," Nick said to himself while sliding off his coat and rolling up his sleeves, "at least breakfast was good."

Seventeen

At first, Nick wondered if there had been a fever going through town to account for the pile of coffins out back of the parlor. Once he got a look at the tools Carmine had to work with, Nick realized that the pile was probably just a backlog of work.

With no horses or wagon to pull the coffins from one place to another, Nick was left with a small cart and his own two hands to haul the heavy boxes to where they needed to be. More than that, Bitter Creek's boot hill wasn't just a clever name. The cemetery was on top of a hill that was steep enough to force a sweat out of him just by climbing it once. As soon as he'd returned from bringing that first coffin over, Nick spotted a note tacked to the backdoor written in a meticulously clean script.

TAKE THE OTHERS TOO

That was all the note said and it was signed with Carmine's name along with a little arrow pointing toward the other side of the doorway where another stack of coffins was waiting. Nick sighed and wiped the sweat from his brow. The combination of such hard work and a naturally hot day was playing havoc with his system. Even so, there was a certain familiarity to it that once again brought his father to mind.

Stasys was a hard man who believed in hard work. The old man probably still could uproot a tree with his own arms and dig through rocky soil or even clay as though it was mulch. Nick had to guess about that since he hadn't seen Stasys for years. In fact, it was often easier for him to think of his father as dead. At least that way, there was no chance of Nick having to explain what he'd been doing since leaving home.

The entire morning along with most of the afternoon was spent loading coffins and hauling them up the side of that hill. Nick figured he'd get done with the lifting part since digging all those graves would seem easy by comparison. After the second trip, the sweat had formed a slick coating over his entire body. His muscles were hot beneath his dirt-caked skin and every bit of hair stuck to him in greasy strands.

He took a moment to catch his breath and saw that the sun was still high. With summer coming right along, that meant longer days. Normally, such a prospect wasn't such a bad thing. That day, however, the prospect seemed downright horrible. But rather than sit around and gripe, Nick stood up and started dragging the cart back to the undertaker's parlor where one last coffin was waiting.

That coffin wasn't the only thing waiting for him.

Leaning against the wall with one foot resting on the coffin, was a man dressed in plain brown clothes and wearing a bowler hat. He wore a simple jacket over a loose-fitting white shirt. All in all, he resembled plenty of other locals Nick had spotted during his stay in Bitter Creek. But if his eyes weren't deceiving him, that man was far from just another local.

"Is that you, Barrett?" Nick asked while wiping more sweat from his brow.

Barrett nodded once and made no secret of the fact that he was getting a kick out of seeing Nick in his current state. "It's me, all right. I was just starting to wonder if that was really you."

Nick walked up closer to Barrett and took a long look at the man. Despite the fact that the two had spent plenty of time over drinks a few nights earlier, Nick felt as if he was only now getting a clear look at Barrett's face. Shadows and smoke had a way of covering plenty of things that daylight could not. That was the reason men like Barrett and Nick preferred spending time in saloons.

Barrett's face seemed to have aged two years for every one that they'd spent apart. It might just have been that Nick's memories were slanted in a certain direction, but he doubted it. The more likely explanation was that Barrett was still living the life that Nick was trying to bury.

Scars covered Barrett's cheeks and chin like a map that had been carved into his flesh. Some of those scars were familiar to Nick and just as many were new. In fact, it seemed that Barrett was just as good at angling his head a certain way or using certain shadows as Nick was at keeping his mangled hands out of sight.

Trying not to dwell too much on the scars on Barrett's face or the coldness in his eyes, Nick said, "I told you I'm in an honest line of work now."

"Yeah, but I didn't think you'd take a job as a mule."

Before he could get too angry, Nick realized that he was dragging a cart while standing between the two poles where a pack mule would normally be hitched. He dropped the poles reflexively and let the cart tip forward as the poles hit the ground. "Some jobs are harder than others."

"Yeah, well you're not cut out for this line of work."

"And how would you know that?"

"Because I've seen what you were born to do."

Hearing that brought plenty of things into Nick's mind. Once again, he saw the dirty, bloody face of that driver from twenty years earlier. He recalled the excitement on everyone's face when they'd all gathered around to get a look at Nick's kill. And he could still smell the mix of burnt gunpowder and urine that would become so many other men's last contribution to the world before moving on to the next.

"Hot damn," Barrett said as though he was thinking of the very same things. "You always were a natural."

"Maybe. But now I —"

"I know, I know," Barrett interrupted. "You mourn."

Walking forward, Nick stepped up to the last coffin and swatted Barrett's foot off of the side of the wooden box. "What do you want? I thought you had another one of your big jobs to do."

"I do. That's why I'm here. Don't you remember you said you wanted in on it with me?"

Nick bent down to take hold of the coffin at the narrower end. "Yeah," he said, lifting the box up and dragging it toward the cart. "I remember."

Barrett walked around to the other end of the coffin and picked it up. Shuffling to keep in step with Nick, he asked, "Then what are you doing here, working like some kind of dog?" They arrived at the cart and both men lifted the coffin to slide it onto the back. "Or did you think that the job I told you about was just going to dry up and blow away?"

Actually, that was exactly what he'd been hoping for. "It's been known to happen," he said with a shrug.

"Sure, maybe back when we were riding together a few of my plans didn't quite work out too well."

"A few? Try most of them."

"Now, that's stretching it just a —"

"What about that stagecoach that was supposed to be delivering a payroll to a ranch out in the middle of Wyoming?"

"What about it?" Barrett asked innocently.

"It was bound for an army post."

"Yeah?"

"And it was guarded," Nick said, amazed that Barrett could still play ignorant so well when it suited him. "Guarded by soldiers!"

"We all knew it was going to be hard."

"*Ten* soldiers!"

Rolling his eyes, Barrett smacked the top of the coffin as he talked. "Dammit, Nick that was years ago!" Suddenly remembering what was inside the box he'd smacked, Barrett looked down at it and rubbed the spot where his hand had just landed. "You moved on to a different line of work. I haven't."

"So that means I should just sign on and put my life on the line?"

"That means that I've gotten better at what I do. Sure things go wrong sometimes, but they do everywhere." Taking a moment, Barrett looked around until his eyes were inevitably drawn back to the ruts Nick had made on his way back and forth from the hill. "I bet when you took this job you didn't expect to be hauling crates like this."

Nick couldn't answer that right away, simply because the first thing he would have said was exactly what Barrett wanted to hear. Rather than make up something just to prevent Barrett from having the satisfaction of being right, Nick shrugged and nodded. After all, there wasn't much Nick could do to refute the man while looking like he'd been dipped in sweat and rolled in a pile of dust.

The look on Nick's face was all the answer that Barrett truly needed. "I didn't mean to say you were a natural killer. You're a natural with the iron, but you're also inclined to keep your head when everyone else loses theirs."

"It all boils down to the same thing, Barrett."

"Does it really?" Barrett's eyes narrowed and he leaned in slightly. "You see the look in most folk's eyes when they work? Some look dead and others look so miserable that they're hoping for death. I say those are the ones who lost their heads. Remember when we used to sit around and ask why more people didn't ride off and rob trains or hold up banks?"

Nick laughed under his breath. "Yeah."

"Well, it's because they're the flock and we're the wolves. It's natural. They don't know any better, but we do. We know what's out there."

"You know what else I recall? I seem to recall that when we were sitting around talking, it was usually in a cave or in the middle of a swamp somewhere because we were on the run from the law."

Barrett nodded. "All right. Fair enough. But that's because we were just starting out. Just like you don't see a young farmer or businessman fairing too well at first. But we build up from there, Nick. The profits get bigger and things happen to make you realize why you stuck through them lean times in the first place."

"My lean times are over," Nick said, settling the coffin in the back of the cart. "Time for me to start something else besides running from the law and living by the gun."

"It sure as hell is and that's why I wanted to make sure you heard me out. At least help you with this while I fill you in on a few details."

Barrett took hold of one of the cart's poles and waited for Nick to take the other. Together, they lifted the cart and started pulling it toward the hill. Neither man spoke for a while because they were too busy dealing with the immediate job at hand. Nick was sweating, but digging his feet into the dirt and doing his part.

"What's the matter, Barrett? You look about ready to keel over."

"Ah, to hell with you," was all Barrett

could get out through his huffing breaths.

They reached the hill in pretty good time and Barrett even helped Nick unload the coffin from the cart. Either he wasn't at all taken aback by the stack of coffins and the stench of dead bodies, or he was too wrapped up in his own thoughts to notice them. Whichever it was, Barrett was right back to his old self as soon as he caught his breath.

"Where the hell have you been the last day or two?" Barrett asked. "I was beginning to think you left town."

"I've been resting."

"Well, that's good because you're going to need it."

"Yeah," Nick said as he picked up a shovel and started to dig. "Tell me about it."

Leaning against one of the sturdier tombstones, Barrett nodded and said, "Not only is this job still on, but it's looking better than ever. After it's through, you'll be writing me letters for years thanking me for —"

"Thanking you for letting me be a part of it," Nick said, completing Barrett's sentence. "I've heard it all before."

"Maybe so, but I've never known you to back out of something once you've already given your word. You said you still need to settle a few things with certain folks. Well, I know exactly what you're after and the men you want to settle up with aren't the easiest to find. You'll need money to fund a hunt like that."

Smiling and shaking his head, Nick drove the blade of the shovel into the dirt hard enough to bury it right up to the handle. "Don't start in, Barrett. I've heard that before too."

But Barrett wasn't about to be put off so easily. Like a predator that had smelled blood in the air, he kept moving toward his target. "I know what happened in Montana. I know what Red Parks did to you. I know why you can't live in any of the towns you've been through these last couple of years and I know what happened between you and Skinner to make things so bad between you both. That's why you should be willing to take help when it's offered."

Nick tossed away one shovel of dirt and slammed the blade into the ground again. Each time he did was harder than the time before it. When he hit a stone in the dirt, he cracked the shovel against it several times just because it felt better than tossing it aside.

"You don't know shit," Nick growled. "You were hardly even there in Montana. You rode off before . . ." The shovel cracked against the stone once more and Nick left it resting against the rock.

"What, Nick? I left before all them others were killed? You're damn right I did. Them vigilantes were out for blood and they didn't give a horse's ass whose blood they got. I tried to find you, but by the time I got back to where you and most of the rest were drinking, it was too late. The vigilantes were there like a bunch of goddamn ghosts with hoods over their faces.

"I was a kid and I didn't want to die. It was the hardest thing I've ever done, but it was either leave or wind up swinging next to the others in that barn." Barrett pulled in a slow breath and shuddered. "I don't know about you, but memories of that barn still hold on to me like a nightmare I can't wake up from."

Nick let the shovel drop from his hands so he could wrap them around the front of Barrett's shirt. When he pulled the other man closer, Nick almost yanked Barrett clean out of his boots. The anger and fury that had been dredged up from the past only added to his already considerable strength.

"I trusted my life to you and everyone else in that fucking gang!" Nick snarled. "We rode into Montana thinking we were just going to get drunk and find some women to screw, but it didn't quite turn out like that, did it?"

"No," Barrett said in a voice that was unusually calm considering his predicament. "It didn't."

"Either one of us could have said the word and we would have chosen any other town. But we let Skinner talk us into Virginia City and we all paid for it. All of us but you, Barrett. You didn't pay for shit because you didn't stick around! You left us to save yourself and as far as you knew, every one of us was going to swing in that barn. Every one of us but you.

"I had to stay there and listen to the likes of Red Parks because I didn't know any better. If I had known what he was capable of, I would have shot him on sight and taken my chances with the rest of them vigilantes. You were the thinker, Barrett. You were the one that kept us out of trouble like Virginia City. I wish to God that you would have been there to tell me what a no-good bastard Red Parks truly was. It would have kept him from driving a knife in my back and tearing me apart when I thought he'd become my friend. And it would have saved me from wasting so many years tracking him down to set things right."

Barrett managed to shake his head. "I knew you weren't going to hang because you were too tough for that. Same with Skinner."

"Really? And how were you so sure about that?"

"Because I was there, Nick. I saw it all."

Nick let go of Barrett and said, "Okay. Tell me something I don't already know."

EIGHTEEN

Virginia City, Montana
1864

The whore had her legs in the air and was reaching up to grab hold of the headboard as Barrett rocked back and forth on top of her. She let out a groan every so often, but she was plainly going through the motions to earn the money she'd been promised. Truth be told, she didn't mind Barrett too much, simply because a kid his age rarely took up much of her time.

Although it had only been a couple of years since ambushing that shipment of guns, Barrett's face looked more weathered and aged than any seventeen-year-old had a right to be. He'd already gotten one of the scars across his face that would stay with him for the rest of his life.

The smile he wore at the moment was deeper than the scar and made him look a little closer to his proper age. Barrett finished up what he was doing and then rolled off the whore's ample body. "God damn!" he breathed. "I ought to marry you after that performance. First, I'd need to know yer name."

Although the dark-haired woman caught the anticipatory glance Barrett shot her over his shoulder, she shrugged it off the way she'd done every other time he'd seen her in the last two weeks. "You can call me any name you want, sugar. It's your money."

Barrett reached out to slide his hand along her thigh. When he did, he was unable to hide the affection that shone through in his eyes. He touched her naked skin gently, drinking in the sight of her until finally pulling the sheet over her as if he was tucking her in.

"It doesn't have to be this way," he said. "You could live a better life."

"With you?" As soon as she said it, a trace of fear flickered over her face like a ripple over water. Her eyes darted to the gun belt hanging over a nearby chair and she quickly put on a smile to make up for what she'd said. "You're leaving town soon. That's all I meant. I want to stay here. Let's just have our fun while it lasts."

She was afraid of him. Barrett knew that with absolute certainty. He'd known that even before she glanced over to his gun. He could smell it on her. "Look, you don't have to —"

But his efforts to swim back upstream were cut off by a commotion that had exploded outside the window of his room. Barrett started to speak again, but was stopped again by a voice that he instantly recognized.

"Go to hell! All of you, either let us go or we'll send you to hell!"

"Nick?" Barrett said as he leapt up from the edge of the bed and practically flew to the window.

The room was small enough for Barrett to make it to the window in about three steps. Even so, he was in such a hurry that he almost managed to trip himself up that same number of times before getting there. Once he could look through the glass at the street below, his eyes widened with surprise at what he saw.

"Holy shit," he whispered.

The brunette had already pulled on her slip and was stepping up behind him. "What is it?" she asked. "What's wrong?"

But Barrett was still shaking his head and staring down at the scene below.

The whorehouse was across the street and down a little ways from the saloon where most of the rest of the gang had been spending their time. The others hadn't been in Virginia City for long and most of the boys had been too busy drinking and raising hell to get any sleep.

Coming from that saloon was a small crowd of people, including Nick and a couple others from the gang. The rest were men with white hoods over their heads carrying every kind of firearm from hunting rifles to shotguns. Once they got outside, the hooded men were joined by even more of their kind. The ones that had been waiting outside were armed as well, but were also carrying torches.

Barrett could hear so many voices at once that he could hardly make sense of them all. Everyone was talking, screaming, or just crying out as bystanders started joining in as well. But over it all, Barrett could still hear Nick's voice, spewing out threats as well as every curse under the sun. Not that it mattered, of course. Nick was being dragged along by the masked men just like the others.

"I've got to get out of here," Barrett said, scrambling around the room for his clothes and belongings. "I've got to do something."

The brunette had been looking over Barrett's shoulder with a mix of confusion and anxiousness. Now that he'd stepped away from the window, she could get a better look at what was going on. Although she seemed a bit nervous at all the ruckus, she didn't really seem too surprised.

"That'd be the Vigilance Committee," she said plainly.

Barrett froze midway through the motions of buckling on his gun belt. "What did you say?"

Without taking her eyes from the window, she repeated, "The Vigilance Committee. They must have gotten a hold of some men who thought they were bad enough to ride in here and do what they pleased."

"Those men are my friends."

"Well, you might not want to say that too loud."

Now that he was fully dressed and had everything that he'd brought into the room with him, Barrett fidgeted in place as if he wasn't quite sure where to go next. "What's this Vigilance Committee?"

"They're the law around here."

"But there's real law. I saw the office down the street."

But she just shook her head. "That office ain't much more than a sitting room. It's been that way for a while. If anyone's gonna deal with anything worse than drunks or vandals, it's the committee."

"What're they going to do with my friends?"

"I don't know for sure," she replied with a shrug.

She was lying. Barrett could tell that much just by looking at her. Making sure that she would have no trouble reading his own intentions, Barrett stepped forward and took hold of her by the shoulders.

"What are they going to do with my friends?"

Squirming in his tightening grasp, she pleaded, "Let go. You're hurting me."

"Then tell me."

"When they round up folks, they usually run them out of town. They give a warning first before they kill anyone. Lots of times, they just take troublemakers out somewhere and scare them."

"Is that all?" Barrett asked.

When she paused before answering, the brunette was shaken just enough to get her talking again. "Not always. Sometimes it's worse. But I never seen them come out this strong before. Usually there's not so many of them."

"What does that mean? Is this what you mean by worse?"

The brunette twisted to get another look

out the window. When she turned back around again, she didn't even want to look Barrett in the eyes. "Yes," she said, keeping her face tucked down away from his. "It looks pretty bad."

"Where are they taking them?"

"I don't . . . I don't know. They usually just drag out whoever they were after and head out of town. It looks to me like they're set to do more than that."

Pushing the brunette away, Barrett took another look out the window and saw that the hooded men were, indeed, forcing Nick and the others down the street in the opposite direction from the Virginia City limit. The hooded men weren't even talking anymore. All the noise from the street was coming from Nick and the rest of the gang. What troubled Barrett was that not all of the gang could even be seen. That either meant they'd gotten away, or had already been dealt with by the committee.

Barrett wasn't too fond of either of those choices since they both meant that he was now on his own.

"Aw, to hell with this," Barrett grunted. "How big is that committee?"

The brunette shrugged. "Hard to tell since nobody knows who they are."

"That's bullshit and you know it. You live

here. You've seen the committee come and go. You've got to know how big it is."

Once again, she shrugged and shook her head. "I can't see through them hoods," she told him, suddenly seeming to have lost all fear of him. "They come and go as they please. With the work they do, there ain't nobody around here who wants to stop them. Not that anybody could."

"Well, maybe it's about time someone tried."

With that, Barrett turned his back on the brunette and pulled in a deep breath. He'd charged into rough situations before, but he'd always had backing from Nick or the rest of the gang. This time, unless he could find a familiar stray or two, Barrett was on his own.

Suddenly, there was a quick knock on the door. Barrett had been poised to pull it open, but now froze with his hand still stretching out toward the handle. Stepping back quietly, he shot a fierce glance toward the brunette while lowering his hand toward the gun at his side. The brunette caught his meaning surely enough and kept quiet while she tried to get as far away from Barrett and the door as the cramped confines of the room would allow.

When he kept his eyes on her, Barrett

wanted to ask if the brunette was expecting anyone or if anybody she knew might be knocking. She looked back at him as though she was staring at a man who was already dead. There was a certainty in her eyes, mixed with a bit of morbid curiosity that someone might get when they were looking at a man standing on a platform with his head in a noose.

Barrett wasn't about to give her the show she was after. He knew there were several ways to handle whoever was on the other side of that door, but since the knocking was getting faster and more insistent, he knew he had to pick one of those ways real quickly.

Drawing his gun and pointing it at the brunette, he motioned for her to walk over to the door. "Ask who it is," Barrett whispered.

Reluctantly, the brunette nodded and walked to the door while Barrett stepped away from it.

"Who's there?" she asked in a well-practiced, breathless voice.

For a moment, there wasn't an answer. Then, there came a voice that struck a nerve in Barrett's mind.

"Open this door," the voice demanded. "It's important."

The voice was a familiar one, and Barrett couldn't have been happier to hear it. Shoving past the brunette, Barrett pulled open the door while still keeping the gun at hip level. Fortunately, the only one in the hall was Joe Cooley.

"They got 'em," Joe said as though he didn't even notice the gun in Barrett's hand. "They got 'em all."

Barrett nodded and quickly checked to see if anyone else was coming. The hallway, leading only to two other rooms on the second floor of the cathouse, was empty.

"I know," Barrett said. "What happened?"

"They were all in the saloon and I was on my way to meet up with them when those others came around the corner like some kind of posse. They just went in and cleaned out the place. I saw it happen, but there wasn't anything I could do. You gotta believe me."

"I believe you. Now we just need to figure out what we can do about it."

NINETEEN

The brunette got her money, plus a little extra to make sure she kept quiet long enough for Barrett and Joe Cooley to make their escape. Barrett wanted to believe that the brunette would be true to her word simply for old-times' sake, but even his young mind knew better than that. It wasn't that he was already so wise to the world. He'd simply gotten a look at the Vigilance Committee and doubted many people could stand up to such a force without proper incentive.

Even Joe was rattled after what he'd seen, and he was more the type to go in with guns blazing rather than admit he was scared. Barrett felt the fear inside of him as well. It was an unfamiliar thing, to be sure, but it was undeniably there. The sight of so many men in their heavy coats and jackets, buttoned all the way up to the bottom of the hoods they wore, was enough to put the fear into anyone.

The two young men slipped out the back door of the cathouse and made their way to the street below. It didn't take long for them to catch up to the hooded men. In that time, Barrett had given Joe a quickly whispered account of what he'd been told by the brunette. When he finished, Barrett was anxious to get moving so he could catch up with the committee. Joe didn't look so inclined.

"Jesus, Barrett. We should get out of this damn town."

"You can't talk that way! We need to get the others."

Joe shook his head as his eyes glazed over with desperate panic.

"They'll kill them," Barrett insisted. "Now, do you want that on your conscience?"

After a while, Joe shook his head.

"Good. Now, let's head over that way," Barrett said, pointing down the street in front of them. "That's the way I saw that committee go before you come to get me."

"All right," Joe said reluctantly. He took a breath and flushed as much of the fear out of himself as he could and nodded again. "All right. Let's go."

No sooner had they stepped out onto the

boardwalk than a voice came from the saloon where the others had been captured.

"That's them!" the voice cried. "That's the others you wanted!"

Barrett and Joe spun toward the voice and found the bartender from the saloon jabbing his finger excitedly at the two of them. Unfortunately, the bartender wasn't alone. There were two other masked men leaving the saloon and looking in the direction the bartender was pointing.

"Son of a bitch," Barrett snarled. "That bastard just gave us up."

Having regained the nerve that had allowed him to outlive his brother in the gang, Joe brought up the rifle he'd been carrying and sighted down its barrel. "Nobody gets away with that," was all he said before taking his shot.

The rifle barked once and sent a bullet across the street and into the bartender's upper torso. The impact knocked the man clean off his feet and into the saloon. One of the masked men looked back and ducked into the saloon's doorway. The other vigilante merely dropped to one knee, lifted his rifle, and sent a shot of his own as a smoky reply.

"Come on," Barrett insisted while tugging

at Joe's elbow. "We still need to find the others!"

Joe's eyes were narrowed and focused so intently upon his target that he barely even flinched when the vigilante's shot hissed toward him. Even so, he managed to pull himself away from his spot and follow his partner.

More shots whipped through the air and punched into walls around them, but the two gang members only moved faster down the street in the larger group's wake. After those first shots had been fired, several voices sounded from around a nearby corner. Although Barrett couldn't make out what words were being said, the voices were muffled enough for him to know that they were probably being spoken from behind hoods.

Joe kept firing his rifle to cover their backs, walking backward while shooting from the hip. The shots weren't even close to accurate, but they were good enough to keep the two vigilantes from the saloon several paces behind them.

Barrett, on the other hand, kept his eyes pointed forward. He wasn't too familiar with Virginia City, but he knew they were headed further into it rather than to its closest border. It wasn't too often that Barrett

Cobb didn't know exactly what was going on and he hated every second of it. Still, he kept going in the only direction that was left open to him.

"Where are we going, Barrett?" Joe asked warily.

"How the hell am I supposed to know?"

"You've been here before."

"Yeah, but that don't mean I know this place inside and out. Just shut up and keep following me."

That might not have been much of an explanation, but it was enough for Joe to keep firing and do as he was told.

The shots echoed through Barrett's ears like thunder, and he knew it was too much to hope for that they'd gone unnoticed. Still, he kept his steps light and quick while doing his best to catch up to the rest of the committee.

"They're getting closer, Barrett."

Before he could respond to that, Barrett stopped short so quickly that Joe ran into the back of his heels. Having just rounded a corner, Barrett found himself staring down a narrow street. Several of the Vigilance Committee members stood in a line while the rest shoved Nick and the other gang members into an old barn.

Suddenly, the line of committee members

was obscured by smoke that seemed to have dropped in front of them like a curtain. That curtain had been spewed from the barrels of the committee members' guns and was followed quickly by a wave of sound and fury. It was all Barrett could do to get down before all that incoming lead chopped him into pieces.

Although Joe was the quicker of the two, he'd also been facing the opposite direction when the shots had been fired. Even so, he still managed to throw himself facefirst toward the dirt before getting his skull split open by the wave of bullets.

All Barrett could see through the grit in his eyes was the ground that was less than an inch in front of him. At that moment, and even looking back on it years later, Barrett would be able to recall each and every grain of dirt he saw. There were a few bits of rock mixed into the dust as well, all of which was soon covered by a thin spray of blood.

Seeing those crimson drops fall brought Barrett right back into the moment. That rude awakening was enhanced by the sound of Joe's pained grunt as he struggled to get up closer to his partner.

"I'm hit," Joe said through tightly clenched teeth. "But it's not so bad."

When Barrett looked up, he meant to get a look at Joe to see how badly his friend was hurt. But before he could do that, he caught sight of that firing line of hooded men moving closer with their rifles pointed directly at him. They moved as one, like a scythe cutting through tall grass, and were upon him before Barrett could do much about it.

Rough hands took hold of Barrett and hauled him to his feet. They got Joe as well and shoved the two young men toward the barn where the others waited. Glancing from side to side as he was moved along, Barrett hardly knew if he was walking or if he was being dragged. At least he did manage to see Joe moving beside him. His fellow gang member was bleeding from the shoulder and neck, but didn't seem to be hurt too badly.

On his way toward the barn, Barrett spotted a familiar face.

"Skinner!" Barrett said as loudly as he could manage. "What's going on? What's happening?"

Skinner was one of the roughest men Barrett had ever known. The man's skill with a blade was legendary and came not only from practice, but from a genuine love of carving flesh from bone. When Skinner turned to look at who'd called out his name, he regarded Barrett with the same morbid look that the brunette had had in her eyes only minutes before.

Stepping past Barrett and Joe, the committee member who'd shot at them from the saloon walked up to Skinner. "Are these two with the others?" he asked through the hood covering all but his eyes.

Skinner actually held Barrett's gaze and nodded. "Yeah. That's them."

Joe struggled against the hands holding him back and kicked at the ground in his haste to make a run toward Skinner. "You dirty son of a bitch! We're in the same gang! We've ridden together for —"

But Joe's angry words were cut short by a chopping blow on the back of the head from the butt of one of the committee member's guns. The impact knocked Joe's head forward and put out the last of the flame that had kept him moving even after catching a few bullets. Joe's eyes remained open as his body slumped forward. His hooded captor kept ahold of him by one arm and allowed Joe to dangle over the ground like a doll in a child's hand.

"How many more of them are there?" the first committee member asked Skinner. When he didn't get a reply right away, he jabbed Skinner in the gut with the barrel of his rifle. "I asked you a question. If you want our deal to hold water, you'll answer me."

Skinner looked into the eyes that peered at him through the square holes cut in the hood. "Six of us rode into town."

"These two here make seven, by my count."

"We haven't seen that one for a while," Skinner replied, nodding toward Joe's limp form. "He must've met up with that one after we got here."

"But they're both with the same gang?"

Skinner paused, shifted his eyes back to Barrett and kept them there. All it took was one glance between them for them both to know that this was Skinner's last chance to do right by the people he'd been riding with and called his brothers. Barrett waited to see what Skinner would say, praying to God that the bad man had even a hint of a conscience.

"Yeah," Skinner said with a smirk. "They're all the same group."

"Good," replied the man in the hood who seemed to be the one calling the shots. "Get them into the barn."

Barrett and Joe didn't say a word as they were dragged into the barn. Joe was struggling in and out of consciousness while Barrett simply knew better than to think he could deal with the hooded men. Once he got into the barn, however, his attitude changed.

"We didn't do anything," Nick said through his fear. "We didn't even leave the goddamn saloon."

Nick and the other gang members were gathered inside the barn. The committee held them at gunpoint beneath a row of nooses that dangled from the rafters. There were five nooses in all and five young men to fill them.

"Yeah. Not yet, you didn't," the committee's leader said as he strolled into the barn. "But we heard about you boys and we don't want your kind around here. You little bastards think you can come through here because we don't have no law. Well, Virginia City does have law and we're it."

Nick glanced around at the faces close to him. His eyes were wide and moving so quickly, that he only seemed to take notice of some of what he saw. When he looked at Barrett, he regarded his friend in the same way that he regarded the others. It wasn't a surprise that Nick hadn't noticed that Barrett had been missing until this point. Having snuck out while his friends were all drinking and gambling, Barrett was surprised that Joe Cooley had been able to find him at all.

Suddenly, Nick got a familiar fire in his eyes as he picked one of the masked men to look at as he said, "Go to hell. Every damn one of you!"

With that, the man who'd knocked Joe in the back of the head used the same rifle butt to crack the side of Nick's skull. Nick tried to fight, but the second blow from that rifle's handle put him down for good.

"Not that one," Skinner said as he stepped into the barn and pointed toward Nick. "Take him out of here. Red wants to have a word with him."

None of the hooded men budged. Instead, a few of them looked over to their spokesman and waited. When that one gave a nod, the others took hold of Nick by the shoulders and dragged him out of the barn.

"What about the rest of 'em?" one of the hooded men asked.

The leader's eyes shifted beneath the roughly cut holes in his hood. They seemed especially bulbous and devoid of emotion since they were the only part of his face that could be seen. In fact, it seemed to Barrett as if those eyes didn't even have any lids and that they floated behind the hood like bubbles coming to the surface of a pond.

Those eyes looked at each of the gang members in turn before finally coming to rest upon Barrett. "Hang them," he ordered. Nodding toward Barrett, he added, "But leave this one here to watch."

And that was all they needed to hear. Once the command was given, the rest of the hooded men started tying the gang members' hands together behind their backs and positioning them under the nooses hanging from the rafters.

Barrett struggled and fought against the man keeping hold of him, but was unable to do more than kick up some dirt and waste a whole lot of breath. Then, and even in the years to come, he didn't have much of a clue as to what he said. All he knew was that he spat out a stream of words as quickly as he could get them from his mouth, all in an attempt to barter for the lives of his friends.

The Vigilance Committee would have none of it.

They simply went about their assigned task as though Barrett wasn't making a sound. One by one, they hoisted the gang members off their feet and forced their heads through the nooses.

The gang members struggled as best they

could. They kicked, squirmed, spat, even bit at the committee, but to no avail. All of their efforts were either ignored or ended with brutal fists and blows from gun handles. Barrett kept up with his fighting as well, only to meet with similar success.

"You shut up and watch, boy," came the voice of the committee's leader from behind him. "I kept you alive because you strike me as the smartest one of this bunch."

"Why?" Barrett asked, unable to peel his eyes away from the gruesome spectacle in front of him no matter how much he wanted to. "What's going on?"

"If you need to ask that, maybe you're not so smart. Or maybe you're just scared. Either way, this is your lucky day. You get to be the one to spread the word about what happened here to your friends. Tell all your other piece of shit outlaw buddies what happens to little pricks like you if they come around here."

"We can spread the word," Barrett said. "All of us can. And I swear that we won't come back."

"I know all of them won't be coming back," the committee's leader said. "That's for damn sure. And if you decide to try your luck here again, I'll make an even bigger example out of you."

"What about Nick? Where are you taking him?"

"Never you mind about that. Just keep watching this show right here."

One of the other committee members stepped past Barrett and stood beside the leader. "They're all set, Red. Just give the word."

Barrett tried to meet the gazes of his friends, but none of the others would look at him. Their eyes were clouded over either from the beatings they'd taken or from the fearful thoughts that filled their minds. The young men stood on their toes upon foot-stools that put them only thirteen inches or so off the ground. The nooses were tight around their necks, however, and there wasn't a bit of slack in the ropes.

"Take a good look, boy," Red told Barrett. "And keep watching."

If Red gave a signal to his men, Barrett didn't see it. All he did see was the committee members beside each of his friends kick the stools out from beneath their feet.

The rafters groaned slightly and the ropes creaked with the added weight of the bodies dangling from them. The gang members kicked and struggled like a gruesome puppet show before their audience. The committee members watched; their eyes blank and unfeeling behind the hoods.

Barrett watched as well. There wasn't anything else he could do.

The barn was devoid of all other noise apart from the creaking of the ropes, the groans from the rafters, and the hacking, final breaths taken by the bulk of Barrett's gang. Every so often, one of his friends' boots would scrape against some straw on the floor, but that only acted as a bit of hope so false that it was downright cruel.

Their bodies swung.

The breath welled up in their throats behind the noose.

The men's eyeballs swelled within their sockets until, finally, the piss started trickling down their legs.

"Remember what you're looking at," Red whispered. "And don't forget to tell whatever friends you got left in this world."

TWENTY

Bitter Creek
1882

Nick stood staring at the ground the way he'd done throughout Barrett's entire story. Even though he'd been there for those events, he felt as if he were hearing about them for the first time. Plenty of it sounded vaguely familiar, but so much of it wasn't. It was as though he'd lived through it the first time by looking through a murky red haze. The nightmares could only show him so much and there had been plenty that had happened out of his sight.

Throughout the entire story, Nick had listened intently. He not only kept his ears open to what was being told to him, but how it was being said. He'd told enough lies himself to hear them in the voices of others. At that moment, he wasn't sure if he was hearing a lie or if he just didn't want to hear the truth. "When I woke up, I was told you'd left Virginia City."

"What reason did I have to stay?"

Despite all the practice he had in showing a cold, blank stare to the world, every so often Nick was unable to maintain it. "I was still there."

Barrett nodded slowly and took a moment to put together the right words. "I thought you were dead. I thought everyone was dead. That's what that bastard told me."

"You mean Red Parks?"

"Yeah. Red. That was his name. You remember him, huh?"

"Yeah," Nick said. "I remember him."

"I heard that you got out of there," Barrett said, "but not until recently. How the hell did you get out of Montana?" Shaking his head as though he was in a state of growing disbelief, Barrett added, "How the hell did you make it through that night, for that matter?"

"It was Skinner's doing. Apparently he thought I had some promise and kept me alive long enough for Red to have a talk with me."

"What did he say? Did he give you the speech he gave me about spreading the word and warning all our no-good friends to steer clear of Montana?"

Nick shook his head. "Nope. He offered

me a job."

Barrett didn't even try to hide the surprise he felt when he heard that. "A job? What did you tell him?"

"I took it. I figured it was either that or die like the others. Besides, I thought I would just have to bide my time until you or one of the others that didn't get pulled into that mess came back and I could tear out of there in a rush. When nobody came, I started to get comfortable.

"Red had me and Skinner working with the Vigilance Committee. It wasn't what I might have chosen for myself, but it was a living. It also was a way for me to be somewhere that it didn't matter if my face was drawn on a reward notice."

"How long did you stay there?"

"Too long. Eventually, Skinner got lazy and let down his guard enough for me to know that it was him who handed over the gang to that committee. He made a pretty good profit off of it, too."

"I'll bet he did," Barrett said while shaking his head. "Skinner never did anything unless he got something out of it."

"Yeah, well, he got to ride with men who were above the law and he pulled me right along with him. I thought I was doing some good work sometimes, but I always knew it couldn't last." Smirking, Nick added, "It's funny because spending enough time with vigilantes made me look at folks in a different way. I even started to see just what a bunch of bloodthirsty pricks we were."

"I guess there's no denying that."

"When I started looking at folks differently, I started seeing more about them as well. Maybe it was because I got older or maybe I just got smarter, but I figured out plenty during that time in Montana."

"Really?" Barrett asked. "Like what?"

Nick paused and took a long look at his former partner. He could tell that Barrett was studying him just as hard, if not harder. There were some things that needed to be said, but Nick decided it wasn't quite time to say them all just yet. "I figured out enough to want out and when that happened, all hell broke loose. Red didn't take to his committee members parting ways.

"He started in on me, friends I'd made in Virginia City, and even Skinner. He even made threats to track down my pa. Skinner made some kind of deal or just found a crack and slipped through it, but he was gone soon, so Red turned in on me even more. He showed me what hell was like up close and personal. And just when I thought he couldn't do any worse . . . he did. When it's all said and done, I never really got away from Montana. Red just let me crawl out when he was through spilling my blood."

Just thinking back to those days made Nick's jaw clench and a snarl form on his lips. He could still feel the pain that had been visited upon him by Red Parks and he had scars that would never heal. Even though Red was lying in a hole in a Nebraska field, Nick still wished he could dig him up and kill him again.

"Jesus," Barrett said after a low whistle. "After what I saw him do to the gang, I can't imagine things getting any worse."

Instinctively, Nick flexed his hands and felt burning pain stab at him from the past until it seemed as though his mangled fingers were burning. "Believe me," he said, curling his ruined fingers into fists, "it got plenty worse."

"Well, I heard about what happened to Skinner in Nebraska. Sounds to me like you paid him back for what he done."

Nick shook his head. "I wasn't after Skinner. I was after Red and Skinner managed to find him first. Skinner started coming after me for calling down the thunder that ruined what he'd built in Montana. Either that, or he just got meaner as he got older and decided to nail my hide to the wall right beside Red's just for a laugh."

"Knowing Skinner, it could have been either of those or both of them. He was always a bit crazy. When I saw him talking to Red that night in Montana, it wasn't a big surprise. You've got to believe me when I say that if I'd have thought you or any of the others were still alive, I would have come back. I saw them hang Joe and the others and thought you were just going to be taken out back and shot."

Having drawn his conclusions by this point, Nick said, "I know. Back then, I had enough money being offered for my head that Skinner would have cashed me in the next chance he got even if we did make it out of Montana alive. The only problem is that the rewards being offered were tripled since I got away from there and those notices are all still circulating. That's more of Red's doing. Even from the grave, that bastard found a way to ruin my life."

"And now you're forced to dig graves for a living," Barrett said, as though he was making the only possible conclusion to Nick's story.

Although Nick didn't exactly see his current occupation as a jail sentence, he also didn't see the sense in going through the trouble of correcting Barrett's statement.

Instead, he simply shrugged. "I made a mistake back then by coming to trust Red Parks. I should have never tried to think of him as anything else but a killer in a hood."

The fact of the matter was that after crawling out of Montana, Nick didn't trust much of anyone for a long time.

"Maybe I can make up for some of that," Barrett offered.

"What do you mean?"

Shaking his head, Barrett reached over and chucked Nick on the shoulder. "Did you forget why we're here?"

"Oh, right. The jewels."

"You're damn right, the jewels. I've got my boys in place and we're ready to roll. How about you?"

"Is that why you came here?"

"I told you the job was still on. We've had a nice talk and all, but that don't change matters as far as that's concerned."

Narrowing his eyes slightly, Nick said, "You told me you knew what happened between me and Red. You said you knew what happened to me and what happened with Skinner."

"I know plenty of things, Nick. And the way I know so much is by keeping my ears open when people feel like talking. Kind of like you did just a few moments ago. I heard some rumors here and there over the years, but not enough to put the entire picture together. Even if I chose to believe half the things I heard, that don't mean I'm stupid enough to go back into Montana when I damn near got myself hung the last time. Call it whatever you want, Nick, but a man's got to save his skin. Maybe now that you've calmed down a bit you can see that."

Nick pulled in a deep breath, held it, and then let it out again. Looking back toward the hill, the cart, and all the coffins stacked neatly there, he felt as if it had been days since he'd been doing the simple task of burying the dead. Now, after going through his past and dealing with Barrett, Nick wished that digging holes was the only thing he needed to worry about.

"So," Barrett said, rubbing his hands together and smirking as though a harsh word hadn't even passed between them. "You ready to start in on your part?"

"What is it you want me to do?"

"For now, we just need to scout out the shop and make sure the owner and his hired guns are where we think they are."

"Hired guns?"

"Sure. You didn't think all this merchandise and money would just change hands without anyone looking after it, did you?"

"It's been a while since I've thought about things like that."

"Which is exactly why you're lucky to have me around. Come along with me and we can scout that store. Along the way, I can fill you in on what I heard about you over the years and you can tell me how close I am to the truth."

Barrett placed his arm over Nick's shoulders and started turning him away from the coffins that needed to be buried. Knowing his hope that the job would dry up and blow away was officially dashed on the rocks, Nick went along with Barrett anyway. In a peculiar way, it did feel good to be reunited with his old friend.

Nick could think of many worse things than riding fast and living outside the law once again. When a man got past the morality of it, committing crimes wasn't such a bad business. If it was done right, it could be lucrative, there were no regular hours, and nobody got hurt.

At the very least, it beat the hell out of digging holes and dragging a cart like some goddamn mule.

Nick stopped before walking past the parlor and turned to shake free of Barrett's guiding arm.

"What's the matter?" Barrett asked suspiciously. "You change your mind already?"

"Nope. I just didn't want to leave without taking this along." Nick reached for a tarp that was folded up and tossed on the ground. The tarp had been covering the coffins to protect them from the elements, but Nick had also used it to cover up something else. The worn gun belt fit around his waist and buckled up with only a few practiced motions of his hands. Once there, the gun provided Nick with an odd mixture of security and dread.

While he still wore the gun belt more often than not, that day it made Nick feel as if he was rekindling something inside of himself that had been buried.

Buried, but not dead.

"I see some things never change," Barrett said, immediately noticing the change that had settled over his old friend.

"Nope. Some things never do."

TWENTY-ONE

Nick had never actually beaten his head against a wall, but talking to Barrett regarding the details of his plan had to have been a similar kind of headache. Barrett talked and talked and talked some more as they walked down the street. All the while, he would try to amend some things he'd said about Montana. He also tried to implant new things that were surely intended to make Nick feel as though teaming up for this job was the best move that could possibly be made.

But Nick didn't fall for any of it.

He'd listened well enough the first time and knew that Barrett was just trying to draw him in even further. There were a few things that stuck in Nick's craw, but none of them came as any surprise to someone who'd heard Barrett go on like this plenty of times before. So Nick simply followed Barrett and enjoyed the scenery while ignoring most of the words being thrown at him.

That didn't mean that Nick wasn't getting anything out of the conversation. Nick knew Barrett well enough to be able to catch plenty by listening between the bragging and promises for wealth and glory.

"I'm surprised you wanted to work with me," Nick said, interrupting at his first opportunity.

Barrett looked confused for a moment and asked, "Why would you think something like that?"

"Because of the rewards out for me. The price that's on my head was put there by Red all those years ago and has been bumped up every year since. That's not too big of a problem for a Mourner, especially since most folks that knew me already thought I was dead. If we start pulling jobs again, it'll be hard to keep my head down so low. Hell, you're the one who said we should never run with men that're too famous. It brings too much heat."

"Not too big of a problem," Barrett scoffed. "Listen to you."

"I'm serious. I can't even use a regular gun any more, Barrett. Why the hell would you want to work with me?"

Barrett nodded as he listened. He did a fine job of keeping his thoughts to himself, but Nick had played enough poker to spot the glimmer of deception in the man's eyes.

Seeing that he wasn't fooling Nick one bit, Barrett let the smile take charge of his face and nudged Nick using his elbow. "Actually, I did check up on you myself and saw that you've got a small fortune tacked onto your scalp. I remember a day when you'd have been proud of that, but you don't need to worry about that bounty. At least not here, anyway."

"Why, Barrett? What did you do?"

"I did you a favor. Actually, I did you one hell of a favor and you'll probably want to spend the next couple years thanking me for it."

"I don't know if I like the sound of that."

Sheriff Trayner stormed into his office as if he was trying to leave holes in the floor. He kept his arms close to his thick torso, only moving them out when he meant to either push open a door or knock someone out of his way.

"What the hell do I pay you all for?" Trayner bellowed to his deputies. "I asked each one of you to do a couple of things and I haven't heard about one of them being finished yet." Turning so he could spread the hell he was giving equally, he snarled, "Not *one*!"

Two of the three deputies in the office had been talking near the cells at the rear of the room. They'd straightened up and tried to appear busy the moment the sheriff stomped inside, but weren't doing a very good job of it.

"You two," Trayner said, signaling out the two younger lawmen by the cells. "Did you find them gun hands I asked you to find?"

Reluctantly, they shook their heads.

"No, sir," the braver of the two replied. "We been out looking and never found hide nor hair of them."

"And why do you think that is?"

Sensing a trap, the first deputy kept his mouth shut. The other lawman taking up space near the cells wasn't so sharp.

"Maybe they all left town," the second deputy offered hopefully.

Trayner put on a wolf's smile, placed his hands on his hips and started moving closer to both of the men at the back of the office. "You think so? You think they just left town?"

The deputy being addressed by the sheriff actually nodded and smirked as though he'd done something right. The deputy standing next to him, however, was already starting to inch away from what he knew to be coming.

Trayner's hand snapped out so fast that it created a gust of wind. His meaty fingers clenched around the deputy's shirt and pulled him close enough to feel the heat when he screamed, "You'd better pray they left town, you ignorant wretch! It's more likely that you two stomped around and gave them so much warning that they found a hole somewhere, dug in deep, and waited until you stomped in some other direction. How's that sound?"

The second deputy was trying to save face at first, but knew it was too late for that now. Before he could make even a sloppy attempt at appeasing the sheriff, the deputy was released from Trayner's grasp and shoved back against the wall. He looked around nervously to double-check that the cells were empty and the other deputy wasn't giving him any funny looks.

"What about you, Matt?" Trayner asked, snapping his finger out to stab toward the man sitting behind his desk. "Did you look through them notices like I asked?"

The deputy behind the desk nodded sincerely. Unlike the other two, he seemed more frustrated with himself than fearful of Trayner. "I did. In fact, I've been through it twice. And that doesn't count whoever went through them before me."

The sheriff seemed to pick up on this deputy's sincerity and lowered his voice somewhat when he asked, "And what've you found?"

"That's just it. I haven't found a damn thing."

"Go on."

Shaking his head, Matt explained, "Something tells me that I *should* find something. It's almost like I've already seen it and just can't find it again."

Despite the fact that he wasn't as angry at Matt as he was with the other two, Trayner's frustration could still be seen in the way he stomped across the room so he could get a look at what Matt was doing. Walking around to the other side of the desk, the sheriff slapped both hands flat down against the desktop and stared down at the book that lay open in front of both lawmen.

The book was bound in beaten leather and contained various reward notices and wanted posters for all kinds of wrongdoers. Some of the notices were marked to show that the bounty had been collected or that the outlaw was no longer at large. Trayner had paid out some of those bounties himself since Bitter Creek was one of the larger towns in the vicinity.

"Show me what you're talking about," Trayner said.

Matt shook his head and shrugged. "That's just it. There isn't anything. That's what's bothering me."

"You want me to point out the fella to you again? Perhaps them other two might be able to track him down if they wanted to keep my boot out of their asses."

"No need for that. I got a plenty good look at the fella's face. I sat and ate with him down at Norm's Skillet."

"Oh yeah," said one of the deputies by the cells. "You know something? Norm's daughter is one fine little piece of —"

"Shut the hell up!" Trayner boomed. The sheriff then turned his attention back to Matt. "You were saying?"

Matt was still flipping backward and forward through the notices, shaking his head. "I was as close to him as I was to you. I can picture his face even now."

"Then maybe I was wrong. Maybe he's not wrapped up in whatever Cobb's got going."

"Something bothered me when I saw him that first time, but I didn't say anything. My wife says I think the worst about folks ever since I pinned a badge to my shirt. But when you mentioned that you thought that man was up to no good, I thought that you were right. The moment I started looking through these notices, I knew I would find something."

"But you haven't found anything?"

Letting out a disgusted breath, Matt shook his head once again. It was almost as if each time he admitted defeat was harder than the last. "No. Not a goddamn thing."

Trayner gave Matt a pat on the back that some might have called a slap. The lawman's beefy hand pounded lightly against Matt's shoulders as he said, "Move aside. You've been sitting there long enough." Looking up to the other two deputies, he added, "At least someone around here's been earning their pay."

"I'd rather not leave," Matt said. "I want to try and find —"

"You're tired, Matt. Go home, visit the wife, and get some sleep. You've earned it. Now that you gave me a notion of what to look for, perhaps all it takes is a fresh set of eyes to find it."

By this point, Matt had already been forced from his chair to make room for the sheriff to sit in his place. The moment he got to his feet and stretched his back, the hours he'd spent hunched over that book seemed to catch up to him all at once. When he turned his head to work out some of the kinks, his crackling bones echoed through his ears.

"Yeah," Matt said. "Maybe getting some rest won't be such a bad idea after all. You sure you don't need me around here?"

The sheriff had thoughts about that, but kept them to himself. Instead, he shook his head and replied, "Just so long as those other two can keep from shooting themselves in the foot, we should be fine."

"Great. I'll be back in a while."

Trayner was already flipping through the book. Suddenly, he stopped and turned a few pages back. The book had been left open to some of the older notices and Trayner sifted through them real quickly as Matt collected his hat and headed for the door. Before his deputy could step outside, Trayner's eyes narrowed and he focused on something that caught his interest.

"What is it, Sheriff?" asked one of the deputies from the back of the room.

Hearing that brought Matt to a stop so he could turn to look at the sheriff. When he saw the expression on Trayner's face, he asked, "You find something already?"

"Before you leave," the sheriff said to Matt, "come over here and take a look at something for me. You other two come over here as well. I need your opinions on something."

All three of the deputies gathered around the desk and looked at the book lying open there. Over the last few days, all of the lawmen had been going through those notices, but Matt had insisted on sifting through them for the bulk of that time. Now, each of the men was staring down at the notice that the book had been opened to. Matt studied it with growing frustration while the other two deputies simply tried to look as though they were thinking about something relevant.

"Take a close look," Trayner said, tapping the book with his finger.

Finally, one of the other two deputies reluctantly said, "I don't recall seeing that fella there. Is he one of the others that's been seen with Cobb?"

"Nope," Trayner answered. "You're not looking close enough."

The only other notice that could be seen had been marked out, indicating that the man pictured there had been shot dead over a year ago.

Unable to wait any longer, Trayner moved his finger to the spine of the book, rather than to either of the notices. "Look here," he said.

Matt peered closely to where the sheriff was pointing and finally saw what the other man had spotted right away. "I'll be damned," Matt whispered.

Poking up from between the notices, less than a quarter inch above the spine, was a ragged line of paper that had obviously been torn rather than cut. In fact, once Matt reached out to pull the shredded bit of paper, he could see the edges of a few letters that had been printed in ink upon the scrap. Although not enough was seen to make out any words, the placement of the ink was identical to every other notice in the book.

"Whatever it was," said one of the other deputies, "it was another notice. Probably just an old one that was tossed out after being collected, huh?"

Trayner shook his head. "Not likely. I keep these notices all together like this for a reason. The old ones stay right here so we know not to pay any expired bounties. It also helps us keep tabs on who's still out there. I check through this book every month myself to make sure it's up to date and I can tell you that this ripped piece wasn't in there the last time I checked."

Matt nodded and let out a breath that was part relieved and part frustrated. "So that means a page was torn out of here recently."

"Yep," Trayner said. "At least one, but I'd guess there's more missing from here as well." Glancing up to the man looking over his shoulder, he said, "Don't get too worked up about it, Matt. You probably would've caught this yourself if you weren't so damn tired."

"That's not an excuse. I sat right in front of that man and for all I know, he could be a cold-blooded killer."

"Or he could be nobody. This page might have shown one of them others Cobb brought into town. Either way, this shows us that we're dealing with one slick son of a bitch. Gutsy, too, since he needed to sneak right in here and take those pages." So far, the sheriff had been keeping his voice calm and level. Although the tone didn't change much, the edge that had been added to his voice was definitely noticeable.

"So that leaves one question," Trayner said, while shifting his eyes among all three men. "Who left this office empty long enough for someone to get in here, mess with this book, and walk back out again? And who," he added in a voice rising to an angry roar, "was too stupid to not even see someone getting near enough to this office to break into it?"

No answer was immediately forthcoming. Finally, however, there came a grumbled curse. It came from Matt.

"It was me, Sheriff," Matt said earnestly. "It had to be. I've been eating supper with my wife every night. I snuck out a few times during the week, but I swear I locked up."

Trayner was obviously pissed, but he managed to hold it back. By the time he met Matt's apologetic gaze again, he smirked crookedly and shoved him toward the door. "It's all right. Go home. Get some rest and don't pull that kind of shit ever again." When he saw the looks on the other deputies' faces, he added, "And if I catch either of you making that big of a mistake, I'll hang you myself."

Walking out the door, Matt wanted to kick himself for the mistake he'd made. Although it had been a simple thing at the time, it had turned into something that might be haunting him for awhile to come.

The other deputies were still griping when Matt shut the door and headed home.

"You did what?" Nick asked. Even though he had no trouble hearing what Barrett had told him, he could still hardly believe it.

Barrett had his hands in his pockets and was walking beside him casually. He most certainly didn't look like the type of person who'd just admitted to breaking into the sheriff's office and taking wanted notices right out from under the law's collective nose.

"You heard what I said."

Nick shook his head. "You sure have come a long way from when we ran together. Used to be I was the one with all the piss and vinegar. Now you're breaking into sheriffs' offices."

"You also used to be the one who never thought more than half a step ahead of himself. You've changed too, Nick. We both have and it's for the better."

"Yeah, but what you did . . . I never would have asked for anything like that."

"No need to ask," Barrett said. "It's a favor. Besides," he added, removing a folded piece of paper from his pocket and opening it for them both to see, "this picture doesn't even do you justice."

Being suddenly faced with that wanted notice was like a hard slap in Nick's face by a cold hand. He stopped dead in his tracks and gazed down at the likeness that had been drawn and copied onto enough similar notices to plague Nick for years. Nick reached out and took the paper so he could get a closer look.

"You look like you never seen one of those," Barrett said.

"It's been a while. I know they're out there, but . . . Jesus, was I ever truly that young?"

The face Nick saw on that notice was definitely his own, but it was also that of a child. Even drawn as a sketch, the eyes in that picture were fiery and mean. The mouth was set in a straight line and the hair was chopped at awkward angles since Nick usually cut it himself back then with a straight razor.

When Nick finally looked away from the picture that seemed like a mirror from the past, several words on the notice caught his attention. They were words like "murder," "bandit," and "ruthless." Those words sat like rocks in his stomach when he read them.

After a while, Barrett broke the silence that had fallen. "You can keep it if you want, but I think you know that would be fool-ish."

"Why'd you do this?" Nick asked, handing over the notice.

Barrett dug in his pocket for a match and struck it against the nearest wall. "So you wouldn't have to worry about being picked out by the law around here. You're not quite the man in that picture anymore, but you're awful close. At least this way, you won't even have to take the chance of having someone look you up."

"Sure. That is, unless this job of yours goes sour and that reward gets raised."

Smirking, Barrett touched the flame in his hand to the bottom edge of the notice. The dry paper went up immediately and Barrett dropped it to the dirt. "Even if that does happen, we'll both be rich enough to make it worth the trouble. Come on. I've got some friends I'd like you to meet."

Nick followed Barrett down the street as his youthful likeness burned behind him. He only wished the nightmares from those days could be dealt with so easily.

TWENTY-TWO

Nick didn't know how Barrett could find places to hole up. Truth be told, Barrett had always been able to get hold of the keys to squalid, rat-infested hideouts and Nick never knew how he'd gotten them. Barrett was just doing his job.

Most folks never really looked for places as dirty and run-down as the ones that Barrett favored. Even if they walked right by a place like that, most folks rarely even saw it. That was probably why Barrett favored them.

Stepping past the door that was propped against a molded frame, Nick pulled in a breath filled with air that reeked of decay and dirt. His feet crunched against rotten lumber and the husks of dead bugs. He couldn't move without kicking up some dust, which made it difficult for him to see if the shapes at the other end of the room were solid or merely tricks of the light.

"Nick Graves," Barrett said while stepping into the room as if he were coming home, "meet your partners for this little endeavor I've put together. Jasper Morrison and Tom Guile."

The shapes Nick had been staring at started to move, revealing themselves to be human after all. Although they were definitely people, neither of them seemed at all happy to make Nick's acquaintance.

The first one to get to his feet was about Barrett's height, but more wiry in build. He appeared to be at least seven to ten years Barrett's junior, but that estimate might have been thrown off because his face was so cleanly shaven that it almost seemed as though whiskers had yet to poke through the surface at all. His scalp, on the other hand, was covered with thick stubble, reminding Nick somewhat of the picture he'd left burning on the ground behind him.

"You said we wouldn't use our names," the younger man said.

Barrett patted the air and gave a reassuring smile. "Nick's an old friend of mine. We rode together in the days when we were both younger than you two. He's all right, so try not to give too bad of a first impression, Jasper."

Jasper Morrison's eyes shifted in their

sockets. The poor lighting in the dirty back room made it impossible to judge what color they were, but it was plain enough to see that they were cold and intense. They were killer's eyes. Anyone in that room could recognize that much.

"Nick Graves, huh?" Morrison asked. "I heard'a you."

"Yeah," said the other man who'd been waiting in the shadows. "I heard he ran with lawmen up in Virginia City."

Tom Guile had a slim build that seemed to have come from being starved to within an inch of his life. He had the meanness to go along with being so hungry, as well as the sunken face. In the dim light, Guile's face looked more like a skull.

Shifting into a frame of mind that was as comfortable to Nick as it was disturbing, he stared down both of the younger men and watched them each back off. Apparently, his own killer's eyes truly couldn't be buried under any amount of honest work. "You want to believe every rumor you hear? Or would you rather keep your mouth shut and stay healthy a while longer?"

Both Morrison's and Guile's eyes took in Nick from head to toe. They lingered at the gun at his side as well as the mangled hand that hovered over it. Although neither of them seemed to know just what to make of Nick, they decided it best to speak to him in a more respectful tone.

"All right," Guile said. "I guess if Barrett can vouch for you, then that's good enough for me."

But Morrison didn't look too sure. While the man beside him had been talking, Morrison had his eyes locked on Nick and his entire body tensed like a cobra that was about to strike. He took another step back, but only so he could square his shoulders and give Nick a look that could only mean one thing.

Having picked out Morrison as the most dangerous of the two, Nick had been expecting something like this to happen. He knew words would do no good, just as he knew that every second he waited to act chipped away at his own credibility in the outlaws' eyes.

After standing as still as a statue, Nick suddenly burst into motion as he flicked back his coat and drew the pistol from his holster. Although nobody else in the room could see the craftsmanship that had gone into aiding him, it was because of his customized pistol and holster working together that he cleared leather before Morrison so much as touched his own weapon.

Morrison froze with his hand just about to make a grab for his pistol when his youthful face burst into a grin. Somehow, he even managed to make that expression look twisted. "No need to get your feathers ruffled, Nick. I was just seeing if you've got what it takes to work with me. Looks like you do."

His face an unreadable mask, Nick lowered his pistol but didn't holster it. "I'm honored," he said dryly.

Guile seemed to be more interested in the iron Nick was holding than any part of the rest of the display. "What kind of pistol is that? It looks like it was a Schofield once upon a time."

"It was," Nick replied while holding the gun so both of the other men could get a clear look at it. "There were some modifications made to it."

"Yeah. By the looks of that hand, I'm surprised you can still even draw. Did you fix up that gun?"

"No. I was just lucky enough to find someone who could do it for me."

The modified Schofield had a handle that looked as if it had been whittled down to a nub. The trigger had been equally tapered, allowing it to be pulled with just the right touch from a shorter than average finger. In fact, every part of the gun had been sculpted to fit Nick's hand. The handle was made to compensate for the awkward balance of his uneven grip and the trigger was made to respond to that awkward balance as well. Even the holster itself was a piece of work.

Crafted by a man who could work leather the way some artists worked with clay or paint, Nick's holster was made so the inside of it perfectly fit the gun itself. Ridges spiraled along the inside of the holster, made specially to fit into the grooves on the outside of the barrel. That way, when the gun moved within the holster, it was turned in a subtle, yet very important, way.

That turning came into play when Nick drew the gun, twisting the handle into the palm of his hand so he had a better chance at wrapping his damaged fingers around it. Of course, the Schofield would have been useless to anyone with a full set of fingers. There was no need to tell anyone about that at the moment, though.

"As long as you can shoot as impressively as you draw," Guile said, "I got no problem with you."

Nick nodded, fully aware at how important that kind of acceptance truly was among the lawless.

Barrett stepped toward the back of the

room, as though he felt more comfortable in the shadows. "If you two are done second-guessing my choice of friends, then perhaps we can move along."

Guile shrugged and pulled a chewed cigar from his pocket. Morrison still had his eye on Nick, but nodded and let his suspicion slither back into its hole.

"We need to take another look at that store," Barrett said.

Clenching the cigar between his teeth without lighting it, Guile said, "We already checked the store. It's still there and so is the fat cat who owns it."

"Well, Nick still needs to get a look so he's not running blind when the time comes. Along the way, you two can tell me whatever it is you found out while I've been gone."

"The law's getting anxious," Morrison said in a low, rumbling voice. "I can tell you that right now. They been asking around about us."

That raised Barrett's eyebrows. "Do they know who you are?"

Guile shook his head. "From what I hear, they got no names. The deputies have just been asking about any unsavory types that have been seen with you. They know you well enough, that's for damn sure."

"That's unavoidable. Here," Barrett said,

pulling another folded piece of paper from his pocket and tossing it to Guile. "Why don't you use that to light your cigar?"

Guile unfolded the paper, smiled at what he saw, and turned it around so the others could get a look at what was printed there. The likeness on the notice made Guile look like some sort of ghoul, but it still wasn't too much of an exaggeration. Nick couldn't read the smaller print, but he could see the writing at the top just fine.

"Wanted for murder, huh?" Nick asked. "That reward isn't too bad."

"It'll go up after this job," Guile boasted while taking the match Barrett handed over to him. One twitch of his wrist against the floor set the match into a sputtering flame. That flame caught on the notice, which Guile rolled up and then lifted to his face so he could lean in close with the cigar.

Barrett shifted his attention to Morrison. "I looked, but couldn't find a notice for you."

Morrison let out a grunting laugh and replied, "That's all right. I don't smoke."

Nick let out a short laugh. At the very least, he could always appreciate a man with a sense of humor.

Barrett, on the other hand, wasn't so appreciative. "Cut the shit, Morrison. If I went to all the trouble of getting into the sheriff's office, I don't want to think I missed anything when I was there."

"Don't worry. You didn't miss anything," Morrison said. "I've kept my nose clean enough so there's no warrants issued for me just now."

"That's even better." Taking a breath, Barrett said, "You see, Nick? I pick my partners wisely. What do you think? Is this starting to bring back some memories of the good old days?"

"I don't know about how good those days were, but I'm getting some memories all right. I see your taste in hideouts hasn't changed."

"Hey, now! Has anyone ever found us in the hideouts I've picked?"

"Do rats count?"

Barrett rolled his eyes. "People think of places like this as already gone. That's why nobody pays any attention to them. Most folks forget these places are here at all. I taught you that."

"You sure did."

The tip of Guile's cigar glowed in the shadows, illuminating the sharp, angular lines of his face. "So are we gonna stand about reminiscing or should we get to work?"

"You boys ready?"

Both Morrison and Guile checked to make sure their guns were loaded before nodding to Barrett.

When he saw that, Barrett swelled up like a proud poppa and draped his arm once again over Nick's shoulders. The gesture seemed as much affectionate as it was meant to push Nick toward the door and back outside. "Then let's get moving," he said. "Ol' Nick here might get in trouble if he leaves his coffins unattended for too long."

TWENTY-THREE

The coffins Nick had left unburied on the hill seemed as far away as the kid that had been staring back at him from that faded reward notice. Simply being in Barrett's presence had brought things to the surface that pulled at Nick like ghostly hands from the great beyond.

Barrett had a way about him that got Nick to agree to put his life on the line so he could buy into one plan or another. Nick wasn't about to blame his lawlessness on someone else. Barrett was damn good at steering people the way he wanted them to go, but he could never push Nick too far.

The boys in their old gang used to kid Barrett by saying he would make a better lawyer or banker. More than once, Nick wondered if he hadn't been the one to steer Barrett onto the road of the outlaw.

Or maybe Stasys was right when he'd warned his son about "the bad kind."

That term had seemed so simple that it had to be wrong. Either that, or Nick just hadn't wanted to believe the words could fit so well upon the boys he'd chosen to call friends. But it had fit, all right. Looking back, Nick wondered if that term was meant for himself or the company he'd kept.

"You're only a boy," Stasys had said all those years back. "What can you do out there that you can't do here?"

The old man was waving a thickly muscled arm out away from the little house that had been given to him when he'd taken his job digging graves in a small Kansas town. He and his son had been moving around through that state as well as Missouri for the better part of the previous ten years. Whenever he spoke about anyplace but where he was, he talked as if it were foreign soil.

Nick was fifteen years old, which meant that he not only knew everything the world had to offer, but that he was ready to conquer it as well. At least, that's what it meant as far as he was concerned.

"I'm not a boy no more, Pa," Nick said. "I'm old enough to make my own way and that don't include digging no more goddamn graves!"

Stasys's hand swept through the air so fast that Nick didn't have time to duck. The older man's palm caught Nick square of the face just hard enough to catch his attention.

"You don't talk that way to your father!"

Although the anger could be seen like a fire reflected in Nick's eyes, he kept it under control. It faded after a second or two, because the boy knew that he'd deserved exactly what he'd gotten.

"Where do you think you go?" Stasys asked in English that remained broken even after all the years he'd lived in America. "How are you putting food on your table?"

"We'll earn our keep."

"We? Who is this we? You mean those thieving friends of yours?"

Although Nick started to fight back, he stopped himself. Part of him not only agreed with the old man's assessment, but liked hearing it put that way.

"I suppose you want to take that gun of yours too?"

Nick hadn't been expecting to hear that. "What gun?"

"The one I find under your bed. Under the boards in the floor."

"How'd you know about that?"

"You think I'm stupid, eh? You think because I dig graves, that I don't know what goes on in my own home?"

"No, Pa," Nick said with genuine regret. "I never thought you were stupid."

"Then maybe you think I just let you keep a weapon in my home? You know you can get yourself killed just as easy as you can kill someone else. I know. I dig the graves for men who get killed with guns."

When Nick rolled his eyes, he quickly felt Stasys's hand clamp around his jaw so his face could be pointed back in the right direction.

"You listen to me, boy," Stasys said once he had hold of his son's face and was staring directly into his eyes. "If you use a gun, it will either kill you quickly or piece by piece. You understand me? Even if you win a fight, you lose."

"That don't make any sense, Pa."

"Then you listen to this. Stay here and learn an honest trade instead of going off with those thieves and committing sins for a living. You understand that?"

Fixing his eyes on his father, Nick knocked Stasys's hand away from his face and stepped out of arm's reach. "I understand. Maybe I want to live my own way. Maybe I want to see more than these goddamn boot hills out my window. No matter where we live it's always the same."

"You don't listen to me, I'll wind up burying you in a boot hill. Think about that while you're off with your friends shooting your guns."

"So you'll let me go?"

Stasys's eyes were narrowed from years of staring through the sun's glare. His skin resembled worn leather and the lines in his face were deep furrows, which made his emotions show even more prominently. At that moment, Stasys showed an emotion that Nick hadn't seen since that day on the boat when his mother died.

Despair.

"You'll go," Stasys said. "Whether I like or not, you'll go."

Nick was too young to admit to the regrets brewing inside of him. In his mind, that would have been admitting some kind of defeat. So, he lowered his eyes from his father's and asked, "Where's my gun?"

Stasys didn't answer right away. Instead, he kept his gaze on his son to watch his boy decide his own fate. The muscles tensed in his jaw and his weathered hands clenched into fists. But since there was nothing to hold on to, his fists tightened around empty air. He started to speak a few times, but struggled as if he'd forgotten both of his languages.

"We're heading out tonight," Nick said. "I'll need my gun."

Wincing at the helplessness he felt, Stasys let out a breath and grumbled, "I take the gun when I found it."

"What did you do with it, Pa? Where is it?"

Stasys pointed his finger toward the gentle slope several yards away from his property. The ground was studded with markers made of stone and wood, most of which were hand-carved by either Nick or his father. Normally, Stasys looked upon that field with pride. This time, however, there was no pride to be found in his weathered face.

"I bury it out there. If you want it, you can start digging until you find. Maybe along the way, you will come to your senses and take pride in honest work."

"Honest work don't make someone known, Pa. It don't make them rich and it sure as hell don't give them more than blisters and some shack of a house to grow old and die in."

And there it was.

Even as he'd spoken those words, Nick could hardly believe they were coming out of his mouth. But there was no taking them back now and he was too proud to apologize. The thought would enter his mind soon after that moment and for years to come, but the words remained lodged in his throat.

Stasys kept his jaw set and his eyes fixed upon his boy. He was no poker player, however, and his expression slowly shifted to reveal what was going on inside of him. When the change was complete, Stasys looked as if he'd been the one to get slapped across the face.

When Nick turned his back on his father and walked away, he did so in an anxious huff. The truth of the matter was that he simply couldn't bear to see that look in his father's eyes for one more moment.

"Dig your own fucking hole, Pa." That was the first time Nick had ever spoken to Stasys that way. After that, the profanity came easier until it was just another nasty habit.

He met up with Barrett and left that night.

He didn't try to find his gun.

He just left.

There would be plenty of guns to be found along the road he'd chosen that day.

"You're awful quiet, Nick," Barrett said as he and the other men he'd gathered walked down the street. "Something troubling you?"

Nick shook his head. "Just trying to think back to how it was when we did things like this every day."

Barrett smiled as though he was remembering a summer breeze. "Those were some good times. Maybe after this one, we can start working together more often. The pay's got to be better than digging graves."

"I thought you said this would be the last job."

Smirking, Barrett said, "There's always another job."

"Before you two start planning a year in advance, why don't you get a look at what's on your plate right now?" Guile said. "Because there it is."

Nick looked to where Guile was pointing and saw what appeared to be just another small storefront in a row of storefronts. The place didn't look like anything special when compared to the other nearby establishments. Compared to the section of town where they'd started, however, the shops could have been palaces.

"And there's our man now," Barrett said.

Hearing that was enough to get both Morrison and Guile to check their weapons to make sure they were loaded. When they reholstered their guns, the two younger men looked to Barrett with a very familiar glint in their eyes. It was the fire that came when a hungry predator could smell blood in the air.

Stasys would have called those two "the bad kind." He'd only been trying to keep his son off the hard road. That was so obvious now.

Nick only wished that he'd been smart enough to listen.

TWENTY-FOUR

Eddison Finch was a small man, but still managed to walk as if he was looking down at everyone around him. He had the fancy clothes and smooth skin of a man who hadn't had to work hard enough to break a sweat for his entire life. In fact, he looked like he barely spent more than an hour out of the shade unless it was absolutely necessary.

He strutted in front of the shop bearing his name like a king touring his castle. All around him, other locals went about their business under the barely tolerant gaze of the dandy with the thinning hair. Finch kept that thinning hair slicked back from his forehead and plastered down with what Nick could only guess was a kind of wax. Whatever it was, it made his scalp glisten like a wet rock even in the fading sunlight.

"Would ya look at that one?" Morrison said. "I bet we can shoot him right now and sell what's in his pockets for a nice profit."

Barrett nodded. "Maybe. But then who would be there to bring in what we're really after."

"None of you should get too twitchy," Guile added. "Because that tenderfoot is the only one who can get into the safe in back. I got a look at it myself and if we need to blast through it, we might as well just set fire to every bit of money that's in there."

"When did you get that close to the safe?" Barrett asked.

Guile shrugged. "You're not the only one who gets to sneak around after dark."

"You see," Barrett said to Nick. "I still know how to put a good bunch together."

The four of them stood across the street and down a little ways from Finch's. When the owner of the shop stood under the sign bearing his own name, it seemed more as though he were being marked by a giant label to make the outlaws' job that much easier. It would have been funny had Nick not felt as if he were stuck in a pool of quicksand.

Going through the motions of his former life, Nick found himself losing track of whether he was there to regain what he'd once had or keep an eye on Barrett and his hired guns.

"He stands out here every day," Barrett said. "His schedule is so regular, that he don't even notice what's around him anymore."

Morrison let out a chuckle. "He's so wrapped up in himself that he don't know what the hell's about to happen. Even if he did, he'd think that his daddy's money would still be able to get him out."

"Poor bastard," Barrett said. "But, if some folks are gonna have a Thanksgiving meal, some turkeys have gotta die."

That went over fairly well with the other two. Nick did his best to laugh along while watching to see if Finch was truly so oblivious that he didn't know he was being fitted for his own coffin at that very moment. Although the dandy looked over at the outlaws, he seemed to be more annoyed that their laughter was intruding on his thoughts than anything else.

Barrett and his hired guns were right. The turkey was ripe for plucking and if there truly was all that cash and jewelry on its way, then it could be taken by any bunch who knew what they were doing and had the sand to pull a trigger.

Nick felt a rush go through him that he hadn't felt in years. It wasn't the sort of feeling he'd ever gotten from digging a grave and it was powerful enough to make him wonder why he'd planned on keeping tabs on Barrett instead of tossing his hat in with the others in earnest.

Barrett nodded toward the storefront and kept a casual look upon his face as he said, "Me and Nick will wait right here until the delivery shows up. You other two can take up the spots in the alley we picked out before just in case our Mr. Finch over there decides to make the exchange out back. Either way, there'll be plenty of time for us to join up once the time is right."

"And when is that?" Morrison asked.

"When I say so. This is my plan, so I'll give the word. Some of this just goes on instinct, so you need to follow my lead."

Morrison and Guile nodded. Nick saw a look pass between the other two gunmen that caught his interest. It wasn't anything unexpected. Just the typical double-dealing among thieves that was thought of as their own brand of insurance.

"We'll hit hard and fast," Barrett continued. As he spoke, he made sure to keep his eyes moving so it didn't look obvious that he was talking about any spot in particular. In fact, anyone who didn't know any better might have thought the group was simply exchanging bad jokes. "Take a good look at this street, because you'll need to know where to go once the smoke starts getting thick. If the law comes, they'll come from that way," he explained, pointing toward the intersection marked by a sign that read, ASHTON CORNER. "That's the way they always come for their patrol and it's the way they'll come when there's trouble."

"Are you sure about that?" Nick asked.

Morrison smirked and replied, "That's the way it went the times when I started trouble."

Barrett patted Nick on the back. "We checked it out. You're just lucky that you weren't here for all the boring work."

Spitting out a piece of stray tobacco, Guile said, "I don't know about the rest of you, but I think this is pretty damn boring."

"Well, you won't have much longer to wait. The shipment should be here tomorrow or the day after. Why don't we just part ways for now and meet up later? If we stay here like this much longer, even ol' Mr. Finch will start to suspect something."

After a few more fake laughs, handshakes were exchanged and the four men split up like any other group of friends who had other things to tend to. Nick made sure to pick the opposite direction from the one in which Barrett walked and eventually headed back to the undertaker's parlor.

As soon as he arrived, Nick was greeted by Carmine's stern face. While it looked like the squat Italian meant to chew Nick's hide for leaving his work, the scolding never came because Nick went straight back to pick up his shovel.

Nick kept his coat on until he knew he was no longer being watched so Carmine wouldn't see the gun strapped around his waist. He worked until long past sundown, making sure that all the coffins were buried before leaving that hill once again. As he worked, Nick thought about what he'd seen and what he'd gotten himself into.

The more he tried to figure out what needed to be done, the more his head started to ache. Some of the problem stemmed from the fact that Nick knew exactly what he should do. He knew it just as plainly as he could still hear his father's voice ringing through his ears.

Barrett needed to be stopped before he got himself or anyone else killed.

Then there was the voice that was even more familiar to Nick: his own. Sure, the voice was a bit younger and overly anxious, but it still held plenty of truth when it told Nick to drop his goddamn shovel and take hold of life once again.

There were men after him and that would never change. Why not give those men something to talk about for the years to come and haul in some real money in the process?

Nick shook his head, knowing only too well how much trouble that youthful voice had gotten him into. Before he knew it, he was patting the ground on top of the last coffin.

It was dark and the air was taking on a definite chill. While summer was approaching, the heat wasn't a steady factor just yet. Some nights still carried the cold teeth of winter and this seemed to be one of them. Nick walked back to the parlor, dropped off his shovel, and checked in with the undertaker.

"Good work today," Carmine said. "You come back tomorrow and I'll put you to work again. But not so long of a break next time, okay?"

"Okay," was all Nick said before heading back out again.

Nick's belly was grumbling, reminding him of the fact that he hadn't had much to eat since breakfast. After all the hours of hard work he'd put in, that meal was long gone. Still, it felt good to get the blood flowing through his muscles after digging those holes. Compared to the other brand of work he'd done with Barrett, digging those graves seemed even better.

His hands burned with fresh blisters and his back ached from lugging that cart up the hill. Dirt caked his hands and filled the spaces beneath his nails and his throat tasted like the underside of a saddle. What got to Nick even more at that moment was the fact that he was all too used to every one of those tastes, aches, and smells.

That was what years of hard work had brought him. That and less money than he'd seen when working for two days in his prime outlaw years.

"Excuse me."

At first, those words weren't loud enough to catch Nick's attention.

"Hello?" came the same voice, which was definitely feminine. "Excuse me? Mr. Graves?"

That brought Nick to a stop. He placed the voice as belonging to Vera Coswell and spotted her a moment later. She was dressed differently since the last time he'd seen her in Norm's Skillet, but she still had on the same beaming smile.

"I got your name correct, didn't I?" she asked while approaching him.

"You did."

"Nick Graves. I thought you'd left town. I wanted to hear from you again after we met up the last time. Have you been busy?"

"You could say that."

"Did you find work?"

Before he could answer that question, Nick found himself walking with Vera right beside him. She kept pace with him easily and waited anxiously for him to speak.

"You could say that too," he told her. "It's not much. Just doing odd jobs for Carmine Minneo."

Vera nodded. "That's wonderful. Are you done with work for the day?"

"Actually, yes. I was just going to head back to my room for —"

Suddenly, Vera threaded her arm around Nick's and said, "If you're hungry, we should probably stay away from Norm's, but they serve a fine steak over at the Texas Rose. At least, that's what they call the place now. There's no reason we can't share a table."

"What about your husband?"

"He's sleeping," she said dismissively. "He's been working so much lately that I barely see him. Actually, Sheriff Trayner's been running all his boys pretty ragged lately," she said, tightening her hold on Nick's arm. "I doubt I'll see any of them anytime soon. Matt's barely been home at all the last couple of days. Tonight, they're just rousting some bunch of troublemakers holing up on Seventh. You ask me, it's just an excuse for the boys to kick up some dust. I'm glad Matt could get some rest instead of bothering with that."

The shack Barrett was using was on Seventh Street. And if the lawmen were headed in that direction, they were in for anything but fun.

Nick's poker face was in rare form as he kept from reacting to that news in the least. "I really should be going," he said without a hint as to how quickly he wanted to leave. "There's still a bit of work I need to do before the morning."

Twenty-Five

No matter how much Nick might have learned from his father, there were some things that Stasys simply could never have taught him. Firing a gun was one and picking the spot to enter a fight was another. Those were things that Nick had been forced to figure out for himself, and he'd done so the hard way.

All this time, Nick had been treading water and biding his time. He'd ridden into Bitter Creek expecting to find someone else who was out for his blood for something that had been done in Nick's past. Instead, Nick had found an old friend and that had thrown him off to such a degree that he'd almost been sucked back into the life he'd vowed to leave behind. There had been something keeping him from making that final leap into lawlessness, however, just as there had been something keeping him from going against Cobb directly.

When Nick heard about the deputies moving in on a place down on Seventh, he knew the time had come to put up or shut up. He needed to pick a side in the fight that was about to happen because it was too late to walk away from it. Nick had never been the sort to stand by and watch if he was able enough to lend a hand.

At least that was something about which Stasys could be proud.

As Nick cut across side streets and bolted through alleyways, he slid into the role that he'd been forced to take when he'd lost the full abilities of his gun hand. That loss hadn't set him back as far as it had been meant, but it did force him to go about things in a different way.

Modifying his Schofield had been part of that readjustment.

Learning how and when to use it had been another.

Where speed and nerve had been good enough in the past, Nick now had to rely on stealth and patience.

Every step he took when drawing closer to Barrett's hideout got quieter. His ears stretched out to pick up on voices or footsteps that might belong to the lawmen while his feet followed the shortcuts he'd been picking out since his arrival in Bitter Creek.

Finally, he heard the very thing he'd been waiting for.

"You head that way," came a gruff, commanding voice from around the next corner. "And we'll cover this spot here. They won't have anywhere to go but through us."

Nick knew he'd found the lawmen.

Letting out a controlled breath, he drew his gun and melted into the closest shadow.

Sheriff Trayner had James Hyde with him while Dave was sent around to the back of the building that was to be the night's target. Trayner watched his other deputy move as quickly as he could around the corner and then waited another few seconds for Dave to get into position. Not wanting to give the outlaws any more time than was necessary, Trayner looked over to Hyde and nodded.

"You ready?" Trayner asked.

Although Hyde returned the nod, it wasn't as confident as the sheriff's. "You sure this is the place?"

"Dave followed Cobb and lost him around here. I've been looking into it myself since then and narrowed it down to that shack right there or the one next to it. The others were too rickety to stand up, let alone serve as any kind of hideout. That's the place, all right. I'd stake my life on it."

"And you're certain we can't just go in shooting?"

"We don't even know what they're up to yet."

"Then why the hell are we doing this?"

"Because if we sit around on our asses much longer, whatever they got planned will happen." Trayner focused his eyes on the shack. "Dave may not be good at much, but he's sneaky. Just give him another few seconds."

Both lawmen hunkered down and watched. After a while, Hyde started to fidget and shift on his feet.

"I feel like a damn fool squatting in the . . ." Hyde stopped himself when he spotted something that made his eyes narrow and his breath catch in the back of his throat. "Did you see that, Sheriff?"

Trayner was already smirking. "Sure did. Something just moved in that shack and it's too big to be another rat."

"I think I hear something. Sounds like there could be more in there." Hyde's hand tightened around his gun and his muscles tensed. "Someone's outside the shack. Maybe they're coming out."

But Trayner reached out and placed his hand on top of Hyde's gun so he could lower it. "That's just Dave. He's trying to get a better look at what's going on inside."

"I think there's someone else."

"You're jumping at shadows. I don't see anyone else, so just shut up before you tip our hand."

Dave maneuvered swiftly through the darkness until he got close enough to the rundown shack for his stomach to tighten. Paying close attention to his instincts, he slowed his steps and even pulled in his breaths so they hardly made a sound as the air came in and out of his lungs.

The temperature had dropped quickly since the sun had gone down, yet it was too early for anyone to have lit any streetlights in that part of town. The shadows were thick and only growing thicker by the moment. While Dave should have taken comfort from that, he just couldn't allow himself to get overly confident.

When he thought about one of the outlaws sneaking into the sheriff's office, Dave felt his teeth gnash. It riled him to think that they'd pulled one over on him like that. It was time for some payback and that made Dave want to perform better than he ever had.

Once he forced himself to put that aside

for a moment, the blood slowed enough inside of him that he could start to hear voices coming from the shack. Dave froze and squatted down so low that his knees started to ache. His gun was in hand, but the pistol was all but forgotten as he strained to hear what was being said inside the shack.

Finally, after what seemed like hours, words began to separate themselves from the rush of wind and the rattle of loose boards.

". . . don't know about him. For all we know, he could . . . kill . . . all."

Dave didn't recognize the voice, but he could already tell that the sheriff's instinct was right. Those weren't the words of transients huddling in a dirty room for the night.

"Don't worry about him," came another voice that had more behind it than the first. "I know him and . . . die than . . . like that."

". . . you really know about him, Barrett? He's been . . . for years."

Dave didn't know exactly what they were talking about, but hearing that one name cast away the final bit of doubt on whether or not they'd come to the right place. Nodding, he let out a breath of air that steamed up slightly in the chill of night. Dave kept low and started to shuffle slowly toward the closest window so he might be able to fill in some of the holes of the conversation.

"What about you, Guile?" came the stronger of the two voices Dave had heard so far. "You got a problem with any of this?"

Now that Dave was picking up more of the words, he wanted to get a little closer so he could hear the answer to Barrett's question. His boot lifted just high enough so that it wasn't scraping against the dirt and he started shifting his weight forward. And just when he was beginning to drop his weight onto his front foot, the conversation inside the shack came to an abrupt stop.

The quiet was so complete that it might as well have been a thunderclap. At least, that's what Dave's boot sounded like when it finally dropped onto the dirt.

Gravel crunched beneath his foot and seemed to echo in his ears. Surprisingly enough, that wasn't the worst thing he heard at that moment. What topped the sound of his own step was that of another step coming from directly behind him. When he turned around to get a look, Dave was just in time to see a figure reaching out for him like a monster from the shadows.

TWENTY-SIX

Nick's positioning was perfect. His steps were well timed and just quiet enough to go unnoticed beneath Barrett's typically overpowering voice. There was always something to mess things up, however, and the sudden unexpected silence had been just that.

When it came, it not only caught the deputy off-guard, but Nick as well. Both steps came in a rush, forcing Nick to take immediate action.

Nick rushed the deputy with both hands outstretched, having holstered his pistol to keep from bumping it against a wall or one of the protruding planks. When he came at the smaller deputy, he was already planning what it would take to put the lawman down and where he would toss him after doing so. Nick took hold of the deputy by the collar so he could pull him away from the shack. The possibility of keeping this quiet was still alive in Nick's mind and he wouldn't give it up unless it was absolutely necessary.

Although he did manage to get a good grip on the deputy's collar, Nick wasn't able to budge the man. It was almost as if the lawman's feet had grown roots into the ground.

The deputy had been caught off-guard, but his instinct was to cover up as best he could when he saw he was under attack. Now that the fight had commenced, Dave was able to get his wits about him and start fighting back. His attacker's grip was strong and his face was still obscured by the shadows, but Dave didn't need to see the man's face to know that he had to have a body to go along with it. With that in mind, he knew exactly where to send his fist when he drove it up in a sharp jab.

The chopping blow caught Nick just below the rib cage and seemed to plow right through his innards. He was too close to the deputy to have seen the punch coming and felt his breath fly out of him in a grunting wheeze.

Now, it was Dave's turn to try and get ahold of the man who'd ambushed him. He still wanted to hear what was going on inside the shack, so he did his best to keep as quiet as possible when he grabbed hold of the other man's shoulder and started to straighten up.

Nick felt the deputy's knee slam into his lower abdomen, just an inch or so above the groin. He couldn't help but let out a grunt that could be heard even over the rush of blood through his ears.

"What was that?" came a voice that Nick recognized as Morrison's.

Before the outlaw could get to the window, Nick dredged up all the strength he could muster and wrapped both arms around the deputy's midsection. All the years of digging those graves finally paid off when Nick was able to lift Dave off his feet just long enough to move the deputy away from the window and push him against the wall of the neighboring shack.

Dave's back slammed hard against the rotting wood. Nick felt the man struggling, but the deputy was too confused for the moment to know how to get out of the hold. By the time he realized what was happening he was being shoved back again.

Now that he'd gotten a chance to stand toe to toe with the deputy, Nick realized just how badly he'd misjudged Dave's size. Dave actually stood about as tall as him, with a bit more bulk around the middle. What surprised Nick even more was the fact that the deputy had still managed to keep hold of his gun throughout the entire scuffle.

That fact hit Dave at the same moment and he started to bring the gun up to end the struggle once and for all. Neither one of them were concerned about stealth any longer. That worry had been replaced by the fight to stay alive and Dave meant to win it with one well-placed bullet.

Seeing the glint of dim light against iron, Nick snapped his hand out and across with the same speed he would have used to draw his modified Schofield. The flat of his hand caught the side of Dave's pistol, knocking the gun to one side while also causing the deputy to pull his trigger.

When the gun went off, it let out a roar that filled the space between the two shacks with thunder and sparks that briefly illuminated both men's faces. The deputy strained to get a look at his attacker, but Nick's first impulse was to turn away from the light to keep himself from being seen.

While he hadn't asked for Barrett's efforts to remove that notice from the sheriff's records, Nick didn't want to waste it either.

The sound of footsteps pounding against floorboards was getting louder by the second. It was a matter of a short time only before the outlaws came spilling from the shack and the entire situation became a whole lot uglier.

There was only one thing for Nick to do to keep the night from being coated in blood. Turning his back on the deputy, Nick drove his elbow into the man's gut and felt it sink in as far as it could go. With his other hand, he drew the Schofield and fired off a quick round at Morrison who was peeking out of the shack.

"Jesus Christ!" Sheriff Trayner grunted. "What the hell happened to that fool?"

Hyde was already moving toward the shack, sighting down the barrel of his pistol even though he didn't have a firm target in sight. He squeezed off a round before Trayner rushed past him. Before he could take another shot, however, he was pulled off-balance as the sheriff took hold of his sleeve and pulled him along.

"Save your ammo for them bastards inside," Trayner growled. "You might just hit Dave, unless he's been hit already."

The sheriff kept hold of his deputy until they were almost across the street. From there, he shoved Hyde in one direction and turned himself toward the other. "Try to get in through the back," Trayner ordered. "And for Christ's sake, look before you fire next time!"

Hyde nodded quickly and kept jogging in the direction in which he'd been shoved. He could hear men's voices coming from within the shack. There was another gunshot, but it was hard to tell where it originated. The gunshot that followed, however, was most definitely from the men inside the shack. That bullet chipped at the corner of one window and hissed through the air as it came toward Hyde like an angry wasp.

It was all Hyde could do to duck fast enough to keep from getting hit. He felt the sting of hot lead ripping through his skin, but it was a grazing wound and no more than a scratch. He reflexively sent a round into the shack, wincing as the sheriff's warning echoed through his mind.

But it was too late to worry about Sheriff Trayner. As far as Hyde was concerned, it was every man for himself. If one of those men was too dumb to duck when the shooting started, then he deserved to get hit. At least, that excuse was good enough to make Hyde feel justified about firing off another shot.

Trayner kept his head down and hustled toward the shack's front door. He kept his gun at hip level and his finger tight upon the trigger. From there, all he could do was keep alert and hope for the best.

When Barrett had stopped talking only moments ago, it had just been to take a breath. Since that single breath, all hell had broken loose.

Looking around the room, he saw that both Morrison and Guile had drawn their weapons and were pressed flat up against a wall. Barrett followed suit and was soon sitting on the floor with the others, wincing as something heavy slammed against the outside of the shack.

"Well," Guile said with a crooked smirk, "it looks like you were right about someone being out there."

Morrison was squatting with his back to a wall. His eyes were staring so hard at a spot on one of the other walls that they almost burned holes through it. "Cover me," he grunted as he thumbed back the hammer of his Colt and moved toward the window to get a look.

The other two nodded and positioned themselves to do so. But before Morrison could get close enough to get a look outside, a gunshot blasted from the darkness and knocked out a section of the window he'd been approaching. That brought Morrison reflexively to the floor and then scooting back to the spot where he'd started.

Once again, Guile smirked. Of all three of the men, he actually seemed to be the one savoring every moment since the chaos had begun. "What's wrong? I had you covered."

The smirk changed shape ever so slightly as Guile's eyes snapped up from Morrison to get a look at the window behind the other man. That window faced the street, which had been quiet so far. What had caught his attention was the face of someone peeking through the glass. He took a shot at that face before he could think twice about it.

"What the hell are you doin'?" Morrison asked, while ducking down and pointing his gun at Guile.

Although Guile was still smiling, there was a bit more tension etched into his expression this time. "We could be surrounded. Some hideout, Barrett. Did you leave our address when you paid the law a visit?"

"Are you sure it was the law?" Barrett asked.

"Who else could it be?"

"It doesn't rightly matter anymore, does it?"

Morrison nodded. "He's got a point. There's two doors out of here, so —"

"Make that three," Barrett interrupted. He gritted his teeth at the sound of another heavy impact coming from the alley around back of the house. By this point, he could also hear Sheriff Trayner shouting orders to one of his deputies. "There's three doors out of here. I'm standing on the other one."

"All right, then," Morrison said. "That's even better. Since it looks like they'll be rushing inside at any moment, I say we beat 'em to the punch."

Guile raised his gun and nodded happily. "You think anyone else knows about that third door?"

Barrett shook his head as a mischievous grin crept onto his face.

"On the count of three, then," Morrison said.

Outside, the sounds of heavy impacts, footsteps, and desperate voices filled the air. Those sounds, combined with the acrid gun smoke, made the air thick as soup.

"One . . ."

Barrett thumbed back the hammer of his own pistol and sucked in a deep breath.

". . . two . . ."

Guile and Morrison each held their guns at the ready. Barrett dug his finger beneath a tattered cloth that had been serving as a carpet and found the notched board that he'd discovered when originally scouting for the hideout. It wasn't so much of a trapdoor as a few planks that were so rotted and loose that they could be pulled up to allow access to the crawl space under the shack.

". . . three!"

TWENTY-SEVEN

Nick might not have known exactly what was going on inside that shack, but he did know Barrett was in there. If he'd learned anything during his years of riding with that schemer, he'd learned what was going on inside of Barrett's head. At that moment, Nick would have bet everything he owned that it was only a matter of seconds before Barrett made his escape from that shack.

Barrett was never one to back off from a fight, but he wasn't the type to charge into a firing squad. After adding a bit of incentive himself, Nick knew that Barrett was making good on his escape at that very moment. He couldn't be so sure about Guile and Morrison, but Nick's guess was that they would follow Barrett's move.

The deputy Nick had ambushed was trying to signal Trayner or one of the other lawmen. "Over h—" was all the deputy could get out before his words were cut off by a quick jab from Nick into his ribs.

Nick pushed forward with both feet and knocked Dave one more time against the wall of the neighboring shack. Although the impact did weaken the deputy a bit, it weakened the wall even more until it finally buckled and gave way, allowing both men to crash right through.

Dave's finger tightened around his trigger upon impact. It was nothing more than a reflexive twitch, but the consequences were much more serious. His gun blasted once, sending a bullet through the bottom flap of Nick's coat. Sparks from the barrel sprayed over the heavy cotton and set the bottom part of the coat on fire. Unfortunately, Nick and the deputy were both too distracted to notice the flicker of little flames beneath their field of vision.

Dull pain flowed through Dave's back after being slammed through the wall. That impact was soon followed by another that was much more solid and made it damn near impossible for him to breathe. It took a few moments before he realized that the world had been set on its side and he'd actually fallen backward onto the ground. Breathing became a chore and only luck could explain how he'd managed to keep from knocking his head any harder than he did.

Nick's hand locked around the deputy's wrist. His only thought was to get the gun away from the man before Dave got a chance to truly take aim. Although he did maintain a decent grip, the deputy merely had to twist his wrist and pull to escape through Nick's mangled fingers.

As much as he tried to get a look at his attacker's face, there was simply not enough light to see much more than shapes and shadows. Enough dust had been knocked loose when that wall came down to fill both men's eyes with grit and set them to burning. Dave didn't need to see much for him to send his gun smashing into the skull of the man who'd attacked him.

Turning his head away reflexively, Nick was barely able to dodge the brunt of Dave's incoming blow. The butt of the deputy's pistol grazed Nick's head and rattled him just enough for the deputy to toss him to one side.

Nick landed with a grunt and felt every bit of broken lumber, trash, or glass that had been littering the ground beneath him. He took a moment to appreciate how much protection his coat had given him, but that appreciation was only too short-lived. It lasted right up until the moment he felt the back of his legs burning.

He was out of the coat in a heartbeat. Jumping to his feet, Nick spun and saw the deputy propping himself up on one arm and swiping at his eyes so he could take a clear shot. When he'd gotten rid of enough of the dirt and tears that blurred his vision, Dave found a burning length of dark brown material being swung toward his head.

Actually, Nick had aimed to swing well over the deputy's head and hoped that the lawman had enough of his wits about him to duck. The burning coat rustled through the air toward Dave as the flames licked out in all directions. The lawman dropped down in plenty of time to let it pass over him, which put him in perfect position for Nick to let the coat go and rush forward.

Nick closed the distance between them in two steps and dropped his boot down onto the man's gun on the third. Using the side of his other foot, Nick pushed Dave over with relative ease. He then stooped down and picked up the deputy's gun, feeling no small amount of pride as he did so. Unfortunately, there was one more surprise in store for him.

Behind the deputy, smoke rose up from the ground as a pile of rubbish and broken shingles coaxed a sputtering flame to life. The coat had landed well away from the deputy, just as Nick had intended, but it hadn't stopped burning. In fact, the flames were now greedily spreading themselves across the back of the room.

Not only had the deputy managed to get up again by this time, but Dave was also reaching for the gun in Nick's holster. Before he could do anything about it, Nick's Schofield was gone and a victorious gleam flickered in Dave's eye.

Breathless from the exertion of the fight as well as the smoke that was joining with the dust to fill the room, Dave raised the gun while squinting through the murky shadow. "Don't move. I've got —"

But that was all the lawman could get out before Nick ducked and moved sharply to his right. He knew the quick movement would probably force the deputy to take a shot at him. Actually, he'd been counting on it.

Sure enough, Dave's finger tightened reflexively upon the trigger. The only problem was that the gun's gnarled handle didn't come close to settling against his palm and the odd, splintered trigger only made matters worse. When the Schofield went off, it sent its bullet well off the mark. Not only that, but the gun was sitting so awkwardly in Dave's grip that the blast nearly jerked the pistol clean out of his hand.

Nick hadn't stopped moving during this time and had even managed to step around the deputy and get behind him. From there, Nick used the gun he'd taken to deliver a quick, chopping blow to the back of the deputy's head.

Letting out a surprised grunt, Dave dropped onto his stomach and let Nick's gun slide from his grasp.

Nick scooped up his weapon, dropped it into his holster and took another look at the fire. The flames were spreading, but seemed to be confined to the pile of junk that had caught the initial spark. If he was going to make that fire work for him without burning down the rest of Bitter Creek in the process, Nick would have to work fast.

At times like these, he wished he would have learned more from Barrett about planning.

Sheriff Trayner had been shouting his orders to Hyde, praying that the deputy was actually listening. It was too late to worry about stealth any longer because the lawmen had been trading shots through the windows with the men inside the shack for a while now. It had reached the point where they hardly thought about firing their guns anymore.

After the first shot came at him through the window, Trayner had been sending in a few of his own every so often. His hope was to keep the problem contained long and wrapped up quickly. The last thing he wanted was a running gun battle to claim any innocent lives.

"Dammit, Hyde, get in there!" Trayner said. "Dave! Where the hell are you?"

Hyde ducked as a shot came through the glass. "They're ready for us!" he replied, doing his best to try and hide the fear that had brought him to the point of paralysis. "Come over here and we'll both go in."

The firing from inside the shack had stopped for the moment, so Trayner took the opportunity to get a look at Hyde. That was the only way he could tell if the deputy was going to be worth anything or if he needed to go it alone. Although the deputy was definitely rattled, he was still at least trying to get a grip on himself.

"All right," Trayner shouted toward the wall at his back. "I know you're in there, Cobb. I didn't come here to kill you, but I'll do it if you force me to. Toss out them guns and come out so we can end this without any blood getting spilled."

The sheriff waited and was about to give another ultimatum when something else caught his attention. Sniffing the air, he started to glance nervously back and forth. "Jesus," he whispered. "That smells like smoke."

"Sheriff?" came Hyde's voice. "Do you smell that?"

"Yeah."

"I think the next building over is on fire."

Trayner, who also happened to be on Bitter Creek's fire brigade, dashed around Barrett's shack to get a look at the source of the smoke. Just as he rounded the corner, he spotted the shattered wall that had smoke trickling out of it. Before he could go any farther, a figure stepped through the smoke and shadows.

The sheriff's first impulse was to raise his weapon, even though his only thought was that the figure had to be someone escaping the flames. There was just something about the figure, however, that made Trayner's hackles rise up. That's when he realized the figure was dragging something behind him.

No . . . actually, he was dragging some*one.*

"I think this one belongs to you," the figure said in a voice that had become rough from the smoke. With that, the figure dragged Dave another step forward and dropped him onto the ground.

The sheriff's face contorted into a mask of rage as he looked at what he thought was his deputy's dead body. Just as he was about to avenge the fallen lawman, the air was filled with the sound of boards rattling and boots pounding against the dirt. Only a split second before that had come Barrett's voice shouting out one word.

"Three," the outlaw had hollered.

Suddenly, armed men came swarming out from beneath the shack like ants. Trayner and Hyde pivoted to aim their pistols at the outlaws as a series of shots filled the air.

Lead hissed from the smoky building next door as sparks leapt from the side of Guile's gun. The bullet came from the shadows and bounced off the steel in Guile's hand. He dropped his weapon reflexively and then stooped down to pick it up again a moment later.

Another shot from the same shadows punched a hole in the dirt next to the lawmen's feet, forcing both the sheriff and his deputy to leap back from the shack.

When Trayner took another look toward the smoky building, the dark figure was no longer there. Instead, Dave lay on the ground, struggling to pull in a breath and get to his feet.

"Dave!" Trayner shouted. "You're alive! Hyde, cover me while I fetch him."

Hyde hadn't heard all of the sheriff's command, but had managed to catch the important part. Lifting his gun, he fanned the hammer to send a spray of lead through the air toward the oncoming outlaws. One of the bullets took a chunk from Guile's side, but the rest blasted holes into the closest wall as the gun was knocked this way and that by Hyde's flailing hand.

When Morrison had left the shack, he found himself in a very tenable position at the lawmen's backs. He took his time and lined up his shot, meaning to kill both of the other two before they could cause any more trouble. The smoke from the fire was getting thicker and just as he was about to pull his trigger, Morrison heard a gunshot blast through the air from the smoke behind him.

Morrison dropped to the ground and rolled toward the other neighboring building, which was when he met up with Barrett.

"What the hell happened here, Barrett?" Morrison asked as they both backed into an alley. "I thought you said this place was safe."

"It was."

"It sure don't look that way to me."

Another series of gunshots blasted through the air, followed by the sound of quickly approaching steps. By the time the steps reached Barrett and Morrison, both men had their guns aimed at the sound and were prepared to fire. When they saw who it was, they relaxed their fingers upon their triggers.

"I gotta hand it to you, Barrett," Guile said with his familiar smirk. "You sure know how to throw a party."

"Shut up, both of you," Barrett snarled. "Let's get the hell out of here."

"What about them lawmen?" Morrison asked.

Guile shook his head. "I wouldn't worry about them. They've got a fire to keep them busy."

"I guess that's it for us in this town," Morrison said angrily as he and the other two started sneaking away from the scene of the fight. When he heard Barrett laughing, he asked, "What's so funny?"

"Nothing at all. It's just that you're thinking exactly what those lawmen are probably thinking."

"And what's that?" Guile asked, panning his gun around as he moved and aiming at any little sound he heard.

"That we'd be fools to stick around here after barely escaping with our lives. At the very least, they won't think we'd be ready to do anything as soon as tomorrow afternoon. And even if they did, they've got themselves a hell of a mess to clean up, which should keep them occupied while we take care of our business with Mr. Finch." Shaking his head, Barrett added, "I only wish Nick could have been here for this."

TWENTY-EIGHT

Nick shook his head as he stood nearby and watched as Sheriff Trayner and his deputies got to work on the fire he'd started. Although he'd done his best to keep anyone from getting killed, Nick sure hadn't meant for things to turn out like this. Even as he'd fired from the shadows to protect the lawmen, Nick couldn't help but send a few rounds to help Barrett as well.

Looking back on it as Trayner rushed to put out the fire, Nick wondered exactly whose side he was on. Just when it seemed that he'd chosen, the opposite part of him reared up and made itself known.

He knew Barrett and those other two gunmen were more than ready to send a sheriff and a few deputies to their graves. That was why Nick had stepped in to prevent the lawmen from stumbling in and poking a hornet's nest.

If they had busted in on that hideout, they

all would have been killed for certain. Barrett wasn't much of a shot when they'd first met up, but he'd learned plenty during his years with Nick and the rest of the gang. That much was certain because Nick had been the one to show Barrett around a piece of iron.

The events of that night had made Nick certain of something else.

Trayner was a good man.

All Nick had to do was watch what a man did to figure what was going on inside his head. Sure, folks may say plenty of things, but it always boiled down to what they did. So far, Nick may not have gotten along too well with the lawman, but Trayner hadn't done much that wasn't outside his appointed duties. Nick had seen plenty of other lawmen who were more concerned about making a profit than actually helping folks.

Not only had Trayner done his level best to keep the fight under control, but he even risked his own skin to put out a fire when most anyone else would have been happy to see a bad part of town get erased from the map.

The lawman was brushing his hands together and clearing out his lungs in a series of hacking coughs as he stepped out through the hole that had been knocked into the side of the run-down building.

"That about does it," Trayner said.

Hyde came out next and was swiping his forehead with the back of his hand. "I didn't think we'd make it, Sheriff."

"It looked a lot worse than it was. From what Dave was saying, it was more of an accident than anything else. Damn lucky, too. If much else had gone up, we'd be standing in the middle of a burning town right about now. If I've told folks once, I've told them a thousand times, that places like this are just piles of kindling. All it takes is —"

Once he saw that the lawmen were alive and well and the fire was out, Nick turned his back on them and headed in the opposite direction. He may have felt some guilt for what happened, but he didn't consider listening to Trayner's tirade as part of his penance.

After putting some distance between himself and Barrett's shack, Nick started in on the task of finding the outlaws themselves. He didn't bother checking anyplace near the hideout since he knew they wouldn't be there. The outlaws would have either left town or found someplace else to hole up.

Barrett still had his job to do, so Nick

didn't have to ponder for too long about which of those choices the other man had taken. Now, the only task that remained was for Nick to find Barrett before any more shots were fired. Despite the difficulty of that chore, Nick couldn't help but feel confident.

No doubt about it, both he and Barrett had learned plenty every time they were lucky enough to live through another crime. One thing that Nick had learned was how Barrett thought. He knew when Barrett would fight and when he would run. He knew when he was bluffing and when Barrett was holding a full house. Hopefully, all of that knowledge would help him find Barrett now.

As Nick walked, he did his best to appear as though he hadn't been fighting for his life only a few minutes before. The people he passed once he got into the better parts of town were involved in their own affairs, so they paid him little or no attention anyway. Even so, Nick's blood was still pumping furiously through his veins and his heart was slamming against the inside of his chest.

His breaths were only just beginning to slow as he thought about what had just gone on. He'd gotten through worse scrapes, and had lived through worse beatings, but there was something different now. It would have been easier if he'd intended to kill anyone who got in his way. The choice to kill was always there, even as a last resort. This time, however, he hadn't wanted to kill any lawmen and he sure as hell hadn't wanted to see Barrett dead.

When he thought about that, Nick stopped in his tracks.

Memories of his outlaw past were bloody ones at best. Most of the people from those days fit on one of two lists: the list of people that wanted Nick dead or the list of people Nick wanted to kill. Barrett, on the other hand, didn't have a place on either list.

Barrett had always been a friend, even when doing his best to lead him astray. Barrett was still a friend, which was why Nick didn't just end the man's proposed crime spree with a quick bullet through the skull.

Nick never had many friends. They were too much trouble. Unfortunately, this time was no exception to that rule. If anything, it proved it.

Before long, Nick found himself in a familiar part of town that wasn't too far from the room he'd rented. The main saloon district was a ways off and the sounds from there filtered down the street to echo like ghosts in the night.

There were plenty of sounds to be heard in the buildings on either side of the street where Nick was walking at that moment. The sounds were of a different sort than the ones that had filled his ears earlier. There was more laughing than piano music and more of women's forced groans than gamblers hollering about being cheated. It was the whoring district, and it was such places that had always caught Barrett's attention. It was also just the sort of place that the old gang used to wind up in when they wanted to kick back and relax without worrying about getting hauled in by the law.

Whores always had a good handle on the law in their town and usually had intimate knowledge of the men upholding it. It was a relationship that kept them in business and nobody appreciated that relationship more than the lawless. The same soiled doves that bedded a sheriff would usually take even more pleasure in spending the night with a wanted man.

As he stepped onto the boardwalk, Nick pulled in a breath that smelled of perfume and cigar smoke. There was another scent in the air, lying just beneath the surface, and it went more along with the groans that could occasionally be heard from the upstairs rooms.

Nick glanced up toward those rooms to find ladies sitting up on the balconies in rockers or just dangling their feet off the side. If he met one of their gazes for long enough, Nick was given a little wave as well as a quick peek up the lady's skirts to go along with it. Deciding that he might as well start looking for his needle in the most likely haystack, Nick stepped into the closest cathouse and was swept into the arms of a full-figured redhead.

"Nice choice, stranger," she said in a sultry voice that came from two full, soft lips that were painted the color of fresh rose petals. "What can I do for you?"

"I'm looking for someone," Nick replied.

She winked and ran her hand flat against his chest. "You've found her."

"Actually, I was supposed to meet up with three men. They're armed."

"Men? Then I'd say you're in the wrong place. We're just a bunch of lonely ladies in here."

"Then you should probably remember these men," Nick insisted, feeling the redhead's hands start to work their way over his back. "They must've come down this street here not too long ago."

"You're armed," she said, easing her hand over his holster. "Should I be worried about you?"

"Well, no. It's just that —"

Before Nick could make a move or even finish his sentence, the redhead slipped her hand between Nick's legs. "I must be losing my touch if you're still thinking about finding some fellas with guns." Her eyes widened and she smiled broadly. "Nope. It seems I'm still doing just fine."

Nick looked around and saw that while some of the other ladies had found their own men to entice, some of them were also watching the redhead ply her trade. One of the women, a blonde, spotted something outside that seemed to catch her off-guard. The smile on her face faded as she walked to the door while pulling her wrap tighter around herself.

When the blonde walked by, Nick's redhead felt a touch on her shoulder and leaned back to catch a quick whisper from her.

"You want men with guns?" the redhead asked. "Maybe you should ask the sheriff."

Casually, Nick turned to look through the door that he'd just stepped through. He didn't recognize the man in the lead right away, but Nick had no trouble spotting the deputy walking beside him. The lawman wasn't moving at his best after his scuffle with Nick, but he was doing pretty well considering what he'd been put through. Sheriff Trayner was across the street, already poking his nose into one of the other cathouses there.

Although the expression on Nick's face hardly changed, his innards were screaming for him to move out of sight. Nick was at least 90 percent sure that none of the lawmen had gotten a good look at his face, but it was that other 10 percent that bothered him.

"What's your name, honey?" Nick asked after putting his back to the door.

The redhead looked away from the approaching lawmen and slipped her other hand around Nick's waist. "Everyone calls me Lizzy. What should I call you?"

Turning so he could step away from the front door, Nick smiled sheepishly and took off his hat. "Call me weak-willed, I guess," he said. "Why don't you take me somewhere we can be alone."

Lizzy took Nick's hat from him and hung it on a hook next to the door. "Right up those stairs and to the left, Will. My room's the first open door. It's the one with the big, soft bed."

Nick's eyes followed Lizzy's hand as she left his hat hanging where anyone in the front room of the cathouse could see it. The brim was a bit charred and the rest of it still reeked of smoke. He didn't make a big production out of getting it back, however, since the two deputies were now coming straight for the front door and would run into Nick at any moment.

Even if Nick meant to stay downstairs, it was doubtful he would be able to get away from Lizzy anyhow. Her fingers had locked around his wrist and she was dragging him up the stairs. When Nick turned to look up at her, the shift of her hips and the way she tossed her hair back to look at him made him want to escape from the redhead even less.

"Just like I said," Lizzy told him while stopping so she could push Nick ahead of her. "First open door that way. I'll be along in a minute. I've just got to tell Nadine that I'll be busy for a little while."

Heading in the direction he'd been shown, Nick waited until Lizzy walked down the hall. After she gave him a little wave and stepped into the room that was probably the madam's office, Nick took another glance downstairs.

One thing he had to admit: those lawmen

had done a hell of a job putting out the fire. They'd gotten the job done quicker than he'd anticipated and had somehow managed to head Nick off at the pass. While those were good marks for the lawmen, they were sore spots for Nick. Already, he could hear one of the deputies asking about any suspicious characters that had come into the cathouse. Nick just managed to pull himself out of sight when the tall deputy shot a glance up the stairs.

"Come on, Will," Lizzy said as she left the madam's room and took Nick by the hand. "I've got some fun planned for you."

"Good," Nick said. "I could sure use some."

TWENTY-NINE

"A lot of men come through here, Dave," said the woman wearing a blouse that hung open just enough to put her generous cleavage on display.

Dave was battered and bruised. He walked with a slight limp, but that was fading with every step. What stuck out about him the most was the fact that his face and hands were covered with a thick layer of soot. He even smelled like a fire, since he'd been the one to spend the most time inside that burning building.

Even so, the deputy did a good job of maintaining his composure. Part of that came from the fact that he was so tired he could barely stand up anymore.

"I know plenty of men come through here, Emma," Dave said. "But the one I'm looking for nearly killed me tonight. What do you think about that?"

The brunette with the impressive body

reached out to tap her finger playfully against Dave's chest. "I think you've got a way of blowing things out of proportion, Dave. Remember that time you said you ran in a bunch of bank robbers single-handed? If I recall, they almost killed you as well."

"That was different."

"Yes," came a voice that cut into the conversation like a warm knife through butter. "That was very different. It's different because I say so." Sheriff Trayner stomped onto the cathouse's front porch. He was covered in soot as well, but he wore his the way a peacock wore its feathers. "When a lawman asks you a question, it's best to answer him. Or would you rather I shut this place down and tell Nadine that you're the reason why?"

The brunette rolled her eyes and said, "Wait here. I'll ask around."

The moment she turned her back on the sheriff, Trayner leaned over to his deputy and uttered, "You can't let whores call the shots. You gotta tell them what to do. That's what they get paid for."

Standing no more than a few feet from the front door, Emma gritted her teeth when she heard those words come from Trayner's mouth. The other working girls had heard them as well and all of them looked to the brunette to see how she would respond. Rather than throw the fit the others had been expecting, Emma took a breath and went over to the small bar in the drawing room.

Dave followed her inside, having noticed that one of the other girls was taking a man upstairs. "Who is that?" he asked, jabbing a finger toward the couple.

The girl closest to him was dressed more conservatively than the rest and kept her brown hair tied in a bun. She was too young to work for the real money, but Nadine kept her on to help clean and make the guests feel comfortable. Looking slowly in the direction Dave was pointing, she said, "Who? Oh. That's Lizzy."

"Who's with her?"

Again, the young girl took an extended amount of time to answer. Finally, she gave him a shrug.

Dave stepped around her and shot a look up the stairs. Although he knew he'd seen someone up there with the redhead, the figure was already gone. When he started to move toward the stairs, he was distracted by the sheriff's voice.

"Dave!" Trayner shouted. "Go see what's keeping that whore."

Some of the other girls were starting to

get anxious. Seeing this, Emma placed a finger to her lips and poured herself a drink. Now that it was obvious she was killing time, the girls closed in behind her so the lawmen couldn't see what she was doing. After she'd finished her drink, she stepped through the wall of perfumed women and put a disarming smile on her painted lips.

"Nobody's seen anyone suspicious tonight, Sheriff," she announced. "What makes you think someone like that would come here, anyway?"

"Because I've been dogging Cobb's trail since he got to town, that's how," Trayner said. "He likes to frequent cathouses and this is one of them."

"What about the place across the way?"

"Already been there."

Just then, a set of footsteps thundering overhead caught everyone's attention and made all the lawmen's hands drift toward their guns. The figure that appeared at the top of the stairs was bulky and wide across the shoulders. However, judging by the massive breasts and rounded hips, was a long cry from being the man Trayner had expected.

"Maybe you should try the place across the street," the large woman offered. "They cater to the sort of clientele that you're usually after, Trayner."

Sheriff Trayner stepped further into the room and even removed his hat when he saw the big-breasted woman at the top of the stairs. "Already tried there, Nadine. In fact, that was the first place I looked."

"Then why don't you try asking what you want to know in a civil tongue? You may get better results that way."

"I'm always civil. Especially to ladies."

The deputy smirked and stepped back to allow the sheriff to step forward.

Walking slowly down the steps, Nadine stopped halfway and leaned against the banister. "Civil? I didn't hear all of what you said, but I heard you call one of my girls a whore. That's not very nice."

But it was true. That's what Sheriff Trayner was thinking and although he didn't say so out loud, the expression on his face said more than enough. After a pause that said even more, he shrugged. "I let you run this place without a hitch, when I could just as easily shut you down. The least I could get is a bit of cooperation. Most men in my position would ask for a hell of a lot more."

Walking down the rest of the stairs, Nadine carried herself like a queen. She kept her head high and when she got to the sheriff, she even backed him down from the few steps he'd climbed. "What is it you want to know, George?" The way she tossed his common name about not only wiped the telling look off of Trayner's face, but made a statement to everyone in that room as well.

Trayner looked past the indiscretion and said, "Tall fella. Scars on his face. Short, brown hair. He runs with a few others. They'd all be armed and in a hurry."

Just then, Dave leaned over to speak directly into the sheriff's ear. When he was done, he stepped back again to let the sheriff continue what he was saying.

"Seems there was another fella as well. Taller. Lean. He's probably covered in as much soot as Dave over here. He's gotta stink of fire. Any of this ringing any bells?"

Nadine shrugged. "Not for me. What about you girls? Have you seen a man fitting that description?"

Both the sheriff and Nadine looked at the girls one at a time. And, one by one, the girls shook their heads or voiced a similarly negative response. When her eyes came back to Trayner, Nadine shrugged again.

"There you have it," she said. "Happy?"

"Not as happy as whoever is upstairs. You think I could get a look for myself?"

"Come on now. A place like this prides

itself on privacy. I can't have folks busting in on the rooms unless they got a good reason. From what I saw just now, you don't have a very good reason."

Trayner stepped onto the same step as Nadine. Now that they were on even ground, it was plain to see just how much taller the sheriff was as compared to the busty madam. "I've tried to be nice here and all I'm getting is a bunch of sass from you and your girls," he said. "If I was short with you or anyone else, it's just because me and my men have been through hell tonight.

"You're a good woman, Nadine. I've never had a problem with you. In fact, we've had some good times over the years. But if you've started giving comfort to outlaws, then I'm afraid I'll have to overlook those good times. Now I'll ask once more. Have you seen the fella I described or any others that were carrying guns or even ones that didn't look familiar. I'm looking for more than one man, after all."

The madam glanced around to the others once more. This time, the look on her face was more sincere. The same thing couldn't quite be said, however, about some of the looks she got in return.

"None of my girls are speaking up, Sheriff," Nadine replied. "So that means they've got nothing to say. And if you want to start barging into rooms, I'd suggest you start at some other place. If I hear you got all the others to agree to something like that, then I'll let you be my guest."

Trayner stopped and listened. He took a look around for himself until his eyes finally wound up on his deputy. "Where'd Hyde go?"

"Down the way a piece to the place down the block."

Trayner nodded. "Then I'll pick up on the other end of the street. We can cover more ground that way."

"So we're taking this who—" Dave was stopped short by a quick, stern look from Trayner. "We're taking her word for it then?"

"For now." Turning to look down his nose at Nadine, he added, "And don't think I won't be back here right quick if I don't find who I'm after. I know well enough that at least one of that gang is holing up in one of these places. They're killers I'm talking about, Nadine. Not the sort of fellas you'd even want to have in your place."

"I'll take your word for it, Sheriff. Oh, and one more thing." Dropping her voice, the madam took hold of the front of

Trayner's shirt and pulled him a little closer to her mouth. "Treat women like ladies and they'll be more apt to help you out. Keep that in mind before you talk to any of the other girls like they were something you'd scrape off your boot."

"I'll try to keep that in mind," Trayner said in a voice to match Nadine's whisper. "And I trust that if you do find out anything, you'll come find me. I wouldn't want to clean up this part of town the way every sewing circle in Bitter Creek's been asking of me."

The two stepped back and headed in their own directions. Dave hadn't been able to hear what Nadine had said to the sheriff and none of the girls had heard how Trayner had talked to her. That was the way it had been intended and it helped both of them to save face in front of those who looked up to them.

"Stay close," Trayner said to his deputy as he headed back down the stairs and out the front door. "You check the places on either side of this one and I'll take the ones at the other end of the street. With all the poker parlors, cathouses, and opium dens around here, we're bound to stumble across the men we're after. If not," he said, glancing over his shoulder to Nadine, who was already at the top of the stairs, "I'll know where to come for the next round of questions. And next time, I doubt I'll be in such a good mood."

Thirty

Nadine kept her face straight as she watched the lawmen move out the front door. Even before the deputy left, she turned on her heels and started moving down the hall. There were eight doors apart from the one leading to her office and she started knocking on them one at a time.

A few were unoccupied, but the rest were locked up tight. When she got close enough to press her ear to a door, Nadine knocked lightly in a pattern that identified her to whichever girl was inside. At each door, she leaned in close and asked the same question.

"Everything all right in there?"

The responses were the same, each one of them containing a specific word to let her know that things truly were doing just fine. Some of the girls rolled their eyes at Nadine's safety measures when they first came to work for her. But that attitude changed very quickly the first time they were able to signal for help when trying to get out from under some cowboy who meant to put them into a world of hurt.

Nadine had been in the business long enough to know that all a girl needed was to be able to get the word out to prevent a whole lot of pain. Once she was done making her rounds upstairs, Nadine was satisfied that her girls weren't in any immediate danger.

Unfortunately, that feeling ended when she heard the footsteps stomping up the stairs. She quickly turned and headed in that direction so she could get there before the deputy started messing up her night's business.

"Can I help you with something, Dave?" she asked.

The deputy was almost on the second floor and appeared to be weighing the possibility of shoving Nadine aside so he could move on. Every time he shifted to get a look past the madam, she shifted right along with him.

"What're you hiding up there?" Dave asked.

"Just keeping you from scaring away my customers. I've got enough competition around here without the law walking in on my clients when they've got their bare asses in the air."

"What were you doing just now?"

"Checking on my girls. If there's anything wrong, they would have told me. Haven't I always cooperated with the sheriff and his boys?"

Dave was still in a foul mood, but nodded all the same.

Nadine took a closer look at him. The deputy was tall enough that, even standing on the second to top stair, she was still looking directly into his eyes. "You look like you've been through hell, Davey."

"I have."

"Then why don't you take a nice bath and have someone rub those shoulders? Wouldn't that feel nice? I think Stormy is free right now. I know how much you like her and I'll just bet she'd be happy to take care of you."

Dave's smile came like a reflex when he thought about Stormy's slender figure and her long, black hair. But he shook it off and tried to get his mind back on to official business. "I don't have time for none of that."

"Then why don't you take a drink downstairs? That should settle your nerves."

For a moment, it looked as though Dave was going to accept the drink as well as everything else that came along with it. Then, his eyes narrowed and he pulled in a quick, sniffing breath. "Something burning up here?" he asked.

Nadine smelled the air before shaking her head. "Just for the paying customers," she replied with a wink. "Only thing that smells like fire up here is you."

"Yeah, but something else stinks. Kind of smells like someone else was up here reeking of smoke."

"I told you that you need a bath."

"And you seem awfully anxious to get me out of here. You used to harbor bad men in here. You and your girls like those types, don't you? You like sharing your bed with gunmen. I know plenty of your girls who'd open their legs for free if they saw a known criminal come through that door."

Nadine placed her hands upon her hips. "Didn't you hear what I said to George? Badge or not, I don't like it when people talk about my girls like that."

"And I don't like it when someone tries to hide something from me. I've had too rough of a night to put up with this shit, so stand aside and let me take a look for myself at what's going on in these rooms."

"Do you really think I'd hide someone from you?"

Dave didn't answer. Instead, he kept his gaze fixed upon the madam and started to move the rest of the way up the stairs.

Rather than try to shove him back, Nadine stepped aside. She knew that putting him off any longer would only add fuel to the fire. Besides, she wasn't about to get her place shut down just to protect some man that Lizzy had taken a liking to. That didn't mean that she was completely helpless, however.

"Go on, then," Nadine said, stepping so that she was blocking off the half of the hall that was more occupied and giving Dave free access to the other half. "But just so you know, I'll be letting the sheriff know anything you do to upset my business. Honest folk don't have to put up with this sort of thing."

"You're right," Dave said as he marched past her. "They don't."

Starting at the end of the hall, Dave walked up to the closest door and tugged on the handle. When he discovered it to be locked, he pounded on it with his fist and demanded to be let inside. Nadine let out a flustered sigh and rushed over to him so she could unlock the door herself before it got knocked off its hinges.

■ ■ ■ ■

"I don't know who you are," Lizzy said with an excited gleam in her eyes, "but you sure as hell got the law plenty riled up."

"What makes you think it was me?" Nick asked as he peered through the room's only window and at the street below.

"Either you've got something to do with this, or you know someone who does. Either way, you don't act like someone would act who isn't involved."

"I guess you've got me there."

Nick had seen the sheriff walk into the cathouse from the street. He'd also watched Trayner storm back out again minutes later, all from the post he'd taken at the window. While he couldn't hear what was being said in the room below, Nick could feel enough tension in the air to guess what all the fuss was about.

The entire time Nick had been looking through the window and straining to hear what was being said on the floor below, Lizzy had been watching him intently. Every so often, she would lick her lips while slowly peeling the clothes from her body. So far, Nick hadn't acted like an interested customer, but she could tell he liked what he saw whenever he did look her way. More than that, however, she felt a certain chill run over her flesh the closer she got to him.

"What did you do?" she asked.

Nick looked over at her. When he saw that she was down to nothing but a flimsy slip and her high-heeled boots, he couldn't help but keep his eyes on her a bit longer. "What do you mean by that?"

"The sheriff's looking for you, isn't he? That's why you're hiding up here instead of letting me get you out of those clothes. Is that why Nadine was checking up on me? Is that why you came here?"

"I just wanted to know if you saw any armed men come through here."

"Yeah?" the redhead asked, slipping up next to Nick and running her hands over him. "Well I'm looking at an armed man right now." Her hand slid down to rub his Schofield before wandering once again between his legs. "You can keep your gun nearby if you like," she purred. "I don't mind."

Despite everything going on, Nick was still a man with a pulse and that meant he had no choice but to react to the attentions Lizzy was showering on him. He felt her hands move along his chest and back down again. He also watched as she lowered herself onto her knees in front of him. Soon, she was taking down his pants while keeping her gaze fixed upon his eyes.

"Someone's coming," she whispered. "I can hear their steps out in the hall."

Nick tried to concentrate on the noises outside the door, but was finding it increasingly difficult.

Smiling at his growing frustration, Lizzy un-tucked his shirt and slipped her hands along Nick's bare stomach. "I can help, but you'll have to trust me."

"Trust you? Why should I?"

Lizzy seemed to grow even more excited when Nick tried to resist her. "Because I can tell a lot about a man just by watching him. A girl in my line of work needs to be able to do that. And I like you a hell of a lot more than any of those limp-dick deputies."

"Is that a fact?" Nick said, allowing himself to be moved closer to the bed. "That still doesn't tell me why I should trust you."

"Because if I didn't like you, I could have handed you over to the law way back when that knock came on my door."

Nick listened for a moment at the sound of heavy footsteps in the hallway. The pounding was getting closer, as was the deputy's familiar, gruff voice. Closing his hand around the specially modified grip of his Schofield, Nick said, "Actually, I think I'd rather handle this my own way."

Lizzy stood up and pressed herself tightly against him. "Please," she whispered intently. "Just give my way a chance."

Dave worked his way from one door to another. Although the first few were difficult to get open, they started coming open faster after that. Most of the action inside the rooms was coming to a stop after all the noise he'd made. Of course, the fact that Nadine was now helping him didn't hurt matters.

Nadine wasn't exactly happy about it, but she was helping all the same.

"Is there any other way out of those rooms?" Dave asked as he stepped into Nadine's office and started poking around.

The madam followed him into her room and tried to cut him off before he started knocking things over. "Like what? Some kind of secret doors?"

"Yeah."

"Come on, Dave! This is a cathouse, not something out of a yellowback novel."

Dave walked behind Nadine's desk and pulled open a closet. There was nothing inside but stacks of papers and a few boxes on the floor. Some clothes hung from a rack, but the rest of the space was taken up with supplies and linens.

When Dave felt a hand pull him away from the closet, he stepped back and spun around to get a look at the madam. "This room looks clean. Only a few more left."

"Are you really going to look inside those others? Is that really necessary?"

"Yeah. It is."

"Fine. Then at least let me unlock the doors myself before you pound on them. You've already done enough damage. Besides, you damn near gave poor old Mr. Adams a fit when you busted in on him."

It had only been a few moments ago, but Dave had already tried to put the image of the old man's naked body on top of that pretty blonde out of his mind. "Okay. But just open the door and step aside."

"Jesus Christ Almighty," Nadine grumbled as she led Dave from her office. "I swear I am going to throw a fit the next time I talk to Sheriff Trayner about this and believe you me I will definitely be talking to him about this."

"I'm only doing my job, Nadine. The men we're after are dangerous and if we don't find them soon, they'll either get away or settle in somewhere until they can't be found again."

"Sure, sure."

"One of 'em almost killed me, Nadine. What do you think about that?"

The madam had already gone past the top of the stairs and was about to unlock the first door when she turned to look at the deputy over her shoulder. "You said these men had guns?"

Dave nodded.

"Then how come they didn't shoot you? If you tussled with one of them how come you didn't get shot? Hell, I bet even I could have shot you if I had half a chance and was this close to you."

Dave's eyes narrowed and he paused as if it was the first time he'd really thought about what had happened. Then, the anger came back to him and he closed his fist around the grip of his gun. "Just open the damn door."

"This is Lizzy's room," Nadine said as she fussed with her ring of keys. "She's got a gentleman in here, so I know she won't want to be disturbed."

"Open it."

"I will, but if all you find is Lizzy and her customer doing their business, then you'll stop this nonsense once and for all. You understand me?"

Dave felt the hairs on the back of his neck

stand on end. Glancing down the hall, he could see that the other two doors were already opening and girls were peeking out. They looked more curious than anything else and the only door still closed was the one Nadine was unlocking.

"Fine."

"I swear," Nadine muttered as she fumbled with her keys, "if I lose business because of this harassment, I will raise more hell than even you could handle."

"Step aside," Dave said, even though he was already reaching out to push Nadine away from the door. He brought his foot up and thrust it straight out. By the time his heel slammed into the wood just above the door's handle, he'd already drawn his gun.

THIRTY-ONE

Dave broke through the door with enough force to send it slamming against the wall. The handle put a hole in that wall and jammed in among the splinters so the door was kept open as he took another step inside. Already, he was sighting down his barrel at the first person he could find.

"Oh my god!" Lizzy screamed.

Funny, but Dave was about to say the same thing.

Lizzy was sitting on the bed, with her back straight and her hair flowing over her shoulders. The dress she'd been wearing was on the floor and her slip was bunched up around her hips. Her long legs were clenched tightly around the man she was straddling who was lying on his back underneath her.

Smooth, milky skin filled the deputy's vision. All he could seem to focus on were Lizzy's breasts as they swayed freely when she turned to get a look at who had just busted into her room. Her pink nipples were fully erect and as soon as he got to see that much of her, Lizzy's hands came up to cover herself.

"What's going on?" she shouted. Although her arms were crossed in front of her, there wasn't much she could do about the rest of her that was still bare.

Dave sputtered and tried to speak as his eyes wandered down along her spine and then over the generous curves of her backside. "I . . . uhhh . . . I was just . . ."

"Nadine?" Lizzy said, shifting on top of her man so she could get a look at the madam accompanying Dave. "What's happening here? Why didn't you just knock, for god's sake?"

"Dave here wanted to see if you were hiding anyone in here," Nadine explained.

Slowly, Lizzy lowered her hands until she could run them over the chest of the man she was straddling. "As you can see, I can't hide too much right about now."

So far, all Dave could see of the man in Lizzy's bed was a pair of legs and one elbow. The rest was blocked by Lizzy's ample frame and just as he was about to step in to get a look at the other man's face, Dave noticed that both Lizzy and Nadine were looking at him expectantly.

"Umm . . . sorry about this, Lizzy," Dave stammered as he felt the heat flush into his cheeks. "I'll just . . . uh . . . let you get back to . . . to what you were doing."

Lizzy shook her hair over her shoulders as she looked back down to Nick. The smile she gave him was that of someone who knew she was on the verge of going too far and loving every minute of it. "Thanks, Dave. I can get to you later, but you'll just have to wait for a while."

Lying on the bed, Nick was doing his best to try and focus on what was going on around him. With Lizzy on top of him, he could only see the deputy's shadow as he fumbled around the doorway. Other than that, it was hard for him to pay attention to much of anything apart from the fact that Lizzy had insisted on him stripping down as well to complete the illusion.

As far as maintaining the illusion went, Lizzy was paying attention to every little detail. Feeling the response of Nick's body to her closeness, she was actually starting to move back and forth with the door still open.

"Jesus Christ, Dave," came Nadine's voice. "You've seen what you needed to see. The rest ain't proper for you to watch.

Come along now. I'm going to insist that you —"

"All right!" Dave grunted.

When Lizzy turned around after taking another look behind her, she had a smile for Nick that remained playful even with everything that was going on around her. She kept her hips slowly moving as her eyes closed and she allowed herself to slip fully into the moment.

"This whore ain't got the decency to cover herself and I'm the one that ain't proper," Dave grumbled as he allowed Nadine to pull him from the room.

Once the deputy was in the hall, Nadine glanced into the room one more time before she shut the door. "I swear, this place is going to be the death of me," she said under her breath.

The door shut, but it didn't stay that way until Nadine turned her key in the lock. Once the latch was in place, both sets of footsteps receded down the hall.

Lizzy smirked and somehow made it look innocent despite her current position. "I think she may be cross at me."

"Are they gone?" Nick asked.

Lizzy closed her eyes and arched her back, expertly diverting Nick's gaze. "Yes. It's just you and me again."

"Good." Nick's hand came up over her thigh and continued moving along the curve of her buttocks. When his hand moved up over her back, he tightened his grip on her shoulder and pulled her down so he was looking directly into her face.

Lizzy's eyes snapped open. She was unable to hide her excitement. That excitement started to fade when she heard the click of a pistol's hammer being cocked back.

"Now, let's pick up where we left off," Nick said while brushing the gun's barrel against Lizzy's ribs. "Since I have your attention, maybe you can tell me what I want to know."

"I already told you. There wasn't any armed men that came through here."

"Then I'm betting you saw them go by or know who they went to see. I know at least one of them's around here."

"If you know, then why don't you just —"

"Don't," Nick warned. Even though he could tell he was having an effect on Lizzy, there wasn't much fear in her eyes. In an odd sort of way, she was still wrapped up in the moment. From what Nick could see, she was even enjoying herself.

"You're a smart woman, Lizzy. You know exactly what you're doing and you know exactly how to survive in the life you've chosen. I can tell that much because I'm not so different myself."

"I know," Lizzy told him. "I could see it in your eyes."

He nodded, but kept the gun pressed against her body. If nothing else, it kept her from moving. "You heard those footsteps and I'll bet you could even recognize every little sound that comes down that hall." Seeing the agreement in her eyes, Nick continued. "That's how I know for certain that you heard all that shooting earlier. And it would have taken a dead man to miss the smoke and fire coming from down the street."

"Oh, that," Lizzy said, allowing her breathy facade to drop a bit. "I remember that."

"I thought as much. Maybe now you'll remember some armed men who headed this way after the shooting."

Leaning down so her breasts brushed against Nick's chest, Lizzy said, "Just one. A fella with scars on his face. Dark hair. He had a gun, but he wasn't waving it about. That's probably why I didn't recall him before."

"All right, then. Where'd he go?"

"He met up with Nadine once or twice before."

"When?"

Taking a breath that she knew Nick could feel, Lizzy chewed on her lip as she thought for a few moments. Even though he knew she was stalling, Nick just couldn't get himself to hurry her along.

"He stopped by a month or so ago," she finally said. "He wanted to rent a room here, but Nadine turned him away. I heard from one of the girls who works down the street that he's been renting a room there."

"Sounds about right."

"There's others that he rides with. I'll bet they're the ones you're after."

Nick looked into Lizzy's eyes and studied her for a moment. Despite the rough role he'd taken on, he still couldn't get himself to be cross at her. "Why didn't you tell me all of this before?"

"Because you're holding a gun on me now."

He shook his head. "You're not scared of this gun and you're not scared of me. Why'd you hide me from the deputy?"

"Because it was the only way I knew I could get you into this bed." Saying that, Lizzy shifted her hips slightly so that she not only brushed against Nick's Schofield, but against the rest of him as well. "Nadine doesn't harbor outlaws anymore. I miss them."

Women like Lizzy were the sources of some of the best times in Nick's lawless youth. They saw a gun around a man's waist the way other women saw flowers in kinder men's hands. They wanted excitement and could sniff out the worst men in any bunch.

"But you still know where to find the outlaws that come to town, don't you?"

Lizzy gave a shrug. "Mostly, they find me." After another few seconds had passed, she looked Nick in the eyes. "If it was just him, I wouldn't have said anything. But it's them others. I saw them a few times, and they're the sort that would be just as happy killing someone like me as doing anything else. I don't tolerate that sort of thing and I don't tolerate them that does it to others."

"That's an odd thing to say considering your love of bad men."

"Then maybe I just like gunmen." She settled on top of him and added, "You're not a bad man. And if you want to know everything I do about the ones I saw, I'll tell you. One thing I know for certain is that wherever they are, I'll bet they'll still be there in a few minutes."

Lizzy looked down at him, waiting for

Nick to reply. Her skin gave off an extra amount of heat while she slowly shifted back and forth. More than that, when she did look at him, she not only seemed to see down to his core, but she didn't seem to mind what she found.

"Aw hell," Nick sighed as he took hold of her hips. "I guess it would look suspicious if I came out right away anyhow."

Lizzy put on a victorious smile, arched her back, and let Nick's hands guide her on the ride that both of them had been wanting since he'd walked in off the street.

THIRTY-TWO

Despite the fact that Nick was distracted for a bit longer than he'd anticipated, he couldn't exactly get himself to be regretful about it. With a distraction as sweet as the one Lizzy had given to him, it would have been a bigger regret to turn it down. On a strictly practical note, she did plenty of talking throughout the rest of their time together and some of it was actually about Barrett's whereabouts.

Nick had never known Barrett to do anything half-assed. Even when they'd first ridden together, Barrett planned things excruciatingly well. He wasn't invisible, however, and plenty of the girls in the entertainment district had noticed him coming and going. In particular, he'd worn a path in the street that ended at Auntie Mable's; a cathouse just down the block from the one Lizzy called home.

None of the cathouses were in competition with each other. They were all on the same street and figured that randy cowboys would make the rounds no matter what. The girls themselves talked plenty. In fact, they'd formed a sisterhood of sorts since they weren't exactly welcome in Bitter Creek's sewing circles. Lizzy recognized Barrett's description and even his name.

"That's Jeannie's boy," she'd told Nick as he was getting dressed. "At least, he's been spending enough time with her that she considers him her own. When one of us gets a regular customer like that, it's not right for any of the others to try and take him away. Well, Jeannie staked her claim on him since he's been telling her about how rich he's fixing to get real soon."

"Where can I find Jeannie?"

"Like I said. Auntie Mable's. Just go back outside, turn right and you can't miss it. Jeannie's a sweet little thing with black hair."

Nick shook his head. "Barrett always was a sucker for brunettes."

"As for any of the others, I can't really help you there. After the shooting and all, I saw Jeannie's boy come down the street with a few others. They split up in a hurry and were gone. Me and some of the other girls had a bet going as to how long it would take for the sheriff to start rousting us."

Nick's gun was strapped around his waist and he was about to put on his coat when he remembered that it was a pile of ash in a run-down shack.

As if reading his mind, Lizzy said, "You might want to cover up that iron since folks will be a bit anxious after the shootout."

"I don't think any stores are open right now."

Smirking, Lizzy got up and walked over to a narrow closet. "Let's just see what I can do about that," she said, opening the closet and rummaging through a row of jackets, vests, and coats hanging there. After picking out a dark brown coat, she held it up to Nick and nodded. "I'd say this ought to be just right."

Nick put it on and although the coat was a little loose around the middle, it fit well enough. He looked at Lizzy who stood in front of him, naked as the day she was born, and eyeing him like an approving tailor. "You sell clothes as well?" Nick asked jokingly.

"Let's just say you'd be amazed at what some fellas will leave behind when they have to get out of here in a rush. I've got plenty of boots in there too."

"No, I think this'll do it. Thanks."

Normally, Nick wore his holster slung

close to his right hand. But no matter how many modifications had been made to the gun or holster itself, he still couldn't draw from there as quickly as he would like.

Over the years, Nick had found that he could remedy that situation by making one more adjustment to his style. Loosening the gun belt, he shifted it around his waist until the holster was closer to his belly and angled so the handle was pointed toward his right arm. Normally, that angle was to prevent a misfire from taking off Nick's foot when clearing leather. Now, it was just another way to even the odds that had been irreversibly skewed after losing his fingers.

"Are you going to kill Jeannie's boy?"

Nick glanced over to Lizzy who was now stretched out on her side on top of the bed. She was still naked and her hair flowed over her shoulder in a soft cascade. Her skin still carried the sweat that she and Nick had worked up.

But Nick didn't look over at her because of how she looked. It was what she'd said that caught his interest. It was something he'd been wondering about from the moment he'd learned who had brought him into Bitter Creek in the first place. "I didn't set out to do him any harm, although I've got plenty of reason."

"Things don't always turn out the way you'd prefer," Lizzy said. "I should know."

"Barrett's my friend."

"Then you're one of the others that are working with him?"

"As far as he's concerned." Pausing, Nick sifted through his memories as well as a few new things that had come to light in recent days.

"Then maybe you should just do it and be done with it. Is it dangerous?"

"Everything he plans is dangerous, but that's not the point. I think he may not be as close an ally as I had always thought."

"How long have you known him?"

"Too long."

"Then maybe that's why you look like you don't want to do what you know you should."

Nick shook the past from his mind and focused on the here and now. Lizzy was a beautiful woman who seemed to see things that most folks overlooked. Although it would have been more poetic to think that she cared for him more than most, Nick knew it was something more than that. She made her living off of being able to look past what was shown to her, much the way that a poker player had to peel back the surface and look at what was underneath.

Still, the spark in her eyes was something beyond professional. Either that, or Nick was just getting softhearted in his old age.

"I've seen men wear their guns like that," Lizzy said, nodding toward the holster he'd recently adjusted. "Not many times, but I've seen it."

Nick pulled his coat over the holster, feeling as though he could almost hear a coffin creaking shut. With that, he put on the face he normally wore when attending a funeral.

It didn't matter whose funeral, because they all got the same, stoic face.

Nick was a professional and he mourned the same for everyone.

Including himself.

Lizzy's smirk faded a bit when she said, "Men who wear their gun like that aim to get into a fight real soon. The last man I saw wear his gun across his belly said it was to make his draw faster."

Flexing his mangled hand, Nick said, "I need all the help I can get."

"No," Lizzy replied while shaking her head. "That's not it. You just want to be ready because you think there's going to be trouble."

"There's already been plenty of that tonight. It's bad enough the law's breathing down my neck again."

"If you were worried about the law, you wouldn't have stayed here as long as you have. I know I'm good, but not good enough to die for. What is it between you and Jeannie's boy? What's got you so tied up?"

"Maybe I don't want to do something even though it should have been done a long time ago."

"Then maybe now's the best time to do it."

"Yeah. It may just be."

"Here," he said, taking some money from his pocket and setting it on the edge of the bed.

Lizzy didn't even look at the money. "Keep it. I told you I like gunmen and if you couldn't tell that I had one hell of a time with you, then you're blind as well as missing a few fingers."

Nick couldn't help but smirk at the snide way she delivered those words. "Then consider it repayment for the coat and your door. I don't think those deputies have any intention of fixing it."

Although Lizzy nodded, it wasn't out of agreement. She simply didn't think that arguing would do any good. "What's your name?"

"Nicolai Graves."

Stepping up to him, she reached out and

adjusted the lapels of his coat. "Take care of yourself, Nicolai."

Most folks didn't call him by his true name. There wasn't anything mysterious about it, but they simply shortened it to Nick because that's what most folks were used to hearing. But Lizzy actually listened to him. That was something unusual.

"I will," Nick said.

"Before you go, could you do me a favor?"

"Name it."

"Show me that gun one more time."

Nick was unable to hold back the smile that broke straight through his stony facade. Their laughter broke the tension that had been filling the room like a thick fog until that point.

With a slight flourish, Nick opened his coat to show his holstered Schofield as if he'd suddenly taken center stage.

"Oooh," Lizzy moaned theatrically. "That's what I like."

After turning the latch, Nick opened the door and took a quick look outside. The hall was empty, so he left the room. Before closing the door again, he took one more look at what he was leaving behind. Lizzy was still there, smiling proudly as though she'd been posing for that very moment.

Nick shut the door and felt as though he'd

been tossed into the cold, cruel world after being diverted by a particularly good dream. Not only did he feel refreshed after the hell he'd been through that night, but he felt that he had a purpose in his steps as he headed for the stairs.

Lizzy had been right. He needed to take care of himself and not worry about trying to fix someone who didn't even know he was broken. Before doing any of that, however, Nick needed to get out of the cathouse without being spotted by the law.

When he approached the top of the stairs, Nick peeked around the corner and got a look at what was waiting on the floor below. There were still a few girls milling about, as well as a few prospective customers. Apparently, the smoke had cleared and the gunshots had faded, leaving the rest of Bitter Creek open for business. Just as Nick was about to walk down the stairs, he heard another door open at the opposite end of the hall.

A man in a rumpled suit staggered out and was stopped by a pair of smooth, feminine hands reaching out from the room. There were some whispered words, an exchange of money, and a few quick kisses before the door was shut and the man was left to find his own way out. The fellow had a smile on his face so wide that even being surprised by Nick couldn't dim it.

"Hell of a night," the man said.

Nick laughed and nodded.

"Did you get a visit from that damn deputy as well?"

"Yep," Nick said. Nudging the fellow with his elbow, he added, "But it didn't slow me down any."

"Heh. I hear that! I better get home, though. Work in the morning, and all."

With that, the man headed for the stairs and Nick followed a few paces behind.

Using the man as a moving shield, Nick kept his head down and his eyes open for any sign of the deputy that had almost found him in Lizzy's room. Apparently, the lawman had either moved on or was hurried out by Nadine because he was nowhere to be found. After plucking his hat from the rack by the door, Nick and his oblivious escort stepped outside and parted ways. The staggering fellow was bound for the quieter side of town while Nick ventured further into the entertainment district.

Sheriff Trayner wasn't in sight, but that wasn't a big comfort. Since standing still would only draw more attention to himself, Nick pulled his hat down low, stuck his

hands in his pockets, started walking, and
hoped for the best.

THIRTY-THREE

Lizzy had been right about Auntie Mable's. The other cathouse wasn't hard to find. Although the sign over the front of the building was written in a fancy blue script that seemed more fitting of a quilt store, the scantly clad women standing outside were a dead giveaway. Even at the late hour of the night, the place was doing steady business. Unfortunately, not all of the men on the street were simply out for a night's fun. A quick look around was all Nick needed to spot the two deputies patrolling the area.

There was a trick to walking without being seen. It wasn't anything fancy, but it worked better than any kind of magic. All a man had to do was keep moving and hold himself as though he was in danger of getting blown away by a stiff breeze. People tended to forget someone who makes so little of an impression and it hardly took longer than a second or two to do just that.

Nick slouched while he walked and made sure to keep his steps down to a quick shuffle. That didn't mean he was at the mercy of the crowd in the streets, though. On the contrary, he used the crowd the same way he'd used the shadows. Nick weaved in and out of the openings he could find while constantly keeping his eye on both deputies as well as his destination.

It wasn't impossible, but it was still a nice little trick. He even used the fact that he had to keep glancing around to make him seem afraid of being pushed aside. While drunkards and randy cowboys made their way from one sin to another, they simply pushed Nick aside and kept on walking without ever really seeing him. In the meantime, those same drunkards and cowboys were making sure the deputies couldn't see him either.

By the time he reached the front door of Auntie Mable's, Nick felt like patting himself on the back for getting there without drawing more than a passing glance from the deputies. But before he could get too pleased with himself, Nick spotted Barrett moving straight toward him with a determined look in his eye.

Still running on instinct, he snapped his head down and stepped aside as Barrett came walking out through the front door. The wide brim of Nick's hat did as good a job as ever in shielding his face, but that hardly seemed to matter. Barrett apparently had plenty of other things on his mind.

"Where are you going, Barrett?" asked a slender brunette wearing a dark red night-gown as she chased after him. "You only just got here!"

"I got business, Jeannie, I told you."

Suddenly, Barrett stopped.

For a moment, Nick thought that he'd been spotted and was about to step forward to deal with the consequences. That's when he realized that Barrett hadn't spotted him, but had spotted one of the deputies instead.

"Dammit," Barrett hissed. "Jeannie, come out here and help me out."

The brunette pouted and stuck her hands on her hips defiantly. "Not till you apologize."

Nick felt as though he was sitting in a darkened theater watching Barrett squirm in front of the brunette. Although he did move away from the door, Nick still kept himself close enough to see what would happen next.

Barrett wheeled around, took hold of the brunette's arm and shoved her back toward the door. "Get out there and say hello," he ordered. Removing a couple folded bills from his pocket, he stuffed them down the front of the woman's nightgown and added, "Please, thank you, and I'm sorry. Now get moving."

The brunette tucked the bills away, kissed Barrett, and smiled broadly. "Apology accepted." From there, she shook out her hair and strutted out through the front door.

Nick, along with every other man outside, couldn't help but watch as Jeannie stepped into the street and headed straight for the nearest deputy. When she got beneath a streetlamp, the light reflected down her figure and played over the silky material of her nightgown. The fabric clung to her and made no secret that the cold air had found its way beneath her clothes.

"Howdy, Dave," she said to the deputy who stared, slack-jawed, straight back at her. "Just out to see if you caught those bad men you were after."

Once the deputy shook some sense back into his head, he fumbled for a response. "Uhhh . . . not just yet, but we're . . . uh . . . still looking," was the best he could do under the circumstances.

She kept talking as she got closer, but her voice had lowered to a more conversational level. Even though they couldn't hear her any longer, that didn't keep most of the others outside from watching her every move. Nick had to fight to keep from falling into the same trap and managed to turn around just in time to catch Barrett heading back inside the cathouse.

The moment Nick started following Barrett, he took on another stance entirely. Rather than try to blend in and be forgotten, he walked like a freight train and put a look upon his face that said he wasn't about to be stopped. Folks tended to step aside rather than get run down by a freight train, which was exactly what happened when Nick made his way through the cathouse.

Ladies who meant to attract him quickly thought better of the idea and let Nick pass. Even the rugged young men whose job it was to protect the working girls let him pass. In fact, Nick wasn't hindered once as he went straight through and to the side door that Barrett had used to make his own getaway.

Stepping outside, Nick froze in his tracks while his eyes readjusted themselves to the dark. It didn't take long for him to see that he was alone in the alley. Barrett was gone as well, but soon Nick's ears picked up the subtle sound of rushing footsteps coming from deeper in the alleyway.

While Barrett was an expert at sneaking, Nick was an expert at tracking and the two performed a dance of sorts with Barrett in the lead. Nick stayed behind, but not far enough to let Barrett get away. Then again, he couldn't get too close or he might as well just announce his presence.

Barrett was up to something. Nick was certain of that much at least. Since he'd gotten this far without being seen, Nick decided to keep going and see just what Barrett had up his sleeve. It was instinct more than anything else that kept him moving silently in Barrett's tracks. Just as it had been instinct that had brought him away from his home more than twenty years ago and down the road that led into the sea of blood that filled his past.

Sometimes, Nick didn't exactly like his instincts too much. Unfortunately, they were all he had.

Nick didn't have to wait for long before he was rewarded for that silent walk through Bitter Creek's alleyways. Barrett began slowing down and checking around him in quick glances as he approached a quieter section of town. Nick wasn't exactly certain where they were, but he knew they were around more large homes than businesses.

Barrett approached one of those homes

and rapped on the door. All the while, he kept checking over his shoulder and searching to see if he'd been followed. Nick shook his head disapprovingly. Apparently, Barrett really hadn't been paying attention when Nick had tried teaching him how to track a man and keep from being tracked.

Suddenly, as if he could sense the thoughts rushing through Nick's head, Barrett stopped and shot a glance in the direction where Nick was hiding. Having found himself a dark spot to settle into, Nick couldn't do anything but keep absolutely still and wait to see if he'd been spotted.

Just when Barrett was about to start walking toward Nick's spot, the door he'd been knocking on was jerked open and a man stuck his face outside.

"What is it?" the man snarled in a voice loud enough for Nick to hear it clearly.

Barrett turned his back to Nick and focused on the man in the doorway. "It's important. I need to talk to you." As Barrett started walking into the house, he was stopped by a stiffly outstretched hand.

"Not inside," the man said distastefully. He kept his hand on Barrett and pushed the outlaw back as he stepped outside to join him upon the porch.

Even though he was dressed as though

he'd been getting ready for bed, the man still kept his thinning, light-brown hair plastered to his scalp with expensive wax. A pointed nose hung down over a narrow mouth that looked as if it had been sliced into his face.

Unconcerned with anyone around him, the fair-haired man walked straight up to Barrett and clasped his hands behind his back. "What is the meaning of this? I thought you were a professional."

Seeing that Barrett was fully occupied by the imperious figure, Nick crept out of his spot and found another one that was close enough to hear the conversation even as it dropped to a more discreet volume.

"I am a professional," Barrett hissed. "Things just got out of hand."

"I suppose that's why you came to pull me out of my home just as I was settling down to read?"

"Yeah. It was either that or wait for you to make a mess out of our arrangement just when it was about to go through."

"Our arrangement?" the man repeated sarcastically. "Our arrangement didn't involve shooting at the sheriff and his deputies for no reason. And if you were half the professional I'd thought you were, you would have been able to stay hidden until it was time for you to do your job."

Barrett shook his head and let out a slow, humorless laugh. Even from his vantage point, Nick could sense the hostility in Barrett's voice as well as the tension in each of his movements. That's why it was no surprise to him when Barrett suddenly pulled the gun from his holster and shoved its barrel under the other man's chin.

"Don't tell me about my job," Barrett seethed. "This whole thing is my job, Finch, and you're just another man working for me. Understand?"

The surprised expression that came over the other man's face was similar to the one worn by Nick the moment he saw that man's face. It was a good thing that he was already well hidden or Nick might have drawn attention to himself when his eyes widened until they resembled saucers.

Barrett was the only one who seemed to be in complete control as he kept the gun under Finch's chin and kept laying down the law. "I could just rob you and be done with it, but I chose to stick to the plan. That makes things easier on me and more profitable for you, but this is my plan and I don't need to keep you in it. Got that?"

"Yes," Finch replied, somehow managing to keep the distasteful look upon his face.

"But you know damn well that you couldn't do this job without my help."

"You want to split hairs now?" Barrett asked, shoving the gun a little harder against Finch's chin. "Well, it's too late for that. "Me and my boys almost got killed tonight. I came here because you need to know why my end of the profits just got raised."

Finch's eyes blinked a few times and he sputtered as though someone had just told him to hand over his firstborn. "What? But that's preposterous!"

"Is it?"

Finch tried to nod, but couldn't do much with the gun still wedged under his chin. "None of this was supposed to happen. This is getting too messy for us to —"

But Finch was cut off by the metallic click of the hammer of Barrett's gun being thumbed back. When he spoke, it was in a steady tone that was colder than the iron in his hand. "I sure hope you're not planning to tell me the job's off. That would waste my time and that would make me very angry. Also, that would make you completely useless to me."

Gulping painfully against the pistol's barrel, Finch said, "A . . . all right. The job's s . . . still on."

"There does need to be one change,

though. I need to set up another location for the delivery."

"What? Why?"

"What you're going to hear sometime soon is that me and my boys were rousted by the law and that we're on the run."

Finch's posture crumpled until it seemed as though Barrett's gun was the only thing holding him up. "Oh God."

"They found us, but we're not going anywhere. So when you hear the talk or rumors or whatever, you just nod and don't twitch a muscle. Got that?"

"I think I'm going to be sick."

Barrett let out a disgruntled sigh and took the gun away from Finch's chin. After holstering the weapon, Barrett offered a hand to Finch and helped the man take a seat on the edge of the porch.

Watching from the shadows, Nick could see a mean glare in Barrett's eyes that looked only too familiar.

"This has gone too far," Finch said. "The jewelry is supposed to arrive tomorrow. Maybe we should tell them to bring the shipment later."

Barrett stood so he could look down at Finch while also watching the street. His eyes were moving much too quickly, however, to notice any odd shapes within the shadows. "It's too late to change the delivery time and even if it wasn't, I don't want to raise any eyebrows. That could just get a few more guards put with the shipment."

"I said I wanted this done quietly. When we talked before, you said this would be quick and easy. You promised me that my father wouldn't —"

"The only thing I promised was that you'd get a percentage of what we stole. This robbery is happening whether you like it or not. I could have just as easily done this the hard way, but I decided to be generous and cut you in. Don't get yourself too worked up, because whatever I give you is profit. Your daddy will just send out another shipment in a bit to replace the first. Hell, I doubt he'll even notice this loss when he tallies up his numbers a year from now."

"That's not the point. This was supposed to be an easy matter. Now, shots have been fired, the sheriff is after you, and lord only knows what might happen once your men draw their guns tomorrow. If Sheriff Trayner happens to find out about this, we'll both end up in jail and nobody will make one bit of profit."

"That's what I'm trying to tell you. We can't hit your daddy's coach in front of your store like we planned," Barrett said. "The law's going to be too riled up for that. All we need to do is change the spot where I meet the shipment. That way, the plan can go as we figured, we all get rich and nobody gets hurt."

"And what about the sheriff?"

"He's worried about this town. I can take those jewels and pull off the whole job without being in his jurisdiction. To tell you the truth, I should have set it up this way to start off."

Listening to Barrett talk, Nick almost found himself convinced that the plan was perfectly sound. Whatever changes Barrett might have made over the years, his ability to smooth-talk had only gotten better. Judging by the look on Finch's face and his more relaxed posture, he was falling right into Barrett's hands as well.

"So how about it?" Barrett asked, circling in for the kill. "Are we still in business?"

After taking another couple of deep breaths, Finch ran his fingers over his hair and nodded. "I'm in this far. Besides, this does sound safer."

"Of course it does."

"I just want your assurance that your men will keep their wits about them and try to work fast. I don't want any lawmen hurt.

That is . . . not unless it's absolutely necessary."

"I don't want that either," Barrett said. "Too messy all around. Sometimes, though, spilling blood can't be helped."

"I realize that. If that does happen, my concern is that none of that blood gets tracked back to me."

"You just worry about your end of the bargain, Finch. Make sure that shipment goes where it needs to go and that it's packed with as much as possible. You'll also need to be sure and bring the money from that safe along with you. That way, nobody can say that you weren't there to make your payment."

"What? Why do I have to be there at all?"

"Got to keep up appearances. You think the driver of that shipment will just stop for me and say howdy? The whole beauty of this plan is how smooth it'll run. Remember," Barrett added, putting a bit more of an edge into his voice, "that's why I'm keeping you around to be a part of it."

Finch nodded slowly and backed toward the door.

Sensing the other man's fear, Barrett smiled and patted Finch on the shoulder. "Don't worry about a thing. I'll take care of my end. Speaking of which, with the changes and all, I'll need to know the entire route being taken by your daddy's driver."

Finch filled his lungs and let the air out in a deep gush. After steeling himself that way, he laid it all out for Barrett, right down to the stops the drivers would make and where they would water their horses. When he was finished, even Barrett seemed impressed.

"There, now," Barrett said. "Now that you're all the way in, it's not so bad."

"One thing still bothers me. It's been on my mind since this whole thing started."

Barrett took half a step back and fixed his eyes upon Finch. Nick recognized that look as one Barrett gave when he was thinking about all his options and which ones would benefit him the most.

"What is it?" Barrett asked.

Finch looked a bit squeamish, but then straightened up and said, "If someone does get hurt . . . I'll want more money."

"And why's that?"

"Because I can do things to throw the law off your trail. I can . . . forget certain things. Or . . . remember others." Finch did his best to draw himself up and puff out his chest. "That way, you'll try to keep yourself in line. Also, the hell I'll catch from my father will mean I'll earn my extra cut."

Smirking, Barrett nodded. "Extra? Since

I'm gonna make sure there's only two cuts on this deal, there won't be any extra."

"So you've decided to cut your other partners from the job?"

"Only after they're done."

Finch swallowed hard and shuddered. "I don't want to hear about any more killing."

"Then don't listen and let me pull the trigger on them other three. Besides, I'm sure you'll be just fine with it once we're the only two left standing to split up the cash. Don't worry, once the smoke clears, this is going to work out for both of us. Take my word for it."

"I'm sure it will, Mr. Cobb. And if it does, we can work together again."

They talked for a while longer, setting up the specifics on locations and times. Once he saw that both men were wrapped up in their planning, Nick eased out of his shadow and worked his way back into the alleys. He'd heard more than enough and it wasn't long before he was heading back toward his rented room.

Suddenly, Nick realized why he'd been waiting and watching Barrett for so long. He knew his old friend would show his cards eventually, and Nick just wanted to be there to see them for himself. With that sight fresh in his mind, Nick was reminded

of why he'd taken up a shovel rather than
stumbled back onto the road where Barrett
still walked.

THIRTY-FOUR

Nick only got a few hours of sleep, but when the knock came on his door, he felt ready and raring to go. The first thing he did when he got out of bed was to check his dented pocket watch. It was about four in the morning and the sun wasn't even starting to peek into his dirty window. As soon as his feet touched the floor, he reached for his gun belt and strapped it around his waist.

"What is it?" he asked, once he'd made certain the modified Schofield was loaded.

"Someone here to see you," came a familiar, if tentative, voice.

"Clark?" Nick asked, barely recognizing the old man's voice. "Is that you?"

There was a pause and when the old man spoke again, it was obvious by the sound of his voice that he was leaning in close against the door. "Some men here to see you, Nick. They look like no good to me."

"How many?"

"Three. Want me to get the sheriff?"

Nick had already pulled on his boots and coat. His things were already gathered and bundled up. When he cracked open the door, the old man in the hall immediately noticed those things with nothing more than a quick look inside.

"You plannin' on leaving, Nick?"

Ignoring the question, Nick skipped right ahead to his own. "Where are those men you mentioned?"

"Oh. They're up front. I can —"

"No need to do a thing, old-timer," Barrett said as he slapped a hand on Clark's shoulder and eased him aside. "I think we can take it from here."

Although the old man wasn't in a position to fight against the grip on his shoulder, he kept his eyes on Nick and waited. When he saw the subtle shake of Nick's head, Clark yanked himself away from Barrett and stomped back down the hall. "No need to shove," Clark grumbled.

As soon as the old man was out of earshot, Barrett opened Nick's door the rest of the way and started to walk inside.

"How'd you find me?" Nick asked.

"I think the better question is why were you trying to hide?"

"I wasn't hiding. Just laying low."

"You hear about what happened last night?"

"The shooting?" Nick replied with a scoff. "Who didn't hear that ruckus? That should also answer your other question about why I wouldn't want to be around your boys. They struck me as the impulsive types."

Barrett's eyes darted toward the front of the building where Morrison and Guile were waiting. "Yeah, but once this job is over, I'm cutting them loose. After that, it could be you and me again. We could handpick our own gang."

"Let's just try to get through this job, first."

"Yeah," Barrett said as he stepped inside and got Nick to step back from the door. "That's what I wanted to talk to you about. Them lawmen found us last night. Folks almost got killed."

"I heard about it. You look all right to me. How are the others?"

"They're fine. What bothers me is how we got spotted in the first place. Anything you can tell me about that?"

Nick shrugged. "Could be I was followed. I'm not exactly as sharp as I used to be."

"Just a victim of circumstance, huh?"

"You always were the planner, Barrett. I

tend to take things as they come. Even at the top of my game, I barely knew what I was doing or why I was doing it half the time."

Barrett had to laugh at that and gave Nick a slap on the shoulder as if they were both a couple of rough-housing teens again. "Ain't that the truth."

"Besides, I knew you'd find me. Hell, all you had to do was ask Carmine at the funeral parlor where I was staying and he would have told you."

"I came to fetch you because we need to get an earlier start than we thought. The ruckus from last night forced me to change things around a bit."

"Is the job still on?"

"As long as you think you're ready for it." Narrowing his eyes slightly, Barrett asked, "Are you still up for it?"

"Sure beats digging holes for a living."

"There's the Nick Graves I remember! Come on. We've got just enough time to collect your horse and get moving. You do have at least one good horse, don't you? I don't think those nags you got pulling that wagon will do much good."

"Rasa just got shooed, so she'll be ready to go."

"All right then. Let's do this."

Nick took hold of the satchel containing all his clothes and followed Barrett out the door. When he got to the front desk, he noticed the look of deep concern etched into Clark's face. Nick stepped up to the old man and lowered his voice so he could get some measure of privacy without raising the suspicions of the others.

"Do me a favor, will you?" Nick said.

Clark nodded, while occasionally glancing at Barrett and the other two. "What is it?"

"I should have a day's wages waiting for me at the undertaker's parlor. Collect them for me and use them to pay whatever I owe for the room and such. Keep whatever's left for yourself."

"You sure you don't want me to bring the sheriff? He's a good man. He can —"

"I know he's a good man. That's why I want him out of this."

"What should I tell him?"

"Nothing. Don't tell him anything."

Reluctantly, Clark nodded.

Nick put his back to the old man and walked out the door.

Outside, Morrison and Guile were already on their horses and bringing them about. Once they saw that Barrett didn't have anything else to say to them, they pointed themselves east and snapped the reins. At that early hour, the sound of hooves beating against the earth was like the clap of thunder echoing down the street.

With the horses gone, the air seemed not only quieter, but colder as well. Barrett and Nick walked briskly down the street, heading for the livery where Nick had left his wagon.

"So, I guess we're headed down to Ashton Corner again," Nick said as he turned onto the next street and headed toward a familiar stable.

"Like I told you, I had to change things around."

"Were you planning on bringing me up to snuff or do I have to guess?"

"After the shooting and all last night, we decided that it's too hot around here to pull the job in town. We're going to meet the wagon on its way into town instead."

"Sounds familiar," Nick said with a grin.

Barrett thought about that for a moment before finally nodding. "Oh yeah. It does. We've robbed plenty of stages that this one shouldn't be much different."

"What about Finch?"

"What about him?" Barrett asked.

"I thought we were going to get the money he was going to pay for the jewelry as well. If we change this up, won't we miss out on that too?"

"It'll still be in his shop. Once things cool off a bit, we can swing back through there and get it ourselves." Snapping his fingers, Barrett added, "We could even take the clothes off the driver and guards and go in like nothing happened. He'll hand over the money and we ride off."

Nick knew when Barrett was making things up as he went along. That wasn't a normal situation for Barrett and it never did suit him too well. At least that made reading his face that much easier. It reminded Nick of watching someone smirk when they were dealt the card they needed to fill out their flush.

"Nice idea," Nick said. "You always were the planner."

"Then you're still in? For the big haul, I mean. There's no reason for us to stop after a job like this. I mean, we could —"

"Take it easy. Let's do one job at a time."

"Oh. Of course."

When they arrived at the stables, Nick stepped inside to make his arrangements with the liveryman. Although it wasn't the same man he'd dealt with before, he didn't have any trouble paying up and making his final arrangements. All that remained was for him to pick up Kazys and the wagon within the next twelve hours to keep from paying another fee.

It was a simple matter of paying a bill, but it felt like something much more than that. Nick was getting the churning in his stomach that he hadn't felt since he'd lived as an outlaw. Every movement became more important when playing such a dangerous game because it could be his last.

The tension had been fading over the years, but it was back in his stomach now. But it wasn't the tension that made Nick uncomfortable. What got to him more than anything was the simple realization that he'd missed that feeling of excitement deep in his belly.

Barrett's offer was still on the table and the road that Nick had been trying to put behind him was still right there for him to choose at any time. No matter what had happened in Montana or Nebraska, no matter what he'd learned about Barrett's plan, there was no denying the fact that Nick missed the excitement and freedom of his past.

He could draw his gun and take Barrett to the sheriff at that very moment.

Nick could also draw his gun, put a bullet through the liveryman's skull and steal every horse in that barn.

The struggle wasn't new, by any means, and chewed at Nick's innards the way some men felt themselves aching to drain whiskey from a bottle.

"That'll be an extra fifty cents for the extra stable time," the liveryman grunted, desperate to get back to his nap.

And to everyone else, it was just another day.

Just another bill to pay.

Nick handed over the money, saddled up Rasa, and climbed onto the horse's back. He would choose his road just like any other man. And, like any other man, Nick would take that road straight to the end.

THIRTY-FIVE

Morrison and Guile had blazed a trail out of town only a few minutes ahead of Nick and Barrett, but it seemed as if they'd been given an entire day's head start. Nick followed Barrett toward the northern edge of the town's limits, taking note at how carefully Barrett was moving. He didn't move an inch without thinking it over and his eyes were darting about so quickly that he thought they might jump right out of his skull.

Finally, once they were out of town, Barrett snapped his reins and led the way. Even though Nick was confident in his own horse's ability to keep up, he was still amazed at how fast Barrett managed to go. They rode out of Bitter Creek as though their tails were on fire and it wasn't long at all before Barrett started turning east toward the main road.

As he rode, Nick reacquainted himself

with the terrain. While the Dakota Territories were beautiful, they were also dangerous and unpredictable. What you saw wasn't always what you got and the faster you rode, the more a man risked slipping down a steep ridge or running smack into a freshly fallen pile of rocks.

After another half mile or so, Nick rode up alongside of Barrett and motioned for him to head toward a stand of trees not too far off the path. Reluctantly, Barrett nodded and they both slowed their horses so they could eventually come to a stop within the cover of the trees. The wind pushed the branches around gently, but soon worked itself up to a whistling howl.

For the moment, there was nobody else on the road. The only thing Nick could hear was the crunch of hooves upon loose dirt and the whine of the breeze through the branches.

"Why are we stopping?" Barrett asked. "We need to get a little farther out than this."

"How much farther?"

"Just another couple of miles. The other two are already positioned out there a ways. They'll start shooting and drive Finch's shipment right into our hands."

Nick couldn't see any trace of Morrison

or Guile. Even when he leaned forward over Rasa's neck to get a look down the road, he could see no sign of movement or even a trail of dust that had been kicked up by their horses. Of course, with the ground swelling into various rock formations and several other clusters of trees about, there were any number of places where the others could be hiding.

"What is it, Nick?" Barrett asked anxiously. "Why'd you want to stop here?"

Without saying a word, Nick climbed down from the saddle and started walking farther into the trees. He kept his back hunched over and his steps light, constantly moving his eyes back and forth in search of something he couldn't quite find.

It didn't take long before Barrett jumped down from his own horse and stepped over to where Nick was searching. By this time, his eyes were flicking to one side and another even though he didn't know what Nick was looking for. When Nick stopped, Barrett waited impatiently for an explanation.

"We're being followed," Nick said, just before Barrett was about to burst.

Barrett's eyes widened and he focused his gaze on the spot where Nick appeared to be looking. "What? Where are they?"

"Behind us about a quarter of a mile, maybe less. One of them skylined themselves a few minutes ago and I didn't have time to say anything. I tried to pick a spot where they wouldn't see us pull off so we could catch them when they came by."

Nodding as though he could see their pursuers with crystal clarity, Barrett whispered, "Damn, it's good to have you back, Nick. I could always plan things out but you were the one to think on your feet. Goddammit. I knew we should have finished off that sheriff when we had the ch—"

Barrett was cut short by the impact of something heavy against the side of his head. The whole world seemed to lurch around him and he struggled to maintain his balance. That battle was quickly lost. He toppled over onto the ground where he rolled onto his back and clenched his eyes shut. A throbbing pain filled his skull, growing worse with every sound and ray of light.

Soon, the pain began to ebb away and numbness flooded through him as if it had been poured in through his ear. Although Barrett couldn't tell exactly where Nick was, he could hear his steps well enough to get a good idea. Every inch of him felt battered from the fall and his head felt about ready to split apart, but he was doing a good job of holding on to consciousness.

Having already gotten a length of rope from his saddlebag, Nick rolled Barrett onto his stomach and pulled his arms around behind his back. "Sorry about the knock to the head," Nick said as he busied himself with getting the rope around Barrett's wrists. "But there's not enough time for conversation."

"Wh . . . wha," were the only words Barrett could form since his brain was still swimming in a painful fog. After focusing a bit more, he forced himself to speak a little clearer. "What's going on here? Why did you do that?"

"Because this has gone on long enough. Too much blood has been spilled over the years and it's got to stop sometime. Might as well be now."

The smile on Barrett's face was uneasy and trembling from pain. It wasn't long before it faded away. His hands clenched into fists just before he felt the rope cinch in tighter around his wrists. "This righteousness coming from the man who taught me to shoot? From the man who taught me to kill? Is that what happened to you in Montana? Did those vigilantes get you thinking that you're some kind of fucking angel?"

"No."

"Is that why you went after Red Parks in Nebraska? So you could show him the error of his ways? I thought you were a Mourner, Nick, not a preacher."

"Red needed to answer for what he done. You don't need to know any more than that."

"Yeah, but Skinner beat you to it and you killed him. Real righteous man," Barrett scoffed. "You're still nothing more than a killer. Just like you always were."

"I spend enough time regretting things I've done. There's nothing you can say to make them any worse. Folks like Red and Skinner have to pay for what they do."

"And what about yourself?"

"I've sinned plenty. Now, it's time to make up for it."

"So what you're telling me is that I need to pay now, too. Is that it?"

Nick shook his head while throwing a knot together and tightening it against Barrett's wrists. "I could have killed you a dozen times by now. We've been through too much hell for me to put you in the same category as Red or Skinner. You're not like them. Maybe I'm getting sentimental, but I'd like to think maybe you could find another path for yourself before you get killed."

"You ever think that it's too late for that?"

Barrett asked through his uncomfortable smirk.

"Yeah, but that don't mean I shouldn't try."

"So you got me tied up," Barrett grunted. "Now what? Fetch the sheriff and collect the reward?"

"I haven't decided yet. All I know for certain is that I'm not going to be part of another one of your plans. They're too bloody and I can't stand by and let any more folks get hurt because of what we want."

"We?" Barrett asked. "Sounds like you might be trying to convince yourself of something."

Nick didn't say anything to that. His hands moved as if they had a mind of their own, even though his eyes didn't seem half as certain. As he tightened the ropes around Barrett, however, Nick's uncertainty faded away and a kind of peace settled over him. It was the kind of peace felt when the choices had been made, the horses were moving in the right direction, and all that remained was to enjoy the ride.

Turning his head so that he was facedown in the dirt, Barrett said, "You could have just passed on my offer."

"Really? And you just would have let it go

at that?"

Barrett didn't respond.

Nick reached down and picked Barrett up by the jacket as though he were lifting a cat by the scruff of its neck. "Yeah. That's what I thought. And that's why I stuck through this thing until I saw a spot where I could jump in and put a stop to it."

"Here we go again. Jesus Christ, Nick I never thought you'd get to be such a —"

Barrett was cut short when Nick drew his gun and pointed it at Barrett's forehead. The modified weapon made a subtle noise that was the unmistakable click of the hammer being pulled back.

"You want to die?" Nick asked. "Because if that's the case then let me know now and save me a whole lot of trouble."

"I'm just making my way in this world. Just like you."

"No, Barrett. I'm not like that anymore. There's plenty of folks I'd like to bury for what they done, but you're not one of them. You might laugh about this considering your predicament, but I consider you damn close to being a brother. That's why I couldn't let those lawmen gun you down, but I also can't just let you go on this way.

"I've seen too many men like us leave this world swinging from the end of a rope with piss dripping down their legs. I've dug their graves and I don't want that to happen to you. You're smarter than anyone I've known."

Barrett lifted his head so he could look Nick in the eyes. "I know you mean well, Nick, but come on. We're not the types that earn our way in this world by digging holes or working in some general store. We're the ones that take what we want from them that're too weak to defend it. You told me that yourself. Don't you remember?"

"I could never forget those days. I killed more men than smallpox and I should'a hung for it. Instead, I wound up paying in a way that made a noose look like the easy way out. Maybe part of my reckoning is to make sure you don't wind up like all them others."

"All right. Untie me and we can walk away from this one. I'll even buy you a drink and we can work out a job where nobody gets hurt and we make enough to retire for good."

"There isn't going to be another job, Barrett."

"What?"

"You heard me. No more! Your days of spilling blood are over. It don't matter if you're pulling the trigger or paying them who do. Even if I have to kill you myself, I swear those days are over."

THIRTY-SIX

The wagon had been thundering along the trail into Bitter Creek for days. Considering the shipment he was carrying, the driver didn't want to make a stop unless it was absolutely necessary and even those stops had been few and far between. The horses were tired and the men on the wagon were even more so. All of them snapped to attention, however, when they saw a man standing in the road directly in front of them.

They had just rounded a bend and cleared a cluster of rocks when they saw him. The man waved his arms in the air and was yelling for them to stop. Although the driver didn't want to slow down, he also didn't want to trample a man to death along the way.

Grudgingly, the driver reined the horses in and took a moment to calm them after the sudden stop. "Whoa, there," he said. Turning to look at the man who'd stopped him, the driver asked, "What's going on here?"

"There's been a change of plan."

Rubbing his eyes, the driver tried to focus and see through the haze that had developed inside his head after so many hours of tedious riding. "Is that you, Mr. Finch?"

Before the man could reply, a few of the others in the wagon poked their heads out. Most of the eyes staring down at the solitary figure were doing so over rifle and shotgun barrels.

Finch tossed his hands up over his head and put on a nervous smile. Although he didn't convince anyone that he was comfortable in his situation, he at least got the gunmen inside the wagon to lower their weapons. "I tried to get ahold of you earlier, but couldn't get a message to you."

"We've been driving nonstop," the driver said. "What's the matter?"

"Nothing's wrong. I just want to conduct our business outside of town. There was some trouble there with outlaws recently and I figured this would be safer." As he said those words, Finch's eyes searched the horizon. Even after they'd fixed upon something in particular, he still looked as if he was about to crawl out of his skin.

The men in the wagon might have noticed

this more if they hadn't already been acting the same way.

The driver relaxed a bit and visibly let out a breath. "That's good to hear, Mr. Finch. This is the most valuable shipment I've ever carried and to tell you the truth, I'll be glad to be rid of it."

"Well, the money is right here," Finch said, patting the breast pocket of his suit jacket. "Can I see the merchandise?"

"Sure thing."

The driver leaned back and spoke to the man beside him. In turn, that man set down his shotgun and twisted around so he could climb onto the roof. The driver then stomped his boot a few times against the footboard, which set the men inside the wagon into motion.

"I didn't want to keep them all in one place," the driver explained. "You know, for security and such."

Finch nodded, watching the wagon anxiously while flicking his eyes to that spot he'd picked out in the distance. "Oh . . . of course."

After a minute or two of the men shifting about inside and on top of the wagon, the driver was handed three metal boxes. Each of those boxes looked to be made of steel at least half an inch thick and were kept shut by a sturdy lock. The driver lined the boxes up in front of him and dug out a chain that had been hanging around his neck.

"These are the keys to the lockboxes," the driver said, holding out the keys dangling from the chain he wore. "I'm supposed to get the payment before handing them over."

"Certainly." Finch took out an envelope from his pocket containing a thick bundle of money. "You can count it if you like."

The driver looked down at the money in Finch's hand and then pulled the chain from around his neck. "And you can look through the boxes to make sure it's all there." Suddenly, the driver stopped and tightened his grip around the chain. "Where's your wagon, Mr. Finch? And didn't you bring any men to guard the money?"

Finch shifted on his feet and struggled to come up with the exact words to put the other men at ease. Instead, he accomplished the exact opposite and all of the men with the wagon started lifting their weapons once again.

"I . . . I'd appreciate those keys now," Finch said. But he could tell that the men were still uncomfortable and growing more so by the second. With nothing else coming to mind for him to say, Finch looked directly at the point he'd been focusing upon in the distance and held up his left hand.

The driver spun around to look behind him but then a gunshot cracked from that direction and a chunk of lead caught him through the meat in his shoulder. The impact of the shot spun the driver around and sent him to the edge of the seat. He teetered there for a slow moment before falling off.

Finch watched the driver bounce against the wagon's wheel as the sound of the gunshot still rattled through his head. One of Barrett's gunmen was already making his way toward the wagon from the opposite direction. Before Finch could take a breath, another shot came from the rifle in the distance and a familiar *crack* sounded through the air.

Even though Finch had thought this through so many times, he never thought it would be like this. Time seemed to slow for him so he could watch the wounded driver smack against the protruding hub of the wheel and try awkwardly to brace himself before slamming into the dirt.

The driver landed with a gut-wrenching crunch; his arm extended to try and break his fall, but only crumpled beneath him with a wet snap. Finch felt as though it had been his own arm breaking and lost all of what remained of his composure. Letting the money fall from his hands, Finch dropped to the ground and covered his head with both arms.

When that body hit the ground, it rattled Finch right down to the core and things started moving all too quickly.

The men inside the wagon fired in every direction. From the spot where Finch was lying, he would have sworn that lead was hissing through the air from every angle. His ears were ringing and every muscle in his body was trembling uncontrollably.

It was all Finch could do to scrape at the ground and try to crawl for cover. The only place he could get to was under the wagon. As poor a choice as that might have been, it was the only one that didn't involve putting himself out in the open. Once he was there, he huddled into a ball and tried to think past all the gunshots and shouting voices that were raging only a few feet away.

"H . . . help . . . me."

The weak voice came from ground level. When Finch managed to turn around on his belly, he found the driver looking back at him.

"I . . . I'm shot," the driver wheezed.

Finch didn't need to be told that. He'd

seen the bullet knock the driver from his seat and could see the blood spilling from the messy wound. "I know," was all Finch could put together by way of a reply.

The driver clenched his teeth together and choked down the pain. "Get me . . . my gun."

Finch's first reaction was to help the man. Then he remembered what was going on and why. Resigning himself to what he'd put into motion, Finch pulled his hand back and shook his head. "I can't do that. I'm sorry."

The driver looked at Finch with utter disbelief. His eyes became wide and then closed as the realization sank in. Sucking in a breath that made his whole body shake, he turned away from Finch as though the other man suddenly stopped existing. He then began the excruciating process of dragging himself toward the gun that he'd dropped after hitting the ground.

In the wagon and above the driver, men swarmed to get a clear shot through a window while also trying to stay away from the bullets speeding toward them. The man on top of the wagon was pressed flat against the wooden roof and had only just gotten into a position where he could get a grip on his shotgun and point it in the proper direction.

"There's one coming right for us!" came a voice from inside the wagon.

At the same time he'd heard that, the man on top of the wagon caught a good look at the gunman making his way toward the road. The man wore a bandanna pulled up over his face and walked as though that cotton mask was enough to make him bulletproof. After calmly lifting his pistol, the masked man took aim at the wagon and squeezed off a shot.

The wagon's shotgunner felt hot lead tear through the skin of his back, forcing him to press his face down even harder against the wooden roof. When he opened his eyes, he could see with such clarity that he thought he could pick out every leaf on every tree. The rush of blood through his veins made him dizzy, but wasn't going to keep him from firing back.

Fumbling with the shotgun, the man on the wagon brought the weapon around and pulled the trigger. The shotgun's roar was soothing to the man's ears and the buck of it against his shoulder felt like a comforting pat from an old friend's hand.

Morrison grimaced beneath the bandanna

covering his face and threw himself to one side when he saw the shotgun being brought around toward him. Launching himself facefirst toward the ground, he let out a grunted obscenity that couldn't even be heard over the roar of the shotgun.

Buckshot filled the air like a swarm of hornets flying past him. Morrison felt some stinging when he tried to get up, but knew that he'd only been clipped by a few stray pellets. He was back on his feet and firing toward the top of the wagon in no time, forcing the shotgunner to pull away from the edge of the roof.

"See what you can do about that asshole on the roof," Morrison shouted over his shoulder. "I'll clear out the inside."

Morrison spotted a face peeking out from beneath the wagon and almost sent a bullet through it before he stopped himself.

"I've got the keys to the strongboxes," Finch shouted from behind a wheel. "There's no need for any more shooting."

Although Morrison didn't say anything to the businessman, he gave his answer clearly enough when he drew a second gun from its holster and took aim at the wagon.

The remaining guards had been firing through the windows the entire time, but were too rattled to take careful aim. Instead, they just pointed their guns out of the wagon and pulled their triggers as quickly as they could. Morrison was barely even flinching as the hastily fired rounds whipped past him.

Morrison was about ten yards from the wagon by this time and starting to take more careful aim. With the supporting fire still coming steadily from the rifle behind him, Morrison stepped around the back of the wagon and reached for a handhold so he could climb onto the roof.

The side door swung open and one of the guards took a look outside.

Without batting an eye, Morrison took aim and put a round through the guard's skull. A crimson mist filled the air behind his head and the guard flopped out of the wagon like a discarded toy.

"You see that shot, Guile?" Morrison shouted.

But Guile didn't answer.

In fact the cover fire had stopped altogether.

Morrison didn't like that one bit.

THIRTY-SEVEN

It hadn't been much of a problem for Nick to find the site of the ambush. Apart from hearing most of the details from Finch and Barrett the night before, all he had to do was ride in the proper direction and then follow the sound of gunshots. Of course, he'd hoped to get there before those shots were fired, but even Nick knew that was hoping for too much.

As it was, he knew Rasa was up to the task of getting him where he needed to be before too much blood had been spilled. Nick wasn't too wild about leaving Barrett back in those trees, but he reckoned the ropes should hold until he figured out what to do with him. As for the answer to that question, Nick was more comfortable dealing with Guile and Morrison. At least he didn't have any second thoughts when it came to those two.

Rasa had a lot in common with some

women Nick had known throughout the years. The horse may have looked like a nag, but she had the legs of a champion. When the horse's age started to show and her breath started coming in labored heaves, she still dug down and responded to every flick of the reins.

"Not much farther to go," Nick said as he listened to the crackle of gunshots in the distance. "Just a little bit more."

It wasn't long before he could see the wagon stopped up ahead. Nick took a quick survey of the land and spotted a steep ridge rising up to the left of the road. Wanting the higher ground for his initial approach, he steered Rasa toward that rise.

That's when he saw the puff of smoke come from the edge of the ridge that looked down on the wagon. The shooting hadn't started too long before and most of it sounded too quick to be more than panic fire. That wasn't the case for the shot which had been taken from atop the ridge.

It was the perfect spot for a sniper. Unless that rifleman was taken care of, he would just clean out the wagon one guard at a time.

After riding just over halfway up the ridge, Nick pulled Rasa to a stop and dropped down from the saddle. He bent his knees

409

the moment his boots hit the dirt and maintained the crouch as he made his way up to the top of the ridge. His hand stayed just over his gun, ready to draw at a moment's notice.

Guile lay on his belly with his legs straightened out behind him and his face leaning against his Henry rifle. He'd just grazed the shotgunner on top of the wagon when he realized that his job was going to be easier than he'd thought. Morrison was working his way up to the wagon and would be close enough to start really doing some damage.

The guards were beginning to poke their heads out a bit more, so Guile sent a few more shots toward the wagon. He got close a few times and even snuck in a few hits, but his main purpose was to cover his partner. Morrison liked the dirty work and Guile left him to it.

Just as he was about to take another shot, Guile felt something press against the back of his head and push him down. His mouth was full of grit and his vision had gone almost totally black before he even knew what the hell was happening. The ringing in his ears became a dull roar once he was mashed up against the Henry's barrel. His hands scrambled for his other gun, but he could barely get his bearings with his face being driven into the dirt.

Something landed heavily beside him and then Guile felt something heavy push against his ribs.

"Now you know how a bug feels," came a hushed voice from less than two feet away. "And if you keep reaching for that pistol, I'll pop your skull under my boot."

Guile's hand froze only a few inches from his holster. He could feel the knife in his boot pressing against his shin, which made it all the more infuriating to be kept from it. "Who the hell is it?" he asked.

Although that hushed voice didn't come back, Guile got his answer another way as the pressure against his head increased slightly and a gnarled hand reached down to take hold of the Henry rifle. He recognized the mangled hand instantly.

"You're Barrett's old friend," Guile said, each word sounding wet and a bit slurred as it came out through lips that were forced to kiss the ground. "Where is he?"

Still leaning forward to pick up the rifle, Nick kept up the pressure against Guile's head and took a look at what was going on down below. The man under his boot tried to keep his grip on the Henry, but with a little pulling and a bit more pressure from his boot, Nick was able to pull the rifle from Guile's grasp.

Nick lifted the rifle to his shoulder and took a moment to let his hands settle around the stock and barrel. "I wouldn't worry about Barrett too much," he said while lining up a shot. "If I were you, I'd be hoping that your skull's as thick as it seems."

Still squirming slightly, Guile alternated between clawing at the ground and reaching up to try to push Nick's boot off of him. But neither action accomplished much. The ground and Nick's boot were too solid.

Speaking through the corner of his mouth, Guile said, "If it's money you're after, you'll get your share! Barrett made it clear that —"

"Shut up," Nick snarled, tapping his foot down quick enough to force some more dirt into Guile's mouth.

"You see that shot, Guile?" Morrison shouted from below.

Nick had seen it, all right. He'd looked up just in time to see a guard's head get blown open before he could do a damn thing about it. Even as he took aim, Nick could feel that death settling in with all the others for which he would hold himself responsible.

One more voice added to the ghostly

chorus that cursed at him from every nightmare.

On the trail down below, Morrison had a
gun in each hand and had turned to look
over his shoulder, directly to the spot where
Nick was standing. Morrison acted with
finely honed instincts and was able to pitch
himself to one side before Nick took his first
shot.

The Henry bucked in Nick's hands. Although the recoil wasn't too bad, it was still
almost enough to wrench the rifle through
the gaps where his missing fingers should
have been. Nick cursed under his breath
and readjusted his aim. He didn't have to
look to know that the shot he'd taken had
been way off the mark.

"Who's up there?" Morrison shouted as
he rolled to his feet and stopped on one
knee. "Guile? What's going on?"

Nick could feel the man under his boot
pulling in enough breath to fill his lungs,
but was unable to keep Guile from shouting
in response to Morrison's call.

Although the words were muffled, they
came through out of sheer force of will.
"Shoot this asshole!" Guile shouted.

Nick dropped back down to one knee,
anticipating Morrison's response while still
keeping Guile under his boot. Sure enough,

the masked man lifted both pistols and sent a short barrage of shots up toward the top of the ridge. Nick didn't even flinch at the incoming fire. Instead, he tightened his grip on the Henry and took careful aim without giving the rest a second thought.

If a pistol round could make it from the ridge to that wagon, Morrison wouldn't have walked all the way down there in the first place.

Nick took his time and did the job right. He shifted his hands upon the rifle so they could grip it more securely without compromising too much balance. He sighted down the barrel, making allowances for such factors as wind and the movement of his target.

Nick pulled in a breath, held it, and then let it out while squeezing the rifle's trigger. The shot exploded from the barrel, kicking the rifle against Nick's shoulder. After a second roared by, Nick saw the spurt of blood pop from Morrison's side.

The bullet tore a messy path through Morrison's ribs and spun him in a tight, semicircle. The gunman was too fired up to feel much of the pain and what little of it did register only made him angrier.

Morrison's rage twisted his features until his teeth were bared in a savage, animal snarl. In response to that snarl, Nick levered in another round and took a moment to feel the weight of the rifle in his hands.

"How many shots left?" Nick asked, hoping that Guile would be worn down enough to answer on reflex.

"Suck on the barrel and see if there's one more in there."

Nick looked down to take a look for himself. He could feel Guile shifting around more than usual, which drew his eyes toward the other man's hands. Before he could tell how many shots remained in the rifle, Nick's focus was drawn to Guile's left hand which was reaching for a scabbard strapped to the inside of one leg.

Letting his instincts take over, Nick lifted the rifle up and angled the weapon so its butt was pointing almost straight down. He then drove the wooden stock toward the back of Guile's head, waiting to move his foot until the last possible second. Even so, Guile was able to roll to one side the instant the pressure was off, allowing the rifle butt to pound into the earth beside him with a solid thump.

Guile's hand flashed down to his leg and plucked a hunting knife from its scabbard. Wearing a victorious smirk, he rolled to one side and onto his feet, coming up with the knife firmly in his grasp.

"All right, asshole," Guile hissed. "Let's see how tough you are now that you can't sneak up from behind me."

Nick wasn't paying attention to a thing that came out of Guile's mouth. Instead, he was busy watching every one of the man's moves and countering them to keep himself out of that blade's striking distance. The rifle was gripped in both hands and held lengthwise across his body.

Guile spat another taunt before lashing out with the blade in a quick swipe. The edge of the knife sailed toward Nick's gut, but was batted away when Nick snapped the rifle barrel down and out. Nick followed up immediately with a jab from the rifle's stock, using the momentum of the block to flow directly into the attack.

Although the blow wasn't hard enough to drop Guile, the look on his face and the wheeze that came from the back of his throat was enough to tell Nick that he'd been caught by surprise. Nick took advantage of this by turning the rifle so the barrel pointed at Guile. Before the trigger could be pulled, Guile was making a quick stab for Nick's hip.

Nick was able to twist the rifle down to block the knife. Guile ran the blade along the rifle a ways before snapping his wrist and pushing forward with his whole arm in a way intended to rid Nick of another finger or two.

The only thing Nick could do at that point was take a step back and try to move the rifle fast enough to keep the blade from getting too big a piece of him. Guile's stab turned up and down in a quick flow, bringing the blade over the top of the rifle and then knocking the gun clean from Nick's hands.

"Well, now," Guile said with a sneer. "This is interesting. Too bad Barrett isn't here to watch me gut his friend like the pig he is."

Thirty-Eight

Barrett waited until Nick was gone before making any move whatsoever.

Waiting for those few minutes was one of the most difficult things Barrett would ever do. Every second that ticked by, Barrett could feel the money and those jewels slip through his fingers. Although he wanted to sit and piece together what Nick's agenda had been, there simply wasn't time. For the moment, Barrett could only pray that he was in time to salvage one of the biggest hauls in his life.

The first thing he did was squat down and drop himself onto his backside so he could roll all the way onto his back. From there, he curled his legs and pulled them tightly against his chest while continuing to roll back until he was on his shoulders. He then pulled his arms down a bit and wriggled until his backside fit over the ropes binding his wrists.

The effort strained at his shoulders and sent jagged trails of pain throughout his entire body as the ropes dug into his wrists while also burning the flesh. That pain served as a splash of cold water to clear his mind after getting knocked on the head. Barrett's shoulders weren't as nimble as they used to be, but they strained to their limits one more time in his favor. What truly put him over the edge was a simple trick that he'd set into motion when Nick had been tying his hands in the first place.

Barrett's fists were clenched into tight balls, just as they had been when Nick had bound his wrists. When he relaxed them and pressed his hands flat together, it created just enough slack for him to pull his hands through the looped rope. Once his leverage was added to the slack he'd created, his hand popped free of the binding altogether and Barrett lay sprawled upon the ground. It was an old trick, but Nick had always been a sucker for it.

His breath came in a few gulps and he took a moment to check that nothing had been pulled from its socket. All that mattered, however, was that Barrett was a free man. After tossing the rope aside, he scrambled to his feet and made a run for his horse.

In the back of Barrett's mind was the possibility that Nick had taken both horses with him just to be on the safe side. Stopping once he was clear of the trees, Barrett froze and spun about in search of any trace of his horse. Just before panic could set in, he spotted his animal grazing a few yards away behind a rock.

Barrett ran to his horse. His steps were still a bit shaky and his vision was a little cloudy around the edges, but the excited pump of his heart was more than enough to make up for all of that.

By the time he was in the saddle and taking hold of the reins, Barrett felt that he could take on the entire world. He was so wound up, in fact, that a part of him was thanking Nick for the experience.

Of course, the rest of him still wanted to see his old partner dead.

Gunshots were once again firing in the distance as Nick and Guile circled each other warily. More than anything, Nick wanted to see how the guards were holding up against Morrison, but he had some serious concerns of his own at the moment.

"Something tells me Barrett would enjoy this," Guile said, whipping his hand forward with a quick slash of the blade.

Nick stepped away from the incoming knife, keeping close watch on the other man's eyes. It was by watching Guile's eyes that he was able to see the same kind of tells that he would look for in a poker game. Only this time, the hints were foreshadowing something more than a busted flush.

Before he slashed, Guile squinted a bit.

Before he stabbed, he blinked.

And before he made a border shift, Guile's eyes widened as if he'd already won the fight.

After a quick feint, Guile made the shift and tossed the knife from one hand to another. His eyes then snapped down toward his gun belt and the two-shot Derringer peeking up from underneath a row of spare bullets. When Guile reached for the gun, he made a lunging swipe with the knife.

Rather then try to block the incoming knife hand, Nick turned to one side and allowed the blade to pass by. The sharpened edge dragged along his midsection, slicing through Nick's shirt as well as through a bit of the skin underneath. Some blood trickled from the wound, but Nick was too busy to notice.

The knife had just raked over his torso when Nick completed his backward step. From that stance, it was a simple matter of reaching up and taking hold of the gun that was strapped across his belly.

When Nick closed his hand around the pistol's grip and started to draw, the curved grooves of its barrel and the matching ridges inside the holster did their work perfectly. The gun twisted into Nick's palm as it cleared leather, making it that much easier for him to aim and take a shot in less time than it took for most men to blink.

Guile's entire body jumped when Nick's Schofield went off. Part of that was surprise, but most of it was from the hot lead that punched through his heart and tore a hole as it came out from between his shoulders. His fingers were touching the Derringer's handle, but he didn't have enough strength to draw the holdout weapon.

Nick was acting on pure instinct when he fired another shot into Guile's chest just to make sure he'd put the man out of his misery.

Guile staggered back a step and dropped to his knees. He could still feel the paths that had been burned through his chest, but the pain only lasted until he fell forward and hit the ground facefirst.

Striding toward the edge of the rise, Nick swept the Henry rifle into his hands and brought it to hip level. All of his attention was once again focused on the wagon and the gun battle still raging around it.

The air around the wagon was thick with smoke and swirled like a black, gritty cloud. Since Morrison wasn't in sight, Nick hurried down the ridge holding the rifle in front of him. Just as he'd turned the weapon in his hands to get an idea of how much ammunition was left, he heard another set of gunshots blast through the air.

Reflexively, Nick dropped down to one knee and brought up the rifle to aim at whoever was coming around the wagon.

". . . by the horses," came a weak trembling voice.

Nick shifted his eyes and saw one of the guards leaning against the inside of the wagon with his head propped against the window frame.

"He's up by . . . the horses," the guard said. "James is . . . taking him on."

Straightening up, Nick glanced into the wagon and saw one guard with half his head blown off lying at the surviving guard's feet. The shots were thinning out, which meant that there wasn't much time left if he was to play any role in the fight. Nick kept himself low and started moving around to see what could be done.

Even though it wasn't more than a few

paces to get around the back of the wagon, Nick felt as if he'd walked miles before getting there. He knew better than to rush in blindly and that patience was rewarded when Morrison came rushing around toward him.

The gunman's mask was pulled askew, but it was still wrapped around most of Morrison's face. He was rushing around the wagon in a sidestep while twisting his upper body to aim both guns at a target Nick couldn't see.

"Stop right there!" Nick shouted, as he lifted the rifle and took aim.

Morrison stopped, but it was more out of shock than to obey Nick's order. For a moment, he squinted at Nick as if in disbelief before flicking his eyes toward his original target. "You're still alive?"

Nodding, Nick replied, "That's right. Too bad your friend up on that ridge can't say the same."

A bit of anger registered in Morrison's eyes, but that was followed by cool acceptance. "You want a bigger slice of this haul? You can have Guile's share. All we need to do is finish off these guards."

Now that the dust had settled, Nick could just barely make out Morrison's current target. It was a man standing up near the horses. That was the man whose life would end if Nick didn't play his hand exactly right.

"This ends right here," Nick said. "Right now. Put those guns down or die where you stand."

Morrison wasn't responding to the reasonable tone in Nick's voice, so Nick put in a healthy dose of venom when he added, "Come on, Morrison. Don't tell me you want to leave this world along with your partner up there. I can still feel the slime the little bastard's hands left on his rifle."

"What did you say?" Morrison snarled as he shifted around and leveled his full gaze upon Nick.

"I'm not saying it again, asshole. If your head wasn't so full of manure you would have heard me the first time."

Morrison brought his guns around as he turned to face Nick.

Now that Morrison was no longer aiming at the guard, Nick dropped his voice to an even tone and said, "Drop the pistols. It's over."

Morrison shook his head. "Not until I blast your head from your shoulders it ain't."

Nick didn't waver from where he stood. The sound of the guard shuffling away from where he'd been pinned meant Nick had already accomplished his goal. All that remained was getting away with his life. Under normal circumstances, Nick would have been fairly confident in his odds of survival.

But these weren't normal circumstances.

In the time that he'd been holding that Henry rifle up to his shoulder, he'd been weighing the weapon in his hands and he laid better than average odds that it was empty.

Either Morrison saw the glimmer of doubt in Nick's eyes or he was feeling mighty lucky himself, because the outlaw set his jaw and started lifting his guns to make good on the threat he'd made.

There was a thunderous roar and smoke rolled through the air. The gunshot came from close range, but it hadn't come from Morrison or even the rifle in Nick's hands. Rather, it had come from the top of the wagon and the wounded shotgunner lying there.

Morrison was hit with the full force of the blast. From that range, he was nearly cut in two and he flew off his feet amid a bloody, pulpy mist. His remains dropped in a meaty pile and both pistols skidded against the ground in separate directions.

The man on top of the wagon let out the breath he'd been holding and looked at Nick, who was still standing in place with the rifle in his hands.

"You hurt, mister?" the shotgunner asked. "Hey. You all right?"

Although Nick's ears were ringing, that wasn't why it took a while for him to respond. There was one question on his mind and a squeeze of his trigger finger was all he needed to answer it.

Clack.

"Yeah," Nick said while finally lowering the Henry. "I'm doing pretty good."

Slowly, the guard who'd most recently been at the wrong end of Morrison's guns poked his head around the horses to get a look at what had happened. The relief on his face was evident, but was also tempered by a certain wariness when he got a look at Nick.

"It's all right," the shotgunner said. "That man there is on our side." Sneaking a nervous look toward Nick, he asked, "Ain't that so?"

"You've got wounded men," was all Nick said to that particular question. "Take them into town before you lose them."

"Our driver was hurt. I can't see where he is."

"I'll look for him and make sure he gets into town."

"But what about the —"

"Just go! Or would you rather talk while your partners bleed to death?"

That choice was an easy one to make and the shotgunner had already climbed down into the driver's seat before the other guard stepped into the wagon. As the reins were snapped, Nick got a look inside the wagon to see the man who'd spoken to him earlier was still moving. When the wagon pulled away, it revealed Finch and the missing driver huddling under it.

It also revealed someone else who'd been standing on the other side of the carriage.

"Hey, there, Nick," Barrett said from behind his drawn pistol. "Looks like we've still got a bit of catching up to do."

THIRTY-NINE

Nick stood in his spot without moving a muscle until the wagon had rolled a ways down the trail. Even then, what few motions he did make were slow and deliberate.

"Watch it," Barrett said. "I'm still a little jumpy after getting knocked over the head. I saw what you did to Guile. Even after all that, he still left me a present." As he spoke, Barrett held out the gun Guile had died reaching for as though it was wrapped with a bow.

The other two men who'd been hiding under the wagon were still huddled in the middle of the road. While Finch remained low to the ground to keep out of notice. The driver was sprawled out on his back and unable to move. His breathing was shallow and labored.

For a moment, Barrett seemed inclined to head back to the horse that waited behind him a little ways and take off after the wagon. Then his eyes flicked down to a few things that he'd spotted on the ground next to Finch.

"Is that what I think it is?" Barrett asked.

Seeing what was in Barrett's sights, Finch flopped onto his backside and started scuttling away from the driver like a crab on a frying pan. "I've got the money right here," Finch said frantically. He then pulled the bloodstained bills from his jacket pocket and tossed them onto the ground. "Here! Just take it! I don't want any part of this anymore. Just take it and let me go."

"You want out?" Barrett asked. "After all we've been through?"

Finch nodded.

Shifting his eyes toward Nick, Barrett put on a sly grin and said, "I'm not the only one that does the planning around here. I'm not the only devil making things wrong in this world."

"I never said that you were," Nick replied. "I just wanted to make up for some of the things that went wrong before."

"Back to the reform talk. Well, I'm sorry but I don't have time for it, Spud. Thanks to you, I've got to live on the run for a while. At least I'll be able to do it in style. I see Mr. Finch was kind enough to keep hold of his merchandise as well."

Even though he was plainly terrified of both men standing on either side of him, Finch reflexively made a grab for the lockboxes that were lying next to the driver. He was stopped by a murderous stare from Barrett.

"Too many men died here today," Barrett said. "But if you so much as touch them boxes, I'll add one more to the list." Glancing back toward Nick, he added, "Make that two."

Finch backed away from both the lockboxes as well as the money scattered out on the ground. Judging by the look on his face, one might have thought he was leaving behind an arm or leg.

Satisfied once Finch was away from the goods, Barrett shifted his gaze back toward Nick. "Might as well drop that rifle." After Nick let the Henry hit the ground, Barrett said, "And toss over that pistol of yours while you're at it."

Nick could see where this was going. Unfortunately, there wasn't a whole lot he could do about it. He used one finger through the trigger guard to lift the modified Schofield gently from its holster and dropped it to the ground.

Nodding in approval, Barrett said, "Now kick it to me. Oh, and if I see you start any

431

kind of fancy move to get that gun back, I'll burn you down."

Nick used the side of his foot to shove the gun toward Barrett. Suddenly, he felt like a fool for sparing his friend's life.

Bending at the knees without shifting his aim from his target, Barrett picked up the Schofield with his free hand. He started to tuck it under his belt, but then got a look on his face as though he'd accidentally picked up a dead rabbit. "Jesus Christ, this is a sad piece of junk. I know you gotta make do with whatever cards you got left, but couldn't you at least have gotten a better gun than this?"

"There's no reason for a good piece of iron unless you can shoot it," Nick said.

"I suppose you're right about that. Still, I'll keep it to remember you by." He tucked the gun under his belt and then aimed his own gun at Nick's head. "You probably don't believe me, but I really hate to do this. Too bad you chose to grow a conscience after all these years, Nick. It really doesn't suit you."

"You can walk away without taking this any farther. Just know that if you were anyone else, you wouldn't even get that option."

"Is that supposed to be a threat?"

"It's too late for threats," Nick said regretfully. "It's too late for anything." The more Nick spoke, the tighter his teeth clenched together. His eyes were burning with an inner fire. "I've been looking out for you your whole life, Barrett. I taught you how to shoot. I taught you how to kill, all so I didn't have to watch you die as you followed me from one goddamn bloodbath to another.

"But it wasn't until meeting up with you again that I realized you were just as responsible for those bloodbaths as I was. You planned them out and I saw them through. But I always thought you were the smart one and I guess that's where I went wrong."

"What?" Barrett snapped.

"I worked to keep those deputies from gunning you down and damn near got killed in the process."

"Nobody asked for your protection. All I wanted was a partner. Someone I could trust."

"Someone you could trust? Is that why you sold me out along with the rest of the gang back in Montana?"

Barrett squirmed in his spot as though he was the one at gunpoint. "What are you talking about?" he grunted. "I told you where I was when that committee came for you."

"Yeah. You told me a bit too much. You said you'd been with that whore in Virginia City for two weeks when the rest of us had only been there for two days."

"Christ, Nick, that was a slip of the tongue."

"Really? Then how did you know about the law in Virginia City? I was with the others most of the time and I sure as hell didn't know about it. How'd you know it was swarming with bloodthirsty vigilantes? You seemed to know a hell of a lot where Montana was concerned." Narrowing his eyes to fix an intense gaze upon Barrett, Nick added, "You always did know a lot where saving your own skin was concerned."

The conflict in Barrett's eyes flared up for a second before dying out altogether. From there, all it took was one more blink and then the smug grin returned to his face. "You know the only ones in that gang that didn't get exactly what they had coming were you and me. You're damn right I saved my skin in Montana. We were all riding toward the edge of a cliff and as far as I knew, you and Skinner were more than happy to take the plunge.

"The only way out of that gang was to die, so I started looking for a way to speed things up before they got out of hand.

Virginia City was the answer to my prayers. I'd been scouting for a place like that for months. A pretty little whore caught my eye while everyone else was too damn drunk to see straight and she told me about that Vigilance Committee.

"Sure I stretched the truth a bit when I told you that story before, but you were always better at lying than I was. I talked to Red Parks. Hell, I even introduced him to Skinner. I'll bet you didn't know that one. Just like I'll bet you didn't know that Red's alive and well and still stewing over the unsettled business between you two."

Nick didn't say a word, even though that last statement dropped on him like a load of rocks. What cut even deeper was the fact that every instinct in Nick's body told him that Barrett was speaking the truth.

"I bargained to try and keep you alive," Barrett continued. "But I never knew until recently that you'd actually made it out of that place."

"Yeah," Nick said sarcastically. "Aren't I the lucky one."

"Well I won't lie to you. I didn't want it to come to this, but we came too far down this road to leave it now."

"So what, then?" Nick asked. "You put a bullet through an unarmed man to set things straight? If that's justice in your mind, then I'm a damn fool for letting you live this long."

"Like I said, the only way out of this gang is to die. Since we're the last two members, then one of us needs to get out before the gang can be put to rest for good."

Barrett stepped over to the side of the road where one of the guard's pistols had been dropped. He snatched it up and snapped the cylinder open to check it with a few practiced motions. Snapping it shut, he started walking toward Nick. "We'll finish this like we would in the old days," he said, jamming the barrel of his own pistol into Nick's gut.

Plenty of things rushed through Nick's head as he waited for fire and lead to come blasting through his innards. Before Nick could decide exactly what to do, Barrett reached forward to drop the guard's weapon into his holster. The pistol snagged on the specially crafted ridges within Nick's holster and hung out at an odd angle.

Barrett stepped back wearing an amused smile. "I know it's not the gun you're used to, but I figure you should be able to make do."

Looking down at the gun that hung half-way out of his holster, Nick could already feel how awkward the pistol would feel when gripped within his fractured grasp. He knew from experience that a heavy piece of iron had a tendency to slip when a man couldn't hold on to it properly and Nick hadn't been able to wield a gun properly for years.

The men who'd taken his fingers had made sure of that.

"I know what you're thinking," Barrett said with a cocky tone in his voice. "You'd like to have your own gun right about now. Well, I don't think it would be all too fair if I handed that over."

"You always were the smart one."

Accepting the compliment with a slight nod, Barrett moved about five paces back and squared his shoulders. After a moment of heavy silence, he said something that was one of the most heartfelt things Nick had ever heard him say. "Good-bye, Nick. I appreciate all you've done . . . and all you tried to do."

Nick took a step back so he could line his shoulders up with Barrett and give the other man a narrower target. His hand drifted toward the gun sticking from his holster, which was almost about to fall out on its own. His heart was churning within his ribs like a steam engine speeding toward the base of a hill.

Although Nick was certain he could draw and fire the gun at a reasonable speed, he was just as certain that Barrett could draw and fire quicker than that. No matter how he thought through it, Nick couldn't think of a way to outdraw Barrett without his specially modified Schofield.

Even if the guard's weapon was nestled in a normal holster, Nick would have had a better chance. As it was, too many things were out of balance and both men knew it.

Barrett could see the frustration building up behind Nick's eyes. That, coupled with the sight of the money and lockboxes lying in front of him made the moment seem all the sweeter. In fact, when he saw Nick's hand snap toward his gun, Barrett truly felt sorry for the poor bastard.

Nick's fingers closed awkwardly around the handle of the gun he'd been given. The weapon shifted uncomfortably in his grasp. He cleared leather quickly, but was unable to get the barrel pointed anywhere close to Barrett.

Thankfully, Nick was still ahead of Barrett by a few fractions of a second when he drew every bit of strength he could muster into his arm and snapped it forward to send the guard's pistol spinning through the air.

In fact, Nick's awkward draw helped his cause by giving the gun some additional rotation as it sped toward Barrett. The pistol knocked into his arm as Barrett was lifting his own weapon and then bounced up into his face.

It had all happened in the blink of an eye and by the time Barrett was about to blink again, Nick was charging toward him with his hands outstretched. In his haste to move before being trampled by the other man, Barrett felt his gun slipping through his bruised fingers.

Barrett was able to move aside as Nick charged him. His grip wavered for a moment, but he managed to keep hold of his weapon even though his fingers were aching almost as much as his chin after getting hit by the flying pistol. Nick had tried to follow up with a punch, but Barrett had stepped aside just in time to dodge it.

When Barrett came to a stop, he honestly couldn't believe that he was still alive. "Nice move, Nick," he said breathlessly. "But it looks like you've lost your touch."

Nick was crouching as he turned around to face Barrett after coming to a stop a few paces away. Now, it was his turn to put on a subtle, sly grin. "Have I?" he asked, letting his gaze drop slightly toward Barrett's gun belt.

Suddenly, Barrett felt the bottom drop from his stomach as his free hand went to the spot where he'd tucked away Nick's Schofield. The modified pistol was nowhere to be found. That is, until he spotted it clutched within Nick's hand.

"Nice move, Spud. Now how about we split up this money and get the hell out of here?"

"Oh," Nick said. "So now you're ready to split it three ways? Just last night you were planning on killing me right along with Guile and Morrison."

Barrett winced as his words to Finch from the night before were thrown right back into his face. "I'd never kill you, Spud. We're friends. Brothers, even."

Rather than let Barrett talk his way out of his mess, Nick decided to give him a moment to show the cards he was truly holding. It wasn't much more than a slow glance downward, but when guns were drawn, it was the same as baring your throat to a hungry wolf.

Barrett pounced on the opening the moment he saw it. The instant he tried to take aim, Barrett was cut short by a single shot from Nick's gun. That bullet whipped through the air between them, punched through Barrett's skull, cleared a tunnel through his brain and exploded out the other side.

Nick stepped forward after Barrett toppled over, knelt down beside him and gently took the gun from his friend's hand. Without looking away from Barrett's wide-open, unseeing eyes, Nick shouted, "If you take one more step, you'll be the next one to fall."

Finch stopped where he was, his arms wrapped around the lockboxes and his pockets stuffed full of money. "Please . . . don't kill me," he whined, unable or unwilling to turn to look at the man he'd been trying to leave behind.

Nick holstered the Schofield, taking no small amount of comfort that the gun was once again in its rightful place. When he walked up to Finch, all he needed to do was slap the businessman on the back of the head to get him to drop both lockboxes onto his own feet.

But Finch didn't dare to wince or pull his toes from beneath the sturdy iron boxes. Even though the pain went away after Nick picked up one of the boxes, Finch was far from relieved.

"Where are you going with that?" Finch asked.

Nick, covered in flecks of blood and stinking of gun smoke, wore an expression that was enough to drain the color from the businessman's face. He dropped the box he'd been carrying so that it was right next to the others. "Unlock those boxes."

Finch obeyed without hesitating, his hands trembling more with every second.

"Now drop the keys and then put all the money into one box and all the jewels into another."

"Wh . . . what?! But this belongs to —"

"The money and the jewels. All of it. Right now."

"So you're robbing me too? And here I thought you were supposed to be helping."

"And I thought you were supposed to be looking out for your father's interests. Just go crying to him and tell him his jewels were stolen. That would've happened no matter what, right?"

Although Finch's mouth trembled with all the words he wanted to say, he couldn't bring himself to speak.

"And as for that little bit of cash you thought you'd keep hidden from me . . ."

Finch sputtered and started to shake. "I don't know what you're —"

After a stern look from Nick, Finch shut his mouth and produced a single stack of bills from his waistband.

"Find those guards and give it to them," Nick said as Finch started to hand the money over.

Nodding, Finch muttered, "For doctor's expenses. That's reasonable."

"No. That's just for the hell they went through. Any doctor's expenses and funeral arrangements would be handled by your company since you're the one that got them into this." Narrowing his eyes Nick added, "Isn't that so?"

"Yes. Of course."

"Now get moving."

When Finch spoke again, his voice came out in a pathetic squeak. "Are you going to kill me?"

"You can either find one of the horses roaming about here or walk back into town. I don't give a damn which it is."

Then, Nick closed the box full of jewels and money, picked it up and turned his back on the businessman. He walked half-way up the ridge before Rasa came down to meet him. After emptying the lockboxes into his saddlebags, Nick scooped up Barrett's body and loaded it onto Rasa's back. He then climbed into the saddle, snapped the reins, and raced back into town.

FORTY

The Badlands
Three days later

After tossing the last scoop of dirt onto the pile, Nick stuck the shovel's blade into the ground and surveyed his work. The hole he'd dug was the right size and the proper depth to keep it from being found by animals or grave robbers. More importantly, it was big enough to hold the simple, sturdy box that lay open not too far away.

It was a warm day and the sun was blazing down on his shoulders. Nick wiped some sweat from his brow and looked down at the coffin he'd constructed earlier that morning. Sneaking in and out of Bitter Creek one last time to fetch his horse and wagon had been easy compared to nailing together Barrett's coffin.

Nick wouldn't exactly miss Bitter Creek.

Barrett, on the other hand, would be missed.

He'd be missed dearly.

His friend lay inside the wooden box with his hands crossed over his chest and his head tilted to one side. The hole in his skull was covered by a handkerchief. It was the best Nick could do on such short notice. He didn't think Barrett would have minded, especially since every jewel from the lockboxes was tucked inside the pockets of Barrett's jacket.

"I guess you earned your share in this job," Nick said to Barrett's pale face. "The rest of the money is my share and Finch will probably get his replacement jewels in a few weeks so I figured this is the best way to split it up. Besides," he added with a grin, "if anyone could figure a way to take it with him, it's you."

Kneeling down, Nick placed his hand flat upon Barrett's chest and bowed his head. After so many years of mourning for others, it should have been easier to do it for himself.

It wasn't.

All of the words he would have said to someone in that situation went through Nick's mind, but none of it did him any good.

There was nothing left to be said and nobody around to listen.

All that was left was for Nick to nail the coffin shut, lower it into the hole and fill in Barrett's grave.

The work of shoveling dirt from one pile onto another gave him something else to do besides mourn. It also gave him time to think about what he could have done to make things turn out any differently. It made him realize that Barrett and Nick were equally guilty in setting each other onto their respective roads.

Nick liked to think that he'd chosen the higher road, even though he knew he'd been forced onto it by circumstances that just so happened to overshadow his own sins. In fact, he couldn't even rightly say if his was the higher road. Sometimes, it sure as hell didn't feel that way.

By the time the grave was filled, Nick was only certain of one thing.

High or low . . .

Right or wrong . . .

Every road led to boot hill.

The employees of Thorndike Press hope you have enjoyed this Large Print book. All our Thorndike, Wheeler, and Kennebec Large Print titles are designed for easy reading, and all our books are made to last. Other Thorndike Press Large Print books are available at your library, through selected bookstores, or directly from us.

For information about titles, please call:
  (800) 223-1244

or visit our Web site at:
  http://gale.cengage.com/thorndike

To share your comments, please write:
Publisher
Thorndike Press
10 Water St., Suite 310
Waterville, ME 04901